SAVAGE DEVOTION

AN AGE GAP, PREGNANCY, MAFIA ROMANCE

AJME WILLIAMS

Copyright © 2024 by Ajme Williams

All rights reserved.

No part of this book may be reproduced in any form or by any electronic or mechanical means, including information storage and retrieval systems, without written permission from the author, except for the use of brief quotations in a book review.

This is a work of fiction. Names, characters, businesses, places, events and incidents are either the products of authors imagination or used in a fictitious manner. Any resemblance to actual persons, living or dead, or actual events is purely coincidental. The following story contains mature themes, strong language and sexual situations. It is intended for mature readers only.

All characters are 18+ years of age and all sexual acts are consensual.

ABOUT THE AUTHOR

Ajme Williams writes emotional, angsty contemporary romance. All her books can be enjoyed as full length, standalone romances and are FREE to read in Kindle Unlimited.

Mafia Mysteries (this series)
Tangled Loyalties | Savage Devotion | Bulletproof Baby

Shadows of Redemption Series (New Dark Mafia Romance Series)
Soldier of Death | Queen of Misfortune | Prince of Darkness | Angel of Mercy

The Why Choose Haremland
Protecting Their Princess | Protecting Her Secret | Unwrapping their Christmas Present | Cupid Strikes... 3 Times | Their Easter Bunny | SEAL Daddies Next Door | Naughty Lessons | See Me After Class | Blurred Lines

High Stakes
Bet On It | A Friendly Wager | Triple or Nothing | Press Your Luck

Heart of Hope Series
Our Last Chance | An Irish Affair | So Wrong | Imperfect Love | Eight Long Years | Friends to Lovers | The One and Only | Best Friend's Brother | Maybe It's Fate | Gone Too Far | Christmas with Brother's Best Friend | Fighting for US | Against All Odds | Hoping to Score | Thankful for Us | The Vegas Bluff | 365 Days | Meant to Be | Mile High Baby | Silver Fox's Secret Baby | Snowed In with Best Friend's Dad | Secret Triplets for Christmas | Off-Limits Daddy

Billionaire Secrets
Twin Secrets | Just A Sham | Let's Start Over | The Baby Contract | Too Complicated

Dominant Bosses
His Rules | His Desires | His Needs | His Punishments | His Secret

Strong Brothers
Say Yes to Love | Giving In to Love | Wrong to Love You | Hate to Love You

Fake Marriage Series
Accidental Love | Accidental Baby | Accidental Affair | Accidental Meeting

Irresistible Billionaires
Admit You Miss Me | Admit You Love Me | Admit You Want Me | Admit You Need Me

Check out Ajme's full Amazon catalogue here.

Join her VIP NL here.

DESCRIPTION

"**Don't even think about running, sweetheart.**" A silken threat, his voice slithers around me.
"**You belong to me.**"

Sold to the Brotherhood. Betrayed by my sister and ex, I clawed my way free, leaving a trail of gunfire and a darkness deeper than the basement cell.

Now, I wake, a captive in a gilded cage.
Damian, Chicago's most ruthless mob boss, claims me with a single word: "**Mine.**"

His touch offers a twisted security, but the danger hasn't ended. Now, with a secret life blossoming within me, the real battle begins.

Can a ruthless mob boss become a father before his world explodes?

Readers note: Savage Devotion is a full-length standalone, spicy, mafia romance. Perfect for you if you love age gaps, pregnancy & a Cinderella-style plot - with kidnapping, of course ;)

1

ALEXIS

The little bell above the door jingles constantly, never getting a moment's rest as customer after customer pushes through. The sweet smells of freshly baked bread and sugar glazes hang heavily in the air, whetting every appetite that passes by the bakery's windows.

Today was Half Off a Dozen Donuts Day, so the line snaked from the front counter, around the glass display case, and out the door. I watch as customers clamor by the display case, thrusting their fingers toward the remaining donuts.

Behind the counter, there's organized chaos. Store employees in their pink and white striped aprons and white hats pull tray after tray of golden donuts from the back, their enticing aroma wafting through the store.

"One dozen chocolate glazed donuts!" a customer barks at me, ignoring my polite 'good morning'.

Okay, then.

My fingers fly across the register as I ring up the customer's order while Julia, a co-worker, hurriedly stuffs the donuts into a pink and white box embossed with the bakery's name, *Cake My Day*, in cursive font.

Even though the morning rush is hectic and the customers are rude, nothing can bring down my mood. Today marks five years since Mark and I started dating.

Five years. I can't believe it.

I wonder what Mark has planned for us. When I saw him yesterday, he acted like he had no idea what today was, but I know he's just teasing me. He's probably planning a *huge* surprise. Maybe he's going to take me to that new Italian restaurant that just opened up. I've been hinting about wanting to go there for *weeks*.

I can't fight the grin on my face as I imagine how the food will taste and how romantic the evening will be. Even though Mark isn't the romantic type, I just *know* he will be tonight. It's not everyday you reach half a decade with someone!

The hours fly by, and before I know it, my shift is nearly at an end and the bakery isn't as busy anymore.

"Are you excited, Alexis?" Julia asks me as we scrub the counters. "You've been staring at the clock all morning."

"Of course she's excited," Daniela calls as she brings out another tray of warm croissants, her round face shiny from the heat of the ovens. "Her boyfriend is most likely going to propose. Our girl's about to be engaged!"

Julia cheers, and my face warms as I continue to scrub the counter. It's nice to be supported by my co-workers.

I really do hope Mark proposes. I mean, it's been five years so it's only natural that I expect it, right? Plus, it would finally give me a real family, and that's been my one wish ever since my mom died when I was six years old. I don't even remember my father, and the authorities were never able to find him, so I was placed in the foster care system.

After bouncing from house to house, Dennis and Suzanne Carter allowed me into their home when I was eight, and I stayed in their house for the rest of my time in foster care. When I turned eighteen, I was terrified they would kick me out, but Dennis and Suzanne (they never allowed me to call them Mom and Dad) allowed me to stay in their home, as long as I cooked and cleaned for them.

"You don't know how to take care of yourself, Alexis," Suzanne would tell me. "Besides, we're the only people who can keep you safe. Do you want the bad men to come and get you again?"

I shiver as I scrub the already clean counter harder. When I was eight years old, I ran away from a particularly *horrible* foster family. After a few days on the streets, I was nearly kidnapped by a group of men. As they dragged me kicking and screaming to their van, Dennis Carter saved me after he witnessed the event.

I've been with the Carters ever since. Although they aren't the *best*, they keep a roof over my head and allow me to eat their food, so I'm grateful.

Besides, I owe them. Dennis and Suzanne frequently remind me how much it has cost them to raise and house me, so I won't leave their house until I've paid off my debt. By my calculations, that won't be for another five to six years if I decide to start giving them my entire paycheck. Ten years if I continue giving them half.

"You trying to scrub a hole into that counter?"

Gasping, I look up into the face of the most handsome customer I've ever seen.

His thick, tousled black hair frames an intensely chiseled face with high cheekbones, and a strong jawline dusted with stubble draws admiring glances. But it is his smoldering dark eyes that truly captivate, their brooding depths hinting at passions beneath his composed exterior.

He smirks at me, a dimple appearing in his right cheek, and I feel my knees weaken. Even standing still, an aura of powerful charisma seems to emanate from him.

"Oh! Uh." My face reddens as I look down at the rag in my hands. "I have to make sure the surfaces are clean. Can't be too careful with all the germs flying around. I don't want this to be called 'Cake My Day and Go To The Hospital Bakery'."

Oh, *God*, that was so bad. I want to melt into the floor.

His chuckle is low and velvety, a seductive rumble that sends tingles down my spine.

"Well, I'm glad this bakery has *you* here to do the health inspector's job," he says. "But can I have a dozen glazed donuts and a coffee?"

Oh. Yes. My job. At the bakery. Yes.

Julia wordlessly hands me the full donut box, and I give it to him along with a steaming cup of coffee. The handsome customer pays in cash and deposits twenty dollars in our tip jar. With a smile to me, he leaves, the bell tinkling as he does so.

"*Wow*," Julia gasps, fanning herself as I lean against the counter, my eyes wide. "That man was *sex on legs*."

I nod, unable to speak. I didn't think it was possible for someone to be *that* attractive, but was I ever wrong.

Suddenly, guilt gnaws in my stomach. How could I be thinking about this customer when I have a boyfriend? Sure, Mark is nice looking, but he pales in comparison to the handsome stranger.

"He seemed to like you, Alexis," Daniela mentions, having watched the whole interaction. "He was definitely flirting."

"He was *not*," I say firmly, feeling nauseous at the thought of inadvertently flirting with someone other than Mark. "He was just a customer making polite conversation with the person standing in the way of his donuts."

Daniela shares a look with Julia but doesn't try to argue with me.

Once my shift ends, I take the train back home. The Carters live right outside downtown Chicago, nestled in a neighborhood full of Cape Cod-style homes. I let myself into the empty house and hurry to the basement that is my room.

Dennis and Suzanne are at work, and I have no idea where Emma—my foster sister—is. I like it this way as I can get ready in my own time.

Looking in the mirror, I quickly fluff out my curly hair, huffing as an errant piece falls into my eye. Although Mark and I don't have plans that I know of, I'm going to surprise him at his apartment.

Putting on my sexiest dress, I apply some red lipstick and darken my eye makeup for a more smoldering look. Shivering, I grab a coat and put it on, hugging myself for warmth.

The Carters were nice enough to let me stay in their home, but once I turned eighteen and my social worker stopped visiting me, I was forced to move out of Emma's room and into the basement.

Even though the basement is cold, drafty, and small, I'm grateful I have my own space and don't have to worry about Emma stealing my clothes or hiding my blankets.

Slipping on my heels, I put Mark's gift in my bag. Even though Dennis and Suzanne take half of my income, I've still been able to scrimp and save enough to buy Mark a beautiful new watch with our anniversary date engraved on the back.

But I have an even *more* important gift to give him.

Myself.

My virginity has always been a touchy subject. Mark's touched me in more ways than I was comfortable with, but I've resisted. Call me old-fashioned, but I've always wanted my first time to be with someone I truly care about and will marry.

But since I *know* Mark is going to propose to me, I've decided this will be another present for him.

I can't *wait* to see his face.

I hope it doesn't hurt.

My face warms at the thought of Mark touching me intimately, and I squeeze my legs together as my heart pounds.

I *really* hope Mark will be gentle with me. Sometimes, he grabs me too hard or squeezes my arms or face too tightly. Those bruises are hard to explain away when I'm at work.

THE COLD WIND bites at my face and legs, and I shiver as I take the train to Mark's apartment. I really should have worn tights, but Mark likes it when I go bare legged.

I can feel the leers from other men, and I try to tuck my legs underneath my seat, but all it does is hike my dress up even more.

Mark picked this dress out for me and told me I had to buy it, even though I didn't want to. It was a *very* expensive dress and was more than I normally could afford.

But I bought it anyway because Mark said that's the type of dress he likes his woman to wear.

Honestly, the style reminded me more of what Emma would wear. My sister loves to wear tight, revealing clothes to show off her figure. I can understand why—Emma is a Pilates instructor and works out constantly. Her body is incredible.

"You meetin' someone, hot stuff?"

Hot breath touches my ear, and I instantly jerk away as a man sits close to me, eyeing me like I'm his last meal.

"Yes, actually." I sit up straighter, trying to appear confident and aloof even though I'm actually terrified. "I'm meeting my *boyfriend*."

The man laughs, which sets my teeth on edge. "I would never let my woman leave the house wearing something like that. Someone might get the wrong impression."

Something about his expression makes me believe he is getting the wrong impression of me. And that scares me.

Emma would have a sarcastic quip or witty comeback, but I say nothing, hoping the man gets the hint and leaves me alone.

Thankfully, I'm the next stop and I hurry off the train with a throng of other people, melting into the crowd.

I breathe a sigh of relief as I tighten my coat around me, wishing I had something to cover my legs.

No matter. I'll steal a pair of Mark's sweatpants in the morning.

All too soon, Mark's red brick apartment building comes into my view. I quickly hurry my pace, my feet throbbing as I totter about in my high heels.

My body starts to thaw as I head inside and step into the elevator. I relish the warmth of the heating even though the elevator smells faintly of weed.

I finger Mark's key as butterflies explode in my stomach at the thought of surprising him. He's going to be *so excited*.

So why do I feel like I'm going to my funeral? Shouldn't I be happy I'm going to lose my virginity?

I unlock his door and step inside the apartment.

Mark is nowhere to be found.

That's strange. His keys are on the counter.

A strange sound floats from Mark's bedroom, and I freeze. It sounds like a bed squeaking.

My heart pounds and my breathing becomes shallow. Moans float from his open door.

I know I should leave and tell myself that Mark had friends over who were taking advantage of Mark's kindness.

But I don't leave.

My feet feel like lead as I cross the length of the room to the door to see the source of the noise.

What I see makes me feel like I was just punched in the chest.

Mark is standing at the end of the bed, his bare ass facing the door, thrusting forward and backward, his hands gripping the hips of a woman crouched over the bed. Mark yanks the woman's hair and slaps her ass as the woman screams Mark's name in pleasure.

I know that voice.

It's Emma, my foster sister.

2

ALEXIS

The sickening realization washes over me like an icy wave. This was no dream, no horrible mistake. Mark's hands roam shamelessly over Emma's bare skin as she arches her back and moans.

A strangled cry escapes my lips before I can stop it. Mark and Emma's heads whip around in unison, faces shifting from ecstasy to... annoyance.

My eyes brim with tears and the pair become blurry. How could Mark *do* this to me? I've been nothing but loyal and loving to him for *five* years.

And Emma—my own *sister*.

"What the fuck are you doing here, Alexis?" Mark demands, his eyes narrowing in the way they always do when he gets angry with me.

I want to scream at him and tell him I'm here to surprise him for our *anniversary*, but I'm incapable of saying anything, only staring at them in horror.

Can they hear the sound of my heart breaking? I know I can.

"Well?" Mark demands as he pulls up his underwear and storms toward me. I tense as he approaches, expecting him to raise his fist. "Are you going to fucking *talk*?"

"I–I... it's our anniversary," I stammer out, my tongue feeling heavy and thick in my mouth.

Mark raises an eyebrow as Emma rolls over on the bed and laughs.

"Oh, this is *hilarious*," she says, leaning up on her elbows to smirk at me. I avert my eyes, not wanting to look at her naked form. "Mark, did you even remember today is your anniversary?"

"Nope," Mark says, his cold blue eyes never leaving my face.

I search his face, desperate to find *any* sort of regret, horror... *something* that will show he feels bad for what he's done.

But there's nothing. He looks at me like I'm *nothing*.

He scans me up and down. "You look like a slut, Alexis."

I gape at him. "Y–You told me to buy this dress—"

Emma laughs again. "Poor Alexis. You came here expecting Mark to take one look at you and finally stick his cock in your frigid vagina, right?" She twirls a piece of blonde hair around her finger. "How would it make you feel to know Mark and I have been fucking for the past five years?"

It makes me feel like I've been punched in the gut. Breathing has become much, *much* harder and the room feels like it's getting smaller.

"How could you do this to me, Emma?" I whisper. Emma's never been the kindest to me, but she's never been so outright cruel before. "I thought we were sisters."

Emma scoffs and rolls her eyes. "We are *not* sisters," she snaps. "I've hated you for years, ever since your disgusting ass came into my house." A sly smile spreads across her face, making Emma's pretty features seem almost grotesque.

"Did you really think Mark was in love with you this whole time?"

I can't breathe.

"You did! Bravo, baby. You've really played this well." She sits up. "Mark and I were already sleeping together when I introduced you two."

I struggle to process Emma's words. Emma watches me intently, her smile growing as she sees the pain written all over my face.

"Have you ever loved me, Mark?" I ask desperately, hoping Emma is just saying this to hurt me. In a perfect world, Mark would denounce Emma's words and tell me that he's been in love with me all this time.

But the truth is staring me in the face with Mark's silence.

He never loved me.

Suddenly, white hot anger courses through me. I've wasted five years of my life on this man, only to find out he's been two-timing me with my foster sister.

"We're over," I whisper through my tears. Mark cocks his head to the side.

"What did you say?"

"I said, we're done—"

"No, you stupid idiot. I heard you say that. What *I'm* saying is that you are not the one who gets to decide when this relationship ends. *I* do."

I shake my head, feeling surer of myself than I ever have. "You don't have a choice, Mark. It's my decision. I never want to see your cheating, lying, scumbag ass ever again—"

My head suddenly snaps back as pain explodes in my cheek. I fly through the air before landing on my back, the wind taken out of me.

Mark stands over me, fury on his face and his hand still in the air. "Don't you *ever*," he growls, "*ever* talk to me like that *again*."

I clutch the side of my stinging face as my ears ring.

Mark has never hit me before.

Physical abuse isn't unfamiliar to me. My previous foster family doled that out in spades, and the Carters utilized spanking as punishment. But I never expected to be hit by Mark.

He was supposed to be my safe person.

"You hit me," I whisper.

Mark rolls his eyes as Emma sidles up to him, her eyes darting between us. "No shit," he snaps. "How fucking stupid are you?"

Any anger I once felt has quickly disappeared. I know I should fight back, but I don't have it in me. I don't know if I have anything in me anymore.

Everything in my body is telling me to run, but I'm not good at listening to my instincts. When conflict unfolded, I normally didn't know how to react. Instead, I would freeze, my body icing over.

"Get out of here," Mark hisses, wrapping an arm around Emma's waist. "I'll deal with you later."

The malice in his voice promises retribution, and I suddenly unfreeze, scrambling up and fleeing. Tears track down my cheeks as I bite back a sob.

I barely remember the train ride home as my heartbreak distracts me. I just want to get home and hide in my bed.

My chest feels hollow, like someone carved out my heart and left an aching void. How could Mark *and* Emma betray me so callously? His anniversary present still sits in my bag, taunting me. While I was busy saving my money to buy him a thoughtful gift, he was fucking my foster sister.

And he didn't even remember our anniversary.

I never meant anything to him.

When I get home, Dennis and Suzanne are waiting for me in the kitchen. Although they've never treated me like a daughter, I at least hope they'll be the slightest bit compassionate about what I've just gone through.

"Alexis," Dennis says, frowning. "What happened to your face?"

I sniffle, wiping away mascara tracks from one side of my cheek. The side where Mark hit me is swollen and painful.

"Mark happened," I croak, fresh tears spilling down my face. "He–he hit me."

Dennis and Suzanne glance at each other, and for a brief moment, I think they're going to be horrified by Mark's behavior.

Instead, Suzanne scowls. "Well, what did you do to upset him?"

I startle, mouth agape. "W–what?"

"Don't play stupid, Alexis," Suzanne snaps. "Mark hit you for a reason. What did you do?"

How could they think this is *my* fault? I stare at them, unable to say a word.

Dennis slams his hand against the well-scrubbed wooden table. I flinch. "Dammit, Alexis! Answer the fucking question!"

"It's because Alexis *finally* figured out Mark and I have been sleeping together," Emma drawls, walking in the door with Mark behind her. "She tried to break up with him."

I truly expect Dennis and Suzanne to be upset by this news, maybe even yell at her.

What I'm *not* expecting is their next reaction.

"Mark!" Dennis yells. "How could you hit her in the face? Don't you realize how long it'll take for that to heal?"

It truly feels like I've just been punched in the stomach, the wind knocked out of me. Instead of being upset that Mark struck me, the Carters are angry that Mark struck me in a place that is hard to hide.

Mark shrugs, an arm slung around Emma. "She deserved it. She pissed me off."

"You knew that Emma and Mark were sleeping together?" I whisper, my body cold.

"Of course we knew," Suzanne bites out. "Mark has needs and Emma was willing to satisfy him, since *you* weren't. But this works out nicely, actually."

My brain is screaming at me to run, but my entire body feels like Jell-O and I can't move.

Mark nods, a twisted smile playing on his lips. "It really does, Suzanne."

"What are you talking about?" I whisper, my heart beating a staccato in my chest. My stomach churns as something inside me is telling me I'm about to hear something horrible.

Emma looks at her nails, bored. "We're going to sell you, stupid."

My brain seemingly short circuits and I find it hard to breathe.

"The Brotherhood will pay a lot of money for you, Alexis," Suzanne says soothingly, as if that'll make me feel better. "Just think of how much you'll be helping us."

"B–but I cook and clean—"

Dennis shakes his head. "That's not enough, Alexis. We have debts—lots of them. And The Brotherhood will pay a pretty penny for your virginity."

I suddenly lunge for the door, desperate to get out of here. The Carters and Mark have lost their minds. There's no way they can be serious, but I don't want to find out if they are.

"Oh, no, you don't!" Mark grabs me around my middle and backhands me as I fall to the ground. I cry out as my back collides painfully with the edge of the wall. Mark crouches down and grabs me by my hair so I'm forced to look into his eyes.

"You listen to me well, Alexis Hartley," he says venomously. "You have no choice in this matter. You *will* be sold to The Brotherhood, where they can do God knows what." He pulls on my hair harder, and I gasp, my eyes smarting.

"It's a good thing you've been such a frigid bitch," he taunts me. "Your virginity will fetch us a very, *very* high price." He glances at Dennis and Suzanne, who watch the situation with no emotion. "Where should I put her?"

"In the basement," Suzanne states. "And lock the door. We don't want her to get out before The Brotherhood gets here."

As Mark carries me, kicking and screaming, to the basement, I barely hear the lock click over the echo of my sobs.

"Let me out!" I scream as I bang on the door as hard as I can.

But it's no use. No one is going to come for me.

I'm all alone.

I curl up on the stairs, hiccupping. My face is throbbing from the force of my cries and from Mark's abuse.

But I don't know what hurts worse. The physical pain or the pain of knowing the Carters *and* Mark have never cared about me.

Have they been waiting until I turned twenty-one in order to implement their plan? Is that why Mark has been dating me for so long?

Was I just a means to an end?

But I have to get out of here. I can't wait for The Brotherhood—whoever they are—to come and get me.

The Carters wouldn't care if The Brotherhood then sold me to someone evil.

I look around the basement carefully. Even though this has been my room for the last three years, I've never really taken a close look at my surroundings. There has to be another means of escape.

There! How have I never seen it before? A grimy, small window is tucked in the upper right corner of the basement. Now, if I could somehow get up there and open it.

My dresser.

I nearly slip down the stairs as I run to seize my dresser and push it against the wall. With a grunt of exertion, I hoist myself up. I'm now at eye level with the window.

To my relief, the window has a rusty latch. Quickly sliding it open, I gasp as cold air slaps me in the face.

But I don't care. I'll take the cold as long as it means freedom.

Biting my lip, I thrust myself forward, squeezing my body through the narrow opening. I'm terrified that the Carters or Mark will decide to check on me and see me halfway out the window.

I wiggle my hips, scrabbling at the dirt and grass to hopefully provide me some stability. I fight back a cry as I pull myself forward, my heart pounding.

I can't afford for the Carters or Mark to find me. They'll throw me in a windowless room then with no means of escape.

"Come on, come on," I whisper. With one almighty push, I wiggle my hips through, scraping my bare thighs on the edge of the rusty window. I fall face first into the dirt.

But I'm out. I'm *free*. I scramble to my feet and run, trying to put as much distance between myself and the Carters.

I don't get very far before someone yanks me by my arm and pulls me to a hard, unforgiving chest. The cold metal of a gun presses against my temple, and I flinch.

This can't be happening, my mind screams over and over again.

"Don't you make one fucking sound," a voice growls in my ear. "If you run, you die."

3

DAMIAN

The pulsating beat of the music reverberates through the walls, the bass line thumping in sync with the lights that strobe in a dizzying array of colors. The dance floor is packed with writhing bodies, moving as one sweaty, undulating mass to the driving rhythm.

At the bar, people jostle for the bartenders' attention, shouting drink orders over the booming bass that seems to rattle my bones. Colorful liquids slosh into glasses, garnished with brightly hued fruit and tiny paper umbrellas.

The thumping beat can be heard all the way into the basement where I lean against the wall, my eyes fixed on a struggling, bloodied Invicta soldier tied to a rickety, wooden chair.

"I'm going to ask you again," I say in a bored tone, picking an invisible piece of lint off my shirt. "What is Invicta planning?"

The soldier spits a bloody gob of mucus at me, and Edo backhands him, the soldier's head snapping back from the force of his hit.

I sigh and remove myself from the wall, circling the Invicta soldier like a predator would their prey.

Although I have an air of nonchalance, I'm raging on the inside. This fucking asshole won't tell us *shit*.

In a recent gun fight against Invicta, one of my soldiers was captured. He was returned to us in pieces, which enraged me.

He was a goddamn good soldier.

This Invicta soldier was caught prowling around headquarters and was swiftly captured and brought to The Underground, where we do our best interrogations.

Normally, Edo's methods extract the best information from our prisoners, but this Invicta soldier won't fucking say a word.

The soldier laughs and smiles at me, showing off bloodstained teeth. "Invicta is always watching you, Damian Iacopelli," he taunts. "The Boss can't wait to finally eliminate you."

My hand curls into a fist.

Invicta's Don claims my father ordered a hit on his girlfriend and daughter fifteen years ago. As revenge, Bobby Shields had my father, mother, and sister killed.

We've been at war with Invicta ever since and it's been escalating in the last few years.

I grind my teeth together. I had nothing to do with my father's hit on Shields's woman and kid, and Shields got his revenge by killing my father, so what the *fuck* is his issue?

Invicta needs to let this fucking go, but Shields is hell-bent on destroying my gang so I have to fight back. It's what my father would have wanted.

Goddamn, Dad. Why the fuck did you eliminate Shields's girl and his brat?

But I can't let this fucking creature know he's annoyed me. Instead, I crouch down by the soldier and look him up and down. Blood runs in rivulets down his body from numerous knife wounds. His one eye is nearly swollen shut and his nose is crooked.

Pathetic.

I glance at my consigliere coolly as I stand up, brushing off my slacks. "Finish him."

Edo smiles with delight. "With pleasure."

The Invicta soldier's screams fill my ears as I leave the room, shutting the door behind me. Once I do, I hear nothing as the soundproof walls prevent anyone from hearing Edo torture the Invicta fuck.

"So, did he squeal?"

My sister, Natalia, leans against the wall outside the interrogation room, one leg bent beneath her and arms crossed.

I shake my head. "Not a fucking word."

Nat scowls and pushes away from the wall. "Goddammit. We can't keep losing men, Damian!"

"I know that!" I snap, running a hand through my hair. "What the fuck do you want me to do, Nat?"

"Something other than what you're currently doing, which is fucking ineffective!"

Before I can rip into my sister, the interrogation room door opens and Edo emerges, splattered in blood.

"Job's done," he says grimly, shutting the door behind him so I can't see what remains of the Invicta member.

Nat glares as Edo cleans off his bloody knife with a white cloth.

"Has the most recent shipment come in?" I ask Nat, wanting to change the subject before we rip each other to shreds.

The filthy look she shoots me indicates she knows what I'm doing and will only let it go for now. I expect nothing less from Nat.

"Yes," she says, tucking a lock of short, black hair behind her ears. "It's all been accounted for. The boys will be here in the next hour to pick it up."

I grunt and pull out my phone, thumbing through recent messages. Uncle Vinny wants to meet with me soon to talk about an important matter.

"How much are we supposed to make?"

"Five hundred thousand," Nat says evenly.

Edo whistles. "That's some good shit."

Nat shrugs. "It's a good batch."

I'm over this conversation. Stuffing my phone back into my pocket, I jerk my head at Edo.

"Let's go. We have matters to attend to at home. Nat, I imagine you'll be staying here to keep an eye on matters?"

Nat shoulders ahead of me. "Of course. I don't trust anyone else with the delivery."

I settle into the buttery soft leather seat, Edo beside me, as my driver closes the door with a solid thunk.

The plush cream leather molds around my body as I stretch out my legs, rolling my neck to try and release any lingering tension. Instead of relaxing, my body feels tense.

I can't stop thinking about fucking Invicta.

For the millionth time, I curse at my father for supposedly ordering the hit. I don't know why he would have done so as

Dad wasn't the type to randomly have people killed—*especially* kids.

As far as I knew, Dad and Invicta didn't have any beef when Shields's family was killed, so Shields claiming Dad ordered the hit baffles me. He has no fucking proof.

But I can't exactly ask my father why he supposedly did what he did considering he's fucking dead.

For as long as I live, I'll never forget the moment Uncle Vinny called me, frantic, telling me I had to get home *now*. I knew something terrible had happened, but I wasn't expecting my parents and baby sister to be executed.

Invicta has no fucking shame. No fucking morals.

Okay, maybe it's a bit rich of me to deride Invicta for not having morals considering I'm the Don of the Iacopelli Mafia, but there's a fucking code we live by.

And one of them is that we don't kill innocents, especially children.

What were you thinking, Dad? I wish you had told me.

I rub my temples as I look out the tinted windows, the city passing by in a blur of lights and towering skyscrapers.

Edo breaks the silence. "Invicta is getting bolder."

"I know," I snap. "I don't need to be reminded."

My phone buzzes, and I pull it out to see a text from Scarlett Rafa. I grimace and stuff it back into my pocket.

I don't have the energy to deal with Scarlett's bullshit right now.

"My concern is that Invicta and The Brotherhood will team up and try to overtake us," Edo continues.

I drum my fingers against the car door. "Mario hates Bobby," I say. "But I have noticed that The Brotherhood is encroaching on our territory. Maybe I need to meet with Mario and tell him to fuck off."

A ghost of a smile plays on Edo's lips. "I bet if you promise to marry Scarlett, he'll agree to whatever terms you want."

I grimace. "I'm not sticking my dick in crazy again."

Edo opens his mouth to respond, but it's cut off by the sound of tires squealing. Edo and I fly forward from the force, my face colliding painfully with the partition.

I hiss as the car jerks to a stop. "What the *fuck*, Jordan?" I roar to the driver, anger coursing through my veins. He'd better have a fucking good reason to pull that little stunt or I'll have Edo deal with him.

"Sir, I'm so sorry, but there's a situation," Jordan's panicky voice fills the back of the car. "There's a girl being held at gunpoint."

Mother*fucker*.

I seize the gun in the side pocket of the door and burst out of the car, Edo doing the same on the opposite side of me.

We're on a residential street full of shitty looking houses, and standing a few feet away is a man holding a terrified woman around the waist, a gun nestled to her temple.

The deafening staccato of automatic gunfire erupts, shattering the silence.

Edo and I dive behind the car as bullets whiz by in a deadly chorus. I snap a fresh magazine into the gun and chamber a round.

"It's Invicta!" I yell as bullets ricochet off my bulletproof car.

I risk a peek around the car's edge, the acrid scent of spent gunpowder thick in my nostrils. The Invicta soldier has his arm around the woman's throat, his gun pointed in our direction before he throws her to the ground. The woman's head hits the ground with an audible crack.

Edo and I glance at each other and Edo nods. Before I know it, Edo stands up and pitches forward, pulling the trigger. A storm of rounds chews through the soldier's body, flinging him backward and away from the girl as he tumbles lifelessly to the road.

I dart around the car, and Edo and I cautiously approach the soldier.

His leg twitches.

The sharp crack of my pistol pierces the air as I drill the Invicta soldier through the forehead.

For an eternal beat, all was still except the shrill ringing in my ears and the expanding crimson pool around the soldier's body. Edo and I heave identical sighs of relief.

"Nice work," I say to Edo, clapping him on the shoulder. He's always been my best shooter.

He grunts as he looks at the crumpled form of the woman the Invicta soldier was holding hostage.

"What do we do with her?" He jerks a thumb in her direction.

I approach the girl's lifeless form and study her. Long, curly brown hair is splayed against the road and her short, nearly indecent dress is hiked up to her upper thighs. One high heel dangles off her foot and the other is a few feet away.

Is she a hooker or something? She must be. Who the fuck wears clothes like that if you aren't selling yourself?

But then why would Invicta be holding her at gunpoint?

I take a closer look at her. She looks oddly familiar, but I can't place where I've seen her.

I don't normally bring home strays, but I know Invicta will be crawling around soon once they figure out there was a fight—and from the lights turning on in the nearby houses, it'll be soon—and I can't justify leaving this girl unconscious on the ground, especially in front of an Invicta gang member.

Nat's going to kill me for this.

I lift her limp body into my arms and head back to the car, sliding into the backseat. She's ridiculously light and her head lolls sideways, pressing into my chest.

"She's coming with us. We're in Invicta territory. She might know something."

4

ALEXIS

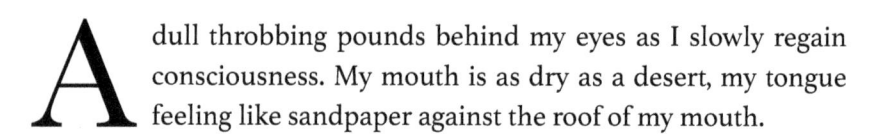

A dull throbbing pounds behind my eyes as I slowly regain consciousness. My mouth is as dry as a desert, my tongue feeling like sandpaper against the roof of my mouth.

I blink slowly, finally managing to crack my eyelids open a slit. Moonlight pours through white curtains, bathing an unfamiliar room in a soft glow. This isn't my room. My heart rate spikes as I take in my strange surroundings.

Cream colored walls with framed landscape photos. An ornate wooden dresser on one wall. Rumpled navy sheets tangled around my legs.

Panic seizes me as I struggle to figure out how I ended up here. I try to push myself upright, but a searing pain rips through my head, forcing me back onto the pillows with a muffled groan.

I'm still wearing that stupid dress and it's hiked all the way to my waist, exposing my ass. My cheeks burn. I hope that happened while I was unconscious in bed. I couldn't bear the thought of whoever rescued me seeing me in such an indecent state.

But, *where am I?*

Fragmented memories start stitching themselves back together. Emma and Mark having sex... the Carters wanting to sell me to some Brotherhood organization... being locked in the basement... escaping and being attacked as gunfire rang out. The feeling of someone pushing me before the ground swallowed me whole. Then blackness.

I swallow as I lift a leaden arm to cautiously probe at my head. There's a large, raised lump at the crown of my head. I hiss at the blossom of pain from the slightest touch.

Okay, so I have a head injury.

I must have been kidnapped after falling unconscious. I can't believe I've been abducted again, but this time, there's no Dennis Carter to save me.

Fear grips my chest as I struggle to stamp down my hysteria. I take deep breaths, trying to calm myself down. I need to look at this situation logically as soon as my muddled mind allows me to do so.

This can't be a kidnapping situation because I seem to be reasonably safe, tucked in a bed and by myself in a room.

But I need to get out of here. Wherever "here" is. Sucking in a sharp breath, I push myself upright, fighting back nausea as the room spins violently. My bare feet sink into the plush cream carpet, and I clutch the edge of the nightstand for support.

My eyes land on the door across the room. My first thought is to bolt through it and figure out the rest later. But what if I end up stumbling right into another dangerous situation? I nibble my lip anxiously as I debate my options.

With a resigned sigh, I realize I need more information before I can make any hasty decisions. Steadying myself, I start poking around the bedroom, keeping an ear pricked for any sounds beyond the door.

I rifle through the top drawers of the wooden dresser, freezing when my fingers brush against a woman's fitted shirt. So this is at least a woman's bedroom. Or at least a woman *lives* here. At least that's mildly reassuring. I withdraw my hand, frustrated that I am not able to unearth any other clues about whose room this is.

Muffled voices drift down the hallway outside the door. I hold my breath, ears straining.

"You have her locked in the guest room?" a female voice asks, dismay evident in her tone.

"Where else was I supposed to put her?" a male voice replies, sounding annoyed.

"A hospital! *Anywhere* but here!"

A beat of silence, then the male voice replies, "We can't take her to a fucking hospital, Nat. I couldn't leave her there. She would have been killed. Or worse."

There's harsh laughter. "Oh, so now you're playing the hero, Damian? Good job. You got your brownie points. Now get her out of here."

"Nat's right, Damian," a third voice states, the tone gruff. "Dump her at the hospital. From that nasty lump on her head, she'll probably be in a concussion for a while and won't ever know she was here."

"No, I think she'll stay right here."

I flinch as I hear something slam against the wall. "Why the *fuck* are you being so obtuse?" the woman snarls.

"We know nothing about her and why she was being held by the Invicta soldier. We should question her first before I decide what to do with her."

"That's stupid, Damian," says the third voice.

There's a heavy pause, and even I take a step back at the venom in the second man's voice. "*What* did you call me?"

"Don't apologize, Edo," the woman says sharply. "He's right, Damian. Ditch the bitch."

"I'll be the judge of that," the second voice retorts.

Heavy footsteps begin approaching the door, unhurried but purposeful. My throat grows dry as the sound grows nearer. I glance around wildly, looking for any weapon I can use to protect myself. I do a double-take as I notice a wooden baseball bat leaning against the wall by the window.

I lunge for the bat just as the door handle slowly turns and opens. Clutching it in my arms, I raise it above my head, my hands shaking.

In the doorway stand two men and a woman. The woman is striking with shoulder-length black hair and bangs framing large brown eyes that are currently narrowed in my direction. Standing next to her is an imposing, incredibly tall man with a thick, tree-trunk neck and shoulders so broad they seem to span the entire doorway. His massive chest strains against the seams of his white button-up shirt, seemingly ready to burst the fibers at any moment.

But it's the man standing in front of the others that makes my heart skip a beat.

It's the handsome man from the bakery. But he looks far scarier now with the scowl on his face, his dark eyes fixed on me.

"Put the bat down," he orders, his voice a rich baritone.

I shake my head, refusing to listen. I'm not sure what's gotten into me as I would have had no problem doing so if Mark or the Carters asked me.

"Put. It. Down," the man snaps, taking one menacing step toward me.

I only grip the bat tighter, my body starting to shake from terror. I've never been the athletic type, but it wouldn't be that difficult to swing the bat at him. Although I'm not sure what to do about the two people still standing at the door. The huge man looks like he could eat me for breakfast, and I'm not about to underestimate the woman.

In the blink of an eye, the handsome man rushes forward, snatches the bat from me, and breaks it clean across his muscular knee. I squeak in fear, my feet frozen to the ground.

"What's your name?" he asks, tossing the baseball bat pieces away from him.

"Where am I?" I whisper.

"No," the handsome man says, his gaze unwavering and intense. "That's not how this is going to work. I ask a question and you answer it. Let's start again. What is your name?"

I swallow hard, my throat constricting with fear. Every instinct is telling me to remain silent, to guard what little privacy I have left.

"I don't want to say," I reply, my voice meek and small.

In a flash, the man is in my face, making me flinch. "That's not an option," he growls. "You don't get to decide what information you share."

My heart pounds in my chest as he leans closer, his face mere inches from mine. I can smell the mint of his breath, and can see the anger in his eyes.

"Now," he says, his voice dangerously low. "Your name."

I open my mouth, but no words come out. Fear has rendered me mute, paralyzed by the threat of his escalating aggression. This is not the same man who tipped Daniela, Julia, and I twenty dollars earlier today.

The man's jaw tightens, and he grabs my arms in a vise-like grip. I whimper involuntarily as his fingers dig into my flesh.

"Damian," the man in the doorway says, his voice full of warning, but the handsome man—Damian—ignores him.

"I'm not going to ask you again," he hisses. "Give me your fucking *name*."

Tears sting my eyes. "A–Alexis," I stammer out, my voice trembling. "My name is Alexis."

Damian releases his grip, a satisfied smirk spreading across his handsome face. "See?" he says mockingly. "That wasn't so hard, was it?"

I say nothing, my body trembling with a potent mixture of fear and shame. I have surrendered my identity to this stranger, and at this moment, I feel powerless.

"I'm Damian. And to answer *your* question, you're at my house. Now that those pleasantries are done, what were you doing with an Invicta soldier?"

Who?

My confusion must be evident on my face because Damian rolls his eyes. "You were held at gunpoint earlier," he says. "By an Invicta gang member. Why was he after you?"

"I–I don't know," I whisper, still scared from Damian's question about my name. I rub my arms self-consciously, painfully aware of the dress I'm wearing. Shame burns at my cheeks and I struggle to hold back tears.

Damian cocks his head to the side, dark eyes studying me. "You don't know?" he repeats.

I shake my head furiously, ignoring the wave of pain from doing so. "No."

He circles me, like a predator stalking its prey. "See, I don't believe that, *Alexis*. You mean to tell me you were just in the wrong place at the wrong time in a neighborhood run by Invicta?" He scoffs, pausing and shaking his head. "Can you see why I don't believe you?"

I don't even know what he's talking about. I don't know who Invicta is and I don't understand what he means when he says the neighborhood is 'run by Invicta'.

"Do you know The Brotherhood?"

I stiffen. Mark indicated that he was planning on selling me to them, but I know next to nothing about them other than their name. "No, I don't."

"So." Damian resumes his circling. "Either you're lying to me—which I highly advise you don't do—or you're a hooker and it was a date gone wrong." He glances at my dress, his eyes lingering on my bare legs.

I gape at him. White-hot anger suddenly courses through me. Before I can stop myself, my open palm connects with Damian's cheek in a resounding slap. "I am *not* a prostitute!" I nearly shriek. "How *dare* you!"

He stumbles back, and when he looks up at me, there's anger flashing in those dark eyes of his that promise retribution.

"Damian!" the woman calls out urgently, seeing the severity of this situation.

I shrink back, my impulsive act suddenly weighing heavily on me. What was I thinking, assaulting this stranger like that? Especially a stranger who has me in his house and has enough strength to break a baseball bat in half?

Damian turns to the door where the woman and man are. "Leave us," he says dangerously.

"But—"

"*Now.*"

The two exchange looks, and I want to shout for them to please stay, but I'm incapable of doing so. Instead, I watch helplessly as the woman and man close the door, their footsteps fading away.

Damian whirls around toward me, a hand raised in the air. The scene is all too familiar to me, and I flinch, my heart pounding.

"P–Please, don't hit me," I plead, tears springing to my eyes. "I'm so sorry. I didn't mean to hit you. It was an accident. I—"

Damian pauses, his hand still in the air, a mixture of anger and confusion on his face. "Hit you? I wasn't about to hit you!"

Staring at him warily, I gesture to his upraised hand. He tracks my movement, and I can see realization wash over him. His tense shoulders loosen and he lowers his hand to his side.

Relief pours through me as I realize I'm not about to be hit again. I close my eyes and breathe out a sigh.

When I open my eyes again, there's a different look on Damian's face as he studies me. It's then that I realize he's staring at the bruise on my cheek from Mark's initial hit.

"Where did you get that?" Damian asks, his voice much gentler than I'm used to.

My mouth dries and I flinch as Damian takes another step toward me. He holds his hands up in surrender.

"I'm not going to hurt you."

"I don't know you," I whisper, backing away from him.

"You're Alexis and I'm Damian," he points out. "See? Now we know each other."

"That's not how this works," I say as I wrap my arms around myself. Damian's eyes fall on the bruises on my arms and his eyes narrow.

"Look, it's clear you're injured, and pretty badly at that," Damian says. "I just want to make sure you're okay."

His personality change is about to give me whiplash. One moment, he's demanding to know my name and breaking a baseball bat, and the other, he's trying to figure out how I'm doing.

"Then why don't you take me to the hospital, like your friends suggested?"

A dark look crosses his face, and I immediately regret my words. He didn't want me to overhear his conversation and I just sold myself out.

"I–I—"

"Can I look at your injuries?" Damian asks again, the tension leaving his body.

Biting my lip, I wrestle with my thoughts. He's a walking contradiction. Damian's a stranger, but I can tell he's being sincere about my injuries. He nearly assaulted me when I wouldn't tell him my name, but he also rescued me from being kidnapped. He can break a baseball bat, but he also tips food workers twenty dollars.

My own feelings surprise me. I feel *grateful* to this strange man for not leaving me on the streets where I probably would have been found by Mark or the Carters.

Is this Stockholm Syndrome?

"Well?" Damian presses.

I nod jerkily, slowly letting my arms fall back to my sides. "Okay," I whisper.

As Damian closes the distance between us, I feel my stomach drop in the same way it did on roller coaster rides. His cologne envelopes me in what feels like a warm hug, and my stomach twists in nerves.

His fingers are light as they touch my face, and my eyes flutter closed. I hiss as he pokes at a particularly tender spot on my cheek, but I also feel warmth and fire, too.

"Who hurt you?" Damian asks, his voice low. "These bruises aren't from Invicta." His hands slide down my face. "I'm going to turn you around to check out your back."

"Okay," I whisper again.

I feel intensely vulnerable, but also, somehow comfortable. This makes no sense. Mark never made me feel this way.

Damian's hands are warm as they press against my back. I flinch at a rush of pain on my left side.

"You have a huge bruise by your ribs," Damian says, his hands stilling at that spot. "That's also *not* from the Invicta soldier. Looks like you were thrown around. I'm going to ask you one more time. Who hurt you?"

Goosebumps erupt along my skin, my stomach swirling with a warmth that trails further down my body, a tingling wetness I'm not accustomed to. It's an uncomfortable feeling, so I step away from Damian's magnetic pull.

I don't want to tell Damian who it is, but I don't think he will allow me to evade the question.

5

DAMIAN

This Alexis girl is driving me fucking insane. I can't figure her out.

One moment, she's trembling and meek as a lamb. The next, she's slapping me across the face for calling her a hooker.

She is frightened of me—that much I can tell from her dilated pupils and her elevated heart rate, but she also stubbornly refuses to tell me *anything* important.

She only responds through threats of violence. She claims to not know anything, especially about Invicta.

And more maddeningly, she won't fucking tell me who gave her these bruises and injuries.

Alexis shivers as she wraps her arms around herself, her already short dress riding up higher so I can nearly see her ass. Her curly hair sways, and it takes everything in me to not wrap a ringlet around my finger.

Can she blame me for thinking she was a hooker? Who the fuck wears dresses like that if they aren't looking for a John?

But why the fuck was she being held at gunpoint by Invicta? It doesn't make any sense. Invicta deals in weapons trading. They aren't about human trafficking like The Brotherhood is. No, there's something else that Alexis isn't telling me, and it's pissing me off.

"So you're not going to tell me who hurt you?" I ask, taking a step toward her.

She shakes her head. "You'll want to hurt them."

Probably, but she doesn't need to know that. I may be a lot of things—Don of the Iacopelli Crime Family, murderer, drug dealer, and a general asshole—but I don't hit women. My mother raised me better than that, and Nat would actually kill me.

"Why are you protecting them?" Another step forward. Her eyes widen at my close proximity, and I can see the flecks of gold in her hazel eyes and her long, black eyelashes. A light dusting of freckles covers the bridge of her nose and she bites her plump, pink lip.

Alexis turns her head away from me, and I scowl, irritation coursing through me.

Who the fuck does she think she is by refusing to answer any of my questions?

Placing one finger under her chin, I turn her head back toward me, forcing her to look me in the eyes.

"Answer my question," I growl. Satisfaction rises in me as Alexis's breathing hikes and she worries her fingers. Good. She should be nervous.

"Please," she whispers, and I nearly snort. Does she really think that's going to work on me?

Her tongue darts out of her mouth to wet her lips, and I can't help but follow that movement, watching as her tongue slides across the seam of her mouth.

I can feel my cock hardening, but I refuse to listen to it. This girl is an enigma, and I'm determined to find out more about her.

"You're making this harder than it needs to be," I murmur, my eyes locked on hers. "Tell me who hurt you."

My hands slip down to her waist and rest at her hips. She gasps and tears her gaze away from me to look down.

Well, that's interesting.

I lean my face closer to hers, my nose skimming her neck. God, her skin is *so soft*. Her body trembles, and she gulps at my close proximity.

Well, if I wasn't convinced she wasn't a hooker, her reactions would have changed my mind. She is too skittish, acting like an animal ready to book at a moment's notice.

Is she a virgin?

The thought shocks me and thrills me at the same time. Even though I have *no* plans to do anything to this Alexis girl, I do imagine dumping her back where she came from and letting her significant other know I took her virginity.

But the bruises tear me away from my reverie, and it's like a bucket of cold water has been poured over my head.

Before I can even allow myself to fantasize further, I need to figure out a few things. One: who gave her these bruises and why. Two: why was Invicta holding her at gunpoint? Three: Do I really want to put myself in the middle of this?

Reluctantly, I pull myself away, resisting Alexis's siren call. I make a show of pulling out my phone and texting Nat.

Damian*: Come back. I need you.*

Alexis seemed to be just as affected as me, and I can see her release a breath she was clearly holding.

I smirk. Good.

The door opens a few seconds later, and Nat appears, frowning at us.

"On time as always, Nat," I say, picking an invisible fleck off my clothes. "Take Alexis to a guest room and lock the door."

Alexis's horrified face nearly makes me laugh. Serves her fucking right for not telling me a goddamn thing.

"But—"

"But, *nothing*. Until I figure out who you are and what to do with you, you aren't going anywhere."

~

I STRIDE into a dimly lit room in the back of The Underground, my expensive suit a contrast to the risqué clothing worn by the clubbers. Edo flanks me closely as I approach the table where my capos are seated.

"What've we got?" I ask, sitting down and snapping my fingers for a scotch. It's immediately placed before me, and I take a sip, savoring the burn of the alcohol as it makes its way down my throat.

Paulie, my oldest capo, slides an envelope toward me. "The shipment came in today from Montreal. Product looks good."

I open the envelope and examine the photos inside, nodding in satisfaction at the bricks of white powder. "Any hassles at the border?"

"Nah, our guys greased the right palms," Paulie says with a grin, revealing a gold tooth. "Feds didn't bat an eye."

"Good, good," I say, closing the envelope and handing it to Edo, who places it in the inside pocket of his suit jacket. "What else?"

This time Nicky, the youngest capo, speaks up. "Heard rumblings that the Colombos are sniffing around our action down on State Street. Might need to remind them of the boundaries."

A predatory smile crosses my lips. The Colombos have been a thorn in my side for a while. The Don defected from The Brotherhood—and somehow didn't end up killed—and created his own Mafia. They've been trying to get a foothold in my territory for a while now.

"Have Buddy and Luciano pay them a visit. Bust up a few kneecaps if needed to get the message across."

The capos nod, knowing my methods are harsh but effective. I drain the rest of my scotch and stand up. "I'm outta here. You guys know what to do."

Edo and I make our way to the secluded VIP lounge where a cocktail waitress in a skimpy outfit materializes and brings over two more glasses of scotch. The pulsating beats of techno music vibrate through the air.

I smile viciously as I settle myself in my seat. This is my palace of vice and sin, and I'm the king.

My massive bodyguards stand by the doors, their shaved heads and bulky frames reminding anyone who passes by to not fuck with them.

Edo touches his ear—a clear signal that he's receiving a message from his earpiece—and leans in toward me.

"Giorgio says Vinny's here with Mario Rafa. They want to speak to you."

I wave an irritable hand, watching scantily clad-dancers writhe to the music. "Bring them up."

Uncle Vinny is my father's brother and was once the underboss for the Iacopellis. After my father's death, there was a power struggle as Uncle Vinny thought it was his right to claim the Don position.

But that position was *mine*. There was a brief skirmish where I brutally put down any of Uncle Vinny's supporters. After that, Uncle Vinny conceded. Nat tried to convince me to have Uncle Vinny killed anyway, but I declined. Maybe it was stupid familial loyalty, but I couldn't have the last ties to my father's family murdered.

So Uncle Vinny has remained on the outskirts of the family and will occasionally be a voice of reason when Nat and Edo haven't convinced me otherwise.

But Mario Rafa—*ugh*.

The Iacopellis and The Brotherhood have a strained relationship. We were once close allies, as I had been engaged to Mario's daughter, Scarlett.

Scarlett. She is as beautiful as she is dangerous. Porcelain skin and big, blue eyes belie the venom lying in wait behind that angelic façade. I fell into her trap once upon a time, only seeing her outward beauty and refined elegance.

We had been in the middle of planning our wedding when Scarlett asked me to do something reprehensible. Enraged after being cut off and given the middle finger while driving, Scarlett hunted down the man responsible for this slight and found that he was a married father of two. Her plan? For me to have my men shoot up the driver's son's school playground as revenge.

I'm a man of principle and we *don't* kill children. Children are innocents, and I do not buy into the bullshit 'sins of the father' adage. So I refused. Scarlett broke up with me shortly after that, claiming I didn't have the "drive" or "commitment" to get things done.

She ended up having the playground shot up anyway, and the driver's son was killed, much to her satisfaction.

Although our relationship is strained, I *do* respect Mario Rafa. He's a vestige of the old guard, a link to the fading days of the Sicilian *omertà*. Mario does his best to restrain Scarlett's more psychotic tendencies, but—as evidenced by the schoolyard massacre—he does turn a blind eye to them.

I get it. Sometimes it's easier to just let Scarlett do whatever she wants instead of dealing with her consequences.

My bodyguards part and allow my guests entry.

"Uncle Vinny," I say, refusing to stand up. "Mario. I trust we're all keeping good health?"

The two men murmur similar pleasantries. I snap my fingers, and two more comfortable chairs are brought forward.

I study Mario as he takes a seat. He looks every inch of the classic Mob Boss straight out of another era. Now in his early seventies, his once-muscular frame has thickened with age, the finely tailored suit straining slightly against his barreled chest. His snow white hair is trimmed in a severe military style, slicked back from his lined face. Despite his age, Mario's eyes still radiate an intense, cunning intelligence.

"I'll get right to it," Uncle Vinny says, plucking up a Cuban cigar and lighting it up. A cloud of blue smoke wafts toward the ceiling. "Mario needs help finding someone."

I raise an eyebrow and turn my glance toward Mario. "Is this true?"

Mario slides a manila envelope toward me. I glance at Edo, who nods and takes the envelope and opens it to reveal a folded up piece of paper and several photographs.

Edo furrows his brow as he hands me the paper, and I skim the contents. It looks like a contract between The Brotherhood and some man named Mark Abernathy.

"What am I looking at?"

Mario leans forward. "Mark Abernathy is our latest recruit," he says, his voice gravelly. "In order to show his loyalty to The Brotherhood and to initiate him as a full member, Mark promised us a young virgin. We fronted him a lot of money in order to ensure he brings her to us."

While my face remains cool and impassive, I internally grimace. The Brotherhood is one of the richest crime families in the Chicago area *because* of their proclivities in human trafficking. It's a distasteful, nasty business and an area I refuse to get into.

Trafficking drugs? Sure. My customers choose to pay money to get high. Trafficking humans? Absolutely not. There's no choice, no agency in the matter for those girls.

"Your first mistake was giving Mark the money before he gave you the goods," I say, tossing the contract down.

Mario's eyes narrow. "You got a problem with how I run my business, Damian?"

I shrug. "Maybe I do."

Uncle Vinny holds up a placating hand. "Easy, fellas. Let's not let tempers get out of hand here. We're all friends."

I want to scoff. Yeah, friends indeed. Rule number one in the Mafia world. You don't have friends. You merely have uneasy truces, and one small spark will reignite a blaze of violence.

"Besides," Uncle Vinny says. "I'm sure Damian didn't mean any disrespect. It's all a little misunderstanding."

I scowl at having to acquiesce, but I understand the game we're playing here. "Yeah, just a little misunderstanding, Mario. It won't happen again."

Mario studies me. "See that it doesn't."

What I wouldn't do to put a bullet through his head right now. But instead of doing so, I wave a hand. "Continue."

"Mark locked the girl up as apparently, the idiot told her what the plan was. He called us so we could come get our artifact. By the time we showed up, the girl had escaped."

I raise an eyebrow. "How did she escape?"

"A window in the basement," Mario spits out. "The idiot didn't bother securing the perimeter."

And this is someone you're willing to let enter your organization? The retort is on the tip of my tongue, but I hold it back. It's clear that Mario is already on edge.

"Mario needs your help in finding this girl," Vinny cuts in, fingers curling around the armrests of his chair. "The Iacopellis have always been excellent in tracking people down."

True, we are, but none of this makes sense. Why is Mario coming to me?

"Why haven't you had Scarlett hunt her down?"

Mario scowls, eyes flashing. "I want this girl brought back alive, not dead," he snaps.

Fair point. I hold my hand out to Edo, and he wordlessly hands me the stack of photographs. "What's in it for me?" I ask casually as I start to flip through the photos. "This will be a lot of manpower, Mario. It's costly."

"If you find this girl and bring her back alive, you'll get a ten percent cut of her sale."

"Thirty," I shoot back.

"Twenty," Mario retorts.

"Twenty-five."

"Deal." We shake hands, preferring to handle situations like these with a gentleman's agreement.

Savage Devotion

"This girl must be important if you're coming to me," I say idly, looking at a picture of a shitty house and a bakery.

Mario shifts in his seat. "Very important. She will be our highest priced artifact."

I raise a brow as I flip to another photo. A girl stands in profile, unaware that she's being photographed. Her long, curly brown hair is clipped back, showcasing a slender neck.

She looks familiar.

"Any reason?" I ask.

Uncle Vinny cuts in. "Unimportant. She just needs to be found as soon as possible."

"Should be easy. The girl's running scared. She'll make mistakes. Tell me—what is her name?" I flip to another photo. This time, the girl is looking straight ahead. Her hair cascades down her back, and her hazel eyes are wide as she stares at something in the distance.

My heart drops to my feet. I now know why this girl looks so familiar.

It's because she's currently locked up at my house.

"Her name is Alexis," Mario says. "Alexis Hartley."

6

ALEXIS

I do my best to prevent this woman—Nat, I think—from dragging me to another room, but she's much stronger than me and basically carries me to my new prison like I'm a sack of flour.

She dumps me unceremoniously on the carpet and stalks toward the door.

"Please don't lock me in here," I beg. "Please let me go. I won't tell anyone. I swear."

Nat pauses at the doorway and turns her head slightly. "You don't get to leave until the Don says you can. I'll be back later with some food."

With that, she shuts the door. I can hear a click as the lock turns into place, and then Nat's footsteps fade away.

Rushing to the door, I pound on it, my knuckles becoming raw and red. "Somebody help me!" I scream. "Please! Let me out!"

Only silence answers my pleas.

I curl up into a little ball, fighting back the terror that's threatening to claw its way out of me. I had managed to escape one captor, only to fall into the arms of another.

But I *had* gotten out of the Carter home. Which means I can get out of here, too.

Giving up on the door, I spin around and survey the room. It's an exact replica of the previous room I was in, just flip-flopped. Plush sheets adorn the four-poster bed, and to the left of the bedroom is a door that leads to a bathroom.

Squaring my shoulders, I rush to the picture window overlooking the bed. Relief pours through me as I'm able to open it, cold air slapping me in the face.

I look down to see that I'm at least on the second floor. Escaping from here wouldn't be as easy as it was at the Carter house. I can't jump without seriously hurting myself.

What to do?

My eyes land on the blankets on the bed, and an idea comes to me. If I knot enough sheets, towels, and blankets together, I should be able to make a makeshift rope long enough to climb down.

I dart around the bedroom, gathering up any cloth I can find—the sheets off the bed, fluffy towels from the bathroom, and an extra blanket located in the bottom drawer of the dresser.

My heart pounds in my ears as I weave the materials into a makeshift rope, glancing over my shoulder at the locked door. Nat had said she would be back with food, but she didn't say *when*.

I'm going to have to work quickly.

I lay two sheets down—marveling at how soft they are—and tie the corners together in a tight knot. I repeat this process with each set of corners, my makeshift rope growing longer and longer.

As I work, my mind can't help but stray to Damian.

He frightens me, but I'm also strangely attracted to him. I don't understand *how* I can be, considering he just took me captive.

But he *did* save me from the person with a gun. He could have just left me in the streets for Mark or the Carters to find. But he didn't. Even if his intentions weren't great, he still brought me to safety.

At least here, I don't have to worry about being sold like cattle. At least I don't think I have to.

I pause my weaving, shivering, although I'm not sure if it's from the cold air coming through the open window.

I can't believe I'm actually considering this place—Damian's *home*—to be safe. For all I know, he could have some dungeon that he plans to lock me into. Or he could have me killed.

But anything would be better than staying with the Carters and being sold to The Brotherhood. I shiver again, feeling nausea rise up in me. It's always been evident that the Carters never truly liked me and they always treated me like a second-class citizen. I was the outsider looking in. My clothes were hand-me-downs from Emma, and Emma always got the bigger portions of food, the better toys. Emma received the fancy vacations while I stayed home. The only time the Carters ever treated me well was when they knew my social worker would be coming for her quarterly visit.

Suzanne always made it crystal clear through her cold indifference and neglectful behavior that I was a burden she resented, and Dennis was too cowed and apathetic to intervene or even show me an ounce of warmth or kindness. So, why do they hate me so much? If they never wanted a second child, why did they rescue me from my would-be kidnappers? And what have I ever done to Emma? Is it because she viewed me as an intruder, a threat to her parents' love and attention?

And through it all, I have done nothing wrong to provoke their dislike that I can comprehend. I busted my ass with chores, got good grades in school, and stayed out of trouble. I was always polite and helpful, hoping against hope that if I just tried hard enough, worked hard enough, proved my worth—maybe then, the Carters would finally accept me. Maybe then, I could have the family I so desperately craved.

Tears burn my eyes. What is so fundamentally wrong or unlovable about me? Why did the Carters hate me so viscerally when I had done everything to be the perfect, grateful foster daughter? Why would they betray me in the worst way possible by trying to sell me to the highest bidder?

I don't understand. Maybe I never will.

It's times like these when I miss my mom so much it feels like a physical ache in my chest. Although I can barely remember what she looked like, I can still remember the way her hands felt as she stroked my hair, the smell of her perfume as I snuggled into her neck, and the warmth of her body as she hugged me.

She loved me unconditionally, and I never felt like a burden or felt alone when with her. When things used to be really bad, I would dream that my mother would knock on the door, ready to take me home to a place where I was safe and wanted.

Sniffling, I stand up, holding my knotted rope in my hands. I can't focus on the past. Right now, my only hope is that this rope is long enough.

Throwing the rope out the window, I watch as it unfurls into the darkness. To my dismay, the rope dangles about ten feet off the ground. I curse under my breath and rush to the dresser. Rifling through each drawer, I triumphantly pull out another top sheet. I rapidly incorporate the sheet into my improvised rope, weaving the ends through the gaps in the sheet knot.

I stretch the rope taut. It looks precarious, like one good stiff wind will untie the knots, but it'll have to do. I have to trust that my knots are tight enough.

Footsteps echo down the hall, and I freeze, my heart thundering in my chest. Even if I could hide the rope, the stripped bed, empty bathroom, and open dresser drawers speak to my deceit. I can barely breathe as I hear the footsteps get louder before growing fainter as the person in the hall walks away.

I release my breath, knees trembling as I lean against the mattress. That was too close. I need to get out of here *now*.

I quickly tie one end of the rope to the solid wooden column closest to the window, securing it as tightly as I can. Giving it a firm tug to test its strength, I move to the window and look down.

Although I've never had a fear of heights, the realization of what I'm about to do hits me like a ton of bricks and my vision suddenly gets woozy. With a deep, shuddering breath, I throw the rope out the window and swing a leg over the windowsill.

The door suddenly opens, and Damian walks into the room.

I freeze, my heart pounding in my ears.

Too late. I'd taken too long.

Damian blinks at me, as if not believing what he's seeing. His eyes scan the bedroom, taking in the stripped bed and me perched on the window sill. His face screws up with rage.

"Going somewhere?" Damian asks, taking a menacing step into the room.

I open my mouth, but no words come out. I can only cling to the window frame, trembling, as he advances.

In a blind panic, I fling my other leg over the ledge, desperately scrambling for purchase on the makeshift rope. But Damian moves with startling speed, closing the distance in four strides. He closes his hands on my wrists, forcefully wrenching me back into the bedroom.

I fall onto the mattress, gasping as the air leaves my body. Before I can take another breath, I'm pinned against the wall, Damian's body pressed against mine to ensure I can't escape, my arms up by my head, his hands wrapped around my wrists.

"Are you *fucking* kidding me?" Damian roars, his face mere inches from mine. "Did you really think you could escape me?"

I should be terrified by his proximity and anger, but I find myself overwhelmed by my attraction to him. It doesn't help that he looks unbelievably handsome right now. The suit he's wearing is undeniably expensive and fits him like a glove, hugging his broad shoulders and tapering down to accent his narrow hips and waist.

"Answer my *fucking* question, *Alexis*," he hisses into my ear, causing me to shiver. Goosebumps erupt onto my flesh.

"Yes, I thought I could escape," I whisper, my head tilted back to expose my throat.

Damian growls, and goddamn, the sound is so unbelievably *sexy*. "I should tie you up to the bed using that fucking rope ladder of yours."

Why does that thrill me so much? My cheeks grow hot as unrequested thoughts of what Damian could do to me while I am tied up flicker through my mind.

Even in Damian's rage and anger, I notice he's careful not to aggravate any of the injuries Mark left. Although I'm pressed against the wall, my back doesn't hurt and he's taking care to not touch my bruised cheek.

He pulls back slightly, his smoldering gaze locking onto mine, and all coherent thoughts sputter to a halt.

"Are you going to run again?" he asks, his voice a whispered caress.

I shake my head. "N–No."

What if I did run? Would he catch me? What would he do to me? My pulse quickens at the thought as the damp heat pooling between my thighs becomes a visceral, instant ache. I want to cross my legs and squirm, but I don't want to draw attention to my arousal.

Damian steps back just slightly and lets go of my wrists, watching as they fall limply to my sides. His eyes never leave mine as he shrugs off his suit jacket and tosses it onto the bed. My jaw nearly drops as I watch his hands work at his collar, stripping off his silk tie with one easy pull before undoing the top button of his crisp white shirt.

That tantalizing glimpse of tanned, taut skin and the promise of lean muscle beneath sends an electric jolt of pure yearning zinging through my veins.

This is worse than torture. My body is hyper-aware of his presence. Who cares if he's a member of the Mafia? Who cares that he's probably murdered and destroyed countless lives? All rational thought has left me, leaving me with an overwhelming need for *him*.

Damian's gaze slowly rakes over me, leaving a scorching trail in its wake, and I can't deny the dizzying effect of being pinned under that intense stare. Those intense eyes miss nothing, taking in every curve, every breath, and every emotion probably playing across my face.

He leans in. "Where did you learn to tie a rope like that?" he growls against the hammering pulse of my throat, his stubble deliciously rough against my oversensitive skin.

I swallow, my core clenching again with wanting. "I–I was taught a long time ago," I whisper.

"By whom?"

I'm surprised I even remember my name at this point. "Some man I worked with. He was an old Navy guy."

Damian moves in closer again, and his body is mere inches from mine. I fight the moan trying to work its way out of my body, resisting the urge to close my eyes and tip my head back. I can feel his warm breath on my face and the smell of his cologne as he leans in. His lips are so tantalizingly close, I think he's about to kiss me.

My heart pounds in anticipation, my lips parting slightly as I angle my head. But instead of kissing me, Damian pauses, his face hovering near mine.

"You haven't been honest with me, Alexis *Hartley*," he hisses. "Why the *fuck* does The Brotherhood want you so badly?"

7

DAMIAN

This girl is a goddamn succubus.

The rage I felt when I looked at Alexis's face in the photograph was indescribable. My jaw was clenched so tightly, it felt like my teeth would shatter. Words failed me in that moment, and coherent thoughts and the ability to articulate went out the window. It was an anger so intense and overwhelming, it transcended the ability to describe it with language.

She fucking *lied* to me. I asked her if she knew about The Brotherhood, and she looked me in the face and *lied*.

Edo could tell how angry I was because he immediately took over the conversation with Uncle Vinny and Mario, leaving me to stew. She fucking played me. And you don't fuck with Damian Iacopelli and get away with it.

On our way back to the mansion, I ordered Edo and Nat to stay the fuck away from Alexis's room as I was going to personally deal with her.

She wasn't going to get away with lying to me. I can't believe I fell for that innocent doe-eyed look of hers as she insisted she had no idea who The Brotherhood was.

Mario Rafa doesn't ask for help if the person he's looking for isn't important. So there's either two possibilities. Either Alexis is a colossal idiot or she's lying to me.

And it's more likely that she's lying to me.

Well, she's going to fucking learn you don't lie to me. I'm the Don of the Iacopellis for a reason, and I *am* going to get my answers or she'll be 'sleeping with the fishes', or whatever the fuck that saying is from terrible Mob movies.

And then I opened her door and saw the room in disarray and Alexis half-hanging out the window, her eyes wide like a deer in headlights. Red-hot fury ignited in my chest as realization sank in. She was trying to fucking escape. And she used fucking *bed sheets* to do so.

That solidified it for me. She definitely isn't an idiot. She's just a liar.

My rage overtook me in that moment as I snatched her away from the window and pinned her against the wall. But when she looked up at me, those hazel eyes flecked with gold wide and innocent, her full lips parted as she caught her breath, I suddenly became hyper aware of how close our bodies were. How the swell of her body felt against mine. The subtle smell of her perfume wafting to my nose. Those pouty lips just inches from mine, begging to be kissed.

That justifiable fury which burned bright just moments ago began to rapidly dissolve until it was nothing but simmering embers. Fury was replaced with an intense need to touch her that left my mouth dry and my heart pounding.

Why did I come in here again? I'm supposed to be pissed at her, but I'm not. Instead, I want to take her to bed and fuck her until she's screaming my name.

I have to pull myself away and make a show of taking off my suit jacket and tie in order to clear my head. I can feel her gaze on me, watching as I unbutton the top button of my shirt. I make a show of looking at her, how that ridiculously short dress is barely containing her breasts as they heave and how the swell of her ass looks as the dress rides up.

She's like an open book, and I can see every emotion play across her face. I smirk as I see her bite her lip, fighting back a moan. Ah, so she's turned on. This I can work with. Desire is the best truth serum outside of alcohol.

Her skin is impossibly smooth as I lean in, my jaw rubbing against her neck, and it takes everything in me to not trail hot kisses down it. My cock twitches, but I have to ignore my baser instincts if I want to get the answers I deserve.

"You haven't been honest with me, Alexis *Hartley*," I hiss. "Why the *fuck* does The Brotherhood want you so badly?"

It's like a bucket of cold water has been poured over her as she gasps, eyes impossibly wide.

"H–How did you learn my last name?" she whispers, pupils darting in every direction.

A satisfied grin stretches across my face as I pull out the manila envelope and toss it at Alexis. "Open it," I say lightly.

She obeys and tears it open, the contract fluttering to the ground. She scans the photos and her body stiffens. She looks up at me fearfully.

"I—where did you get these?" she demands, waving a photo of herself at me. "Who took these?" Her voice is getting louder as hysteria starts to take over.

"No. You don't get to ask the fucking questions here, Alexis Hartley," I snarl. "Why does The Brotherhood want you so bad?"

"I don't know!" Alexis shouts, bringing her hands to her face in frustration. "I'd never *heard* of them before until today when Mark—" She stops short, looking horrified at the partial revelation she's let slip.

My grin turns vicious. "Mark Abernathy, right?"

She stills, her face paling. "How do you know who Mark is?"

I gesture to the contract lying on the floor and tsk unsympathetically. "So defensive over someone who tried to sell you to The Brotherhood." I bark out a laugh. "Did you really think I wouldn't find any of this out, Alexis? Did you really think I am that much of an idiot?"

Alexis shakes her head frantically, wrapping her arms around herself as she tucks her chin into her chest. "No."

I roughly tip her chin up with my finger so she's forced to look into my eyes. The huge bruise on her cheek reminds me of my earlier question.

"Who hurt you, Alexis? Was it Mark?"

Alexis squeezes her eyes shut but quickly nods.

I stamp down the anger rising in my chest. We're finally getting somewhere, and I'm not about to let this moment slide.

"Tell me everything that happened before Edo and I found you on the street," I growl. "And leave *nothing* out. I *will* find out if you do, and I don't think you'll like what happens if I find out you lied."

She flinches at that statement but takes a steadying breath. Suddenly, it's like a dam has been unleashed and she tells me *everything*. From her mother's death to being placed with the Carters to meeting Mark. When she tells me how Mark hit her while her foster parents and foster sister did *nothing* and how they all conspired to sell her to The Brotherhood, I have to clench my fists in order to not hunt them down and take them out myself.

"So I escaped from the basement," she whispers. "And I was so, *so* close to freedom when that guy attacked me. That's when you found me."

Her story is horrifying, but it still doesn't answer the question as to *why* she's so important to Mario Rafa. She only shrugs helplessly when I ask her.

"I don't know how many times I have to tell you that I don't know," she says tiredly. "This is the first time I've ever heard the name Mario Rafa."

For whatever reason, I believe her. Nat would kill me for that, but there's a resigned hopelessness to Alexis right now that can't be faked.

It's not exactly a secret that The Brotherhood dabbles in human trafficking, but this is the first time I'm actually interacting with a potential victim. My stomach twists as I wonder how many other Alexises have been sold to unsavory customers.

Uncle Vinny would tell me to turn Alexis over *now* so we can get our cut, but I don't want to. Whoever The Brotherhood sells Alexis to will do their best to permanently remove that fire from her. I don't buy for one second that Alexis is naturally meek and mild. She's quick to anger, as demonstrated by her slapping me when I accused her of being a prostitute, and she's cunning and intelligent, as evidenced by the fucking rope ladder she created.

No, this timidity is a survival technique. Bland people fly under the radar much easier than passionate ones.

"What are you going to do with me?" Alexis asks, her voice trembling. "Please don't send me to The Brotherhood or the Carters. I'll do *anything*."

I really don't know what I'm going to do. While I don't want her to be sold, I also know keeping her here is dangerous. If Mario gets wind that his missing person has been hiding out here, he'll declare a war to get her.

And we can't afford a war, not when Invicta would probably join up with The Brotherhood to ensure our destruction.

"I don't know," I admit, frowning as I watch her face fall and as she shrinks into herself. Why does my honesty make me feel like a piece of shit?

My phone suddenly rings, a welcome distraction from some potential unpleasant introspection. I swiftly bring my phone to my ear, turning my back on Alexis so I can't see her crestfallen and scared expression.

"Damian," I say shortly.

"Boss!" A frantic voice bellows, and I have to pull my phone back so my eardrum isn't blown out. "Boss! Invicta is here and shootin' up the place!"

I can hear a round of gunfire in the distance, and the man yells before the line goes dead.

"FUCK!" I shout, causing Alexis to jump in fright, but I don't care right now.

I need to get to my warehouse *now* and end this fight before the police get wind of this. The last thing I need is for the pigs to find our drugs.

The door bursts open, and Edo and Nat appear, their faces white and their cell phones in their hands. They must have also gotten phone calls as well.

"Edo, let's go," I order, grabbing the guns that Edo tosses at me. "Nat, you stay here and keep an eye on Alexis."

"*What?*" Nat hisses, dropping her phone to curl her hands into fists. "I'm not a fucking *babysitter*, Damian! I'm your underboss. Are you having me watch her because I'm a female?"

Is my sister really accusing me of misogyny? Fucking seriously?

I gesture toward Alexis who is cowering at the wall. "She just tried to fucking escape using a goddamn rope ladder. You're the only one who could potentially stop her if she decides to be stupid enough to try again."

Nat looks unconvinced, but I really don't care. I have more important things to worry about.

I jerk my head toward Edo. "Bring the men and get the car ready. We have no time to lose."

∼

I STEP through the door of my warehouse, my bodyguards and Edo flanking me with drawn guns. My eyes narrow as I survey the dim interior.

"I have a bad feeling about this," Edo murmurs, his eyes scanning the perimeter. "It's too quiet."

I can't help but agree. Where are my men? Shouldn't there be dead bodies littered on the floor?

Suddenly, the *rat-tat-tat* of machine gun fire erupts from the catwalk above. My men drop in a hail of bullets as Edo and I dive behind a stack of wooden crates.

"It's a fucking trap!" I roar over the sounds of bullets. I pull out my .38 from my shoulder holster. Edo and I blindly fire back, the gunfire deafening in the enclosed space.

"Go left!" Edo shouts as he rolls out from behind the crate and kneels on one knee, firing his gun multiple times.

Gritting my teeth, I dart out from my hiding spot to another one, quickly firing off a round. I can see several people fall from my aim, and I grin in satisfaction.

This *has* to be Invicta. There's no one else who would be stupid enough to start a gunfight with me.

I reload my gun and pop up again, pressing the trigger multiple times as bullets whiz past me. *Bam, bam, bam.* More Invicta soldiers go down.

A searing pain tears through me and I grimace, clutching the bleeding wound. Blood pours around my fingers and I sway on the spot. I'm hit with another searing pain and I collapse on the cement ground, staring up at the ceiling. The pain is indescribable, and the edges of my vision grow fuzzy.

This is what it must be like to die, I think before the world goes black.

8

ALEXIS

Once Damian and the other man—Edo, I think—rush out of the room, Nat kicks the bed in anger and I shrink back, worried she will turn that fury on me.

"Fucking *Damian!*" she snaps. "He named me as his underboss but still treats me like a goddamn babysitter! I'm going to fucking *kill* him. If he tries to pull this shit again, I'm going to drown him."

Although I'm scared, curiosity is the dominating emotion. Nat is the first woman I've seen so far, and I want to know a little more about her. Maybe she would be able to help me? Something in me tells me I wouldn't get very far if I tried to escape again. Nat is all lean muscle with not an inch of fat on her.

"Who are you?" I finally ask, wincing as Nat whirls around to glare at me, her brown eyes narrowing. "Where am I? Why are you keeping me here?"

Maybe I'll get more answers out of her than Damian.

Nat cocks her head to the side, black hair spilling across her neck. "What's it to you?" she asks rudely.

I do my best to not apologize as I don't think Nat would appreciate that.

"I–I just want to know what's going on," I admit. "I know next to nothing other than Damian's name and that I'm at his house."

"Well, then one of your questions has already been answered," Nat snaps. She suddenly shivers as she stands by the open window, the rope ladder still hanging on the window sill. As she goes to shut the window, she pauses and fingers the rope. Spinning around, she scans the room, taking in the disheveled bed and open dresser drawers.

Nat snatches the rope ladder and closes the window before turning to me. She points to the rope. "Did you do this?"

I quickly nod, unable to speak. She intimidates me more than Damian does. There's something about the way she walks and speaks that exudes power and confidence.

Nat looks mildly impressed and she pulls on the rope. "Nice work. You did an excellent job with the weaver's knot, especially under pressure."

Is... is she complimenting me?

Nat studies me again, as if seeing me in a new light. I feel like her gaze pierces through my soul and that she can somehow read my mind.

"I'm Nat," she finally says. "It's short for Natalia, but *no one* calls me that unless they want to die a painful death."

I don't think that's a joke.

"Damian's already told you where you are, so I'm not going to repeat myself. And why are you here? Well, that's something you need to tell us."

"I don't *know* anything!" I burst out. "I've never heard of Invictus—"

"Invicta," Nat cuts in.

"Or The Brotherhood! You guys keep accusing me of knowing things and not believing me when I say that I don't know!"

"Can you blame us?" Nat asks loudly, walking around me like a predator would its prey. "Two of the most powerful Mafia families are after you, and you somehow don't know who they are? That's very hard to believe."

My blood runs cold. "M–Mafia? I thought those ended with Al Capone."

Nat tips her head back and laughs loudly. "No."

Suddenly, some pieces fall into place. Damian in his suit. The guns. The fancy car. Nat calling herself the underboss. My stomach twists and my mouth dries. "You're part of the Mafia too, aren't you?"

"Very good, Alexis," Nat says, her eyes alight with cold amusement. "You've finally figured it out. A-plus work. Haven't you ever heard of *The Godfather*? We're kind of similar."

Horror bubbles up in me and my hands start to shake. "I–Is Damian going to kill me?"

Instead of assuring me that Damian would never, I'm horrified to see Nat shrug instead. "Depends."

"Depends on what?" I ask fearfully.

Nat smirks and folds her arms across her chest, clearly enjoying my discomfort. "Depends on whether you'll be an asset or a liability. You're worth quite a bit of money to The Brotherhood, and I imagine to Invicta, too. It would be very easy to turn you over to either organization and let them duel to the death for you."

"Have you killed anyone?" I don't know if I want an answer. Somehow, I think getting killed by Damian would be less painless than a death by Nat.

Her smile unnerves me. I'm going to throw up. My stomach heaves, and I press a hand to my mouth. A bead of sweat trickles down my back.

"But you've asked too many questions. Now, it's my turn." Nat perches on the bed, ignoring my distress. "You claim you know nothing about The Brotherhood, but can you think of any reason they want you so badly?"

"No," I answer honestly, my mouth tasting like pennies. "I don't know. I'm nobody."

Nat snorts and impatiently gestures to the rope ladder. "I highly doubt that based on your rope work. I also don't buy your 'poor little old me' act. You're a wolf in sheep's clothing, Alexis. Fucking embrace it."

I don't know what to say to that. I want to tell her she's wrong, but I don't think she would appreciate it.

"Is your boyfriend trying to sell you?" Nat asks bluntly, gesturing to my bruised face. "The Brotherhood is known for their human trafficking proclivities."

She says this all so matter-of-factly, like she's discussing the weather instead of talking about organizations using human beings as chattel. I envy her—not for how she's discussing something as abhorrent as human trafficking—but for her confidence and self-assurance. It's a fire I wish burned within me, instead of feeling meek and timid.

"Well?" Nat asks, eyes searching mine. "Are you going to answer my question or not?"

Irritation courses through me. What is it with everyone fucking demanding answers from me? They don't deserve to know everything.

"Maybe if you shut up for five goddamn seconds, I'll feel obligated to answer one," I shoot back before I realize what I'm saying.

Silence envelopes the room as I snap my mouth shut, my heart beating a staccato in my chest. Fuck. Nat's going to *kill* me for that.

Nat's eyes widen at my outburst before a wide, unnerving smile breaks across her face. "Very good, Alexis," she purrs. "See? You *are* more than a wallflower."

I again don't know what to say. I'm relieved that Nat didn't take offense to my retort, but I'm also not sure whether she insulted me or complimented me.

"Based on that *very* defensive response," Nat continues, her smile similar to a Cheshire cat, "I'm going to say yes, your boyfriend was trying to sell you."

My shoulders slump, and it suddenly feels like the weight of the world is pressing on me. The full understanding of what Mark and the Carters tried to do finally hits me, and I burst into tears. I feel so small, so insignificant, and I suddenly miss my mother more than anything. What I wouldn't do to be wrapped in her arms and her telling me everything was going to be okay.

I feel a presence standing next to me and a hand rests on my shoulder. Nat gazes at me with compassion. Suddenly embarrassed, I swipe away the tears at my display of emotion. What must Nat think of me…

I don't know why I suddenly want Nat's approval. Maybe it's because Nat is poised and confident, everything I aspire to be, or because Nat has an aura of authority that came not just from her position as the underboss, but from an inner strength and self-assurance.

"It wasn't just your boyfriend, was it?" Nat asks gently.

I don't know how she's so damn perceptive, but I nod, sniffling. "My foster parents, too," I admit, my voice quaking.

Nat's fingers tighten on my shoulder before she retracts them, balling her hand into a fist. "Your *parents* tried to sell you along with your boyfriend?" she asks, horrified.

"Foster parents," I correct her. "But yes."

Nat gapes at me, her cool façade breaking. Her face suddenly clouds over with anger, her eyes narrowing into slits. I take an instinctive step back as Nat looks *terrifying*.

"Would you like them to be taken care of?" Nat asks casually, staring at her nails with measured indifference.

Taken care of—*oh*.

I shake my head wildly, ignoring the throbbing from doing so. "No! No. Please don't hurt them. I can't have that on my conscience."

"On your conscience?" Nat splutters. "Alexis, they tried to sell you as a *sex slave*! Why are you still loyal to them?"

I don't expect Nat to understand my situation, and frankly, I don't find it to be any of her business. But maybe if I tell her why I feel this way, maybe she'll stop asking me so many damn questions.

"I've been in foster care since I was six," I say, feeling as though I'm stripping myself raw in front of Nat. I don't like to talk about my past. "I was in a pretty terrible situation. My previous foster family abused me, and I ran away. After a few days on the streets, I was nearly kidnapped. Just before I was shoved into the car, my current foster father rescued me. I've been at their home ever since. They protected me when no one else would."

"They're bad people, Alexis!" Nat points out, and I can't help but laugh.

"Isn't that the pot calling the kettle black?" I ask, watching as Nat's face screws up in annoyance that I called her out on her hypocrisy. "I mean, you're in the Mafia. I don't think that gives you some moral high ground."

Nat scowls. "I may be a lot of things and have done some unspeakable acts, but I've *never* tried to sell my loved ones to sexual slavery. There's a line, Alexis."

I shrug, finding her reasoning to be pretty flimsy. "I owe them my life. You don't have to understand why, but you need to accept it. No one is to hurt them."

An alarm suddenly blares, its wailing tone high-pitched. The hair on the back of my neck stands up as I jump, looking around. Nat's face pales.

"What's going on?" I ask fearfully, but Nat's already scrambling for the door and wrenching it open. She disappears down the hall, leaving the door ajar. I hear men shouting and see a gaggle of men rush past my door.

Whatever's going on isn't good. But this might be the distraction I need to get out of here.

Poking my head out the door, I see the hallway is empty. This is my chance.

I rush down the hall and come to a staircase that leads to a front door. My heart leaps into my throat. *Freedom.*

I nearly throw myself down the stairs, my feet making quick work as the door gets closer and closer. I reach out to grab the door handle, almost tasting the night air, but someone grabs me from around my middle and hoists me backward.

No! Not again! I flail in my captor's arms, trying to sink my elbow or knee into something soft, but all I meet is hard flesh. "Let me go!" I shriek.

"You aren't leaving until Damian says so," a deep voice rumbles into my ear as I'm carried back upstairs. Tears prick my eyes as I see my freedom slipping away with each step back toward my prison.

I was so close. *So close.*

My captor deposits me outside a bedroom and opens the door, keeping a tight hand around my wrist to prevent me from escaping again. He pushes me in and shuts the door behind him.

The bedroom I'm in is incredibly spacious, with vaulted ceilings and large windows that let in plenty of natural light during the day. However, the room has a distinct lived-in feel, with clothes and magazines strewn about haphazardly.

Framed photos of classic sports cars, like the Ford GT40, Lamborghini Countach, and Ferrari Testarossa adorn the walls. Along one wall is a massive wooden dresser, its top covered in diecast model cars. The open closet door reveals a tumbled mess of clothes, shoes, and car detailing supplies.

A plush dog bed sits in another corner, surrounded by an assortment of well chewed toys. But my attention is fixated on the king-sized bed in the center of the room, where Damian lies on rumpled red sheets, his chest wrapped in white gauze and bandages. A small dachshund is curled in the crook of his arm. The dog perks up when my captor and I enter the room, a warning growl coming out of its tiny body.

Nat is sitting on a chair beside Damian's bedside and scowls at the dog, her face pale. "Quiet, Biscotti," she orders.

Although the situation looks serious and I should be frightened, I fight a smile when I hear the dog's name. Maybe I've seen too many Mob movies, but I would have expected a Mafia Don to have a pit bull or a German Shepherd, not a lap dog named after a cookie.

"You doing okay, Damian?" my captor asks, concern etched on his face. It's the same man who argued with Damian and Nat about what to do with me.

Damian waves an irritable hand, but I can see how pale his face is and the bags under his eyes. "I'm fine," he says. "Just a flesh wound. I don't even know why I'm lying in bed."

"Because you were shot in the shoulder *twice*," Nat snaps, her voice trembling.

"I was *grazed* by the bullets," Damian corrects her. "Fucking Invicta idiots don't even know how to shoot. How embarrassing. If I were Shields, I would get rid of them."

Damian's dark eyes finally slide onto me, and a wry smirk spreads across his face as he lazily pets his dog. My heart hammers at his smoldering gaze.

"Did you really think you could escape me, Alexis?"

9

ALEXIS

Something snaps within me at Damian's smug expression. I've fucking *had* it with everyone. For the last God knows how many hours, I've been locked in a basement, escaped, nearly taken by gunpoint, rescued by a Mafia Don, *imprisoned* by a Mafia Don, tried to escape *twice*, and still ended up stuck in the same goddamn place.

I didn't ask for any of this. I didn't ask for the Carters and Mark to sell me like I'm a fucking piece of property, and I certainly did not ask to be trapped in a Mafia Boss's house, unable to leave because someone says so. What about my agency? I have the right to come and go as I please, dammit!

"How did you know I was trying to leave?"

Damian laughs, petting the dog's long body. "This is my house. Not much happens here without my knowledge."

"Why can't you just let me *leave*?" I snap, folding my arms tightly across my body.

He cocks his head to the side. "Oh, I'm sorry, Alexis. Is my home not comfortable for you?"

I don't appreciate his mocking tone and I scowl. "Why won't you just let me go home?" I ask again, my hands curling into fists. "I don't want to be anyone's prisoner. I just want to be left alone."

Damian laughs again. "What *home*, Alexis? From my understanding, once you escaped from that basement, that house stopped being your home. Your foster family *and* boyfriend are pretty pissed at you and are currently trying to hunt you down. You have a dangerous Mafia also searching for you. You and I both know the moment you step foot in that house, you'll be carted off to The Brotherhood and never seen again. I can't allow that."

He stops scratching Biscotti's head, his face turning unnaturally serious. "Unless you *do* want to be sold as a sex slave. Then, by all means, I'll happily send you back and get my cut."

Time seems to freeze at his words and my chest constricts painfully. "Y–You're in on this, too?" I whisper, horrified. Every instinct in me is screaming to run, but my captor—Edo—stands behind me. I'll never make it past him.

Damian rolls his eyes. "Are you not listening to a word I'm saying? I've been tasked with finding you and delivering you *alive* to The Brotherhood. This was all agreed to after we rescued you from Invicta when I had no idea who the fuck you were. If I was really in on this, I would have dumped you at Mario Rafa's feet already."

I can breathe again, and I exhale, my body shuddering as I come down from a near panic attack. For one horrible moment, I thought Damian was going to betray me.

Is betraying even the right word considering we aren't even allies? I'm his prisoner.

"Do you want to go back to your foster family?" Damian asks me, his gaze never leaving mine. "Say the word and it'll happen. You'll be stupid as fuck for doing so, but you do have a choice in this matter."

The thought of going back to the Carter house and being whisked away to my worst nightmare makes me shiver, and I rub my arms, goosebumps erupting all over my flesh. "No," I admit in a small voice. "No, I don't want to go back."

"That's probably the smartest decision you've made all day," Damian remarks, ignoring the flash of anger that crosses my face. Did he seriously just call me stupid?

"Then let me disappear," I blurt out, desperate to just get away from *him*. Although I hate being a prisoner, I'm finding that being in the same room as him is like touching a live wire.

Damian raises an eyebrow, an amused smile playing at his lips. "No offense," he says, when it's clear he *does* mean offense, "but you're not the disappearing type."

"What is *that* supposed to mean?"

"It means you have the street smarts of a fucking infant. You wouldn't even last a few days out there before you'd make a fucking stupid move, be captured, and never seen again." He shrugs, ignoring my squawk of outrage. "So, as you can see, the safest place for you is right here at my house."

He smirks. "You could at least say you're welcome," he taunts, looking smug.

I see right through Damian's barb. He's offering me a lifeline, a chance to survive, maybe even thrive if I play my cards right. All I have to do is keep my head down, do as I'm told, and stay out of sight. It's what I'm used to with the Carters. But I'm finding myself to be repulsed by my own meekness and timidity.

Nat's words run through my head. *"You're a wolf in sheep's clothing, Alexis. Fucking embrace it."*

I think about Mark and Emma laughing as I shrank back from whatever biting retort they threw at me. Or how Dennis and Suzanne treated me as little more than a skittish rabbit, useful for my skills but otherwise dismissible.

No, a small voice inside me whispers. *You don't have to be a victim anymore. You can be something great. Start acting like it.*

Nat said my ability to survive rests on whether I would be an asset or a liability, and I choose to be an asset.

Suddenly, it feels like fifty pounds have been released from me. Although I'm scared of The Brotherhood finding me, I know I have to do whatever I can to ensure my safety. I can't just rely on Damian, Nat, and Edo.

Something like approval flashes in Damian's eyes. Was he seeing my internal struggle playing out all over my face? Does he realize what I've decided?

"*What*?" Nat snaps, jerking me out of my introspection. Her cheeks are pink as she jumps out of her chair. "You've got to be fucking kidding me, Damy."

He raises an eyebrow. "I never kid, *Natalia*."

"Damian, be serious. While I agree Alexis should not be turned over to The Brotherhood, you're putting us in grave danger by allowing her to stay here. For fuck's sake, we already have Invicta on our asses and they nearly killed you today!"

"They barely grazed me!" Damian says loudly, but an irate Nat plows on.

"The last thing we fucking need is The Brotherhood to sniff out that Alexis is here, especially when our relationship with them is tenuous at best! Do we really want Invicta *and* The Brotherhood to ally for the sole purpose of destroying us?"

At first, I feel a pang of hurt and rejection at Nat's words. She's just another person who finds me a burden and unwanted. But, at the same time, I also recognize that Nat is speaking out of fear and protectiveness over her family.

If I had a family, I probably would do the same thing, so I don't take offense to her harshness.

"Then what should we do with her?" Damian asks.

"Send her far away," Nat retorts before rounding on me. "Where do you want to go, Alexis? We have more money than God and we can get you fake papers to go anywhere you want. Italy? Greece? Spain? You name it, we can send you there."

Her offer *is* tempting, and I have no doubt that with the right amount of money, I could disappear and never be seen again. But then I would spend the rest of my life looking over my shoulder, waiting for the other shoe to drop.

"She's not going anywhere," Damian says flatly. "And my decision is *final*, Nat. Wouldn't you have wanted someone to do the same for Alessandra?"

The temperature in the room immediately drops by a few degrees, and even though I have no clue who Alessandra is, I can tell Damian's words hit their intended mark. Nat's face turns white before growing rosy with anger, the veins in her neck protruding. She takes one menacing step toward Damian, and for a second, I'm afraid she's going to strike him.

"Fuck you, Damian," Nat snarls before she whirls around, pushing past me and Edo. She slams the door so hard, the pictures on the walls shake and Biscotti growls.

Edo sighs, glancing at Damian with an exasperated look. "Low blow, bro," he mutters before following Nat.

Leaving Damian and me alone.

"Alexis," Damian says, his voice a low rumble that sends tingles down my spine. "Come here."

He pats the empty space beside him on the bed, and I feel my mouth grow dry. I barely know him, and he's asking me to join him in bed. I don't care if we are both fully clothed and he's injured. It just seems so *intimate*.

But how can I refuse him when he's looking at me with those intense, dark eyes?

Swallowing hard, I cross the room, acutely aware of every step on the plush carpet. As I near the bed, my gaze traces the hard lines of his body beneath the thin sheets. I silently berate myself for letting my thoughts wander in that direction. The man is injured, for God's sake!

"How are you feeling?" I ask, proud I'm able to keep my voice steady as I perch on the edge of the bed.

"I'm fine," he says. "Shallow wounds bleed like a motherfucker, but they aren't dangerous so long as they don't get infected. This isn't the first time I've been shot at, and it won't be the last." He looks thoughtful for a moment. "Although this *is* the first time I've ever had someone bungle a shot so badly. Maybe I should hire Nat out to be a sharpshooting teacher."

"Nat can fire a gun?" I blurt out, immediately regretting it the moment the words leave my lips. She's a damn underboss for a Mafia family. Of course she is a skilled marksman.

But Damian doesn't find it an offensive question. "My best shooter," he says. "She's always been better at it than me, although I'll deny it to my dying day."

I wince at his poor excuse of a joke. Shallow wound or not, he *was* in grave danger today.

"Who is Alessandra?" I ask, thinking about the look on Nat's face.

Underneath all the anger lay devastation. Whoever Alessandra was, she had meant a great deal to Nat.

He ignores my question. Instead, he reaches his hand out, fingers brushing my arm, leaving a trail of electric tingles in their wake. My breath catches in my throat as he wraps one of my curls around his fingers.

"So soft," he murmurs, running his fingers through the bottom of my long hair. My heart pounds, and my insides turn to liquid as he plays with my curls. "You have the most beautiful hair."

I'm incapable of speaking, watching with wide eyes as Damian coils a curl around his finger, the brown strands gleaming in the lamp's light. It's getting harder to ignore my throbbing core, and I try to adjust myself, crossing my ankles.

"It's a pity we're going to have to cut and dye it." Damian sighs, looking disappointed.

"*What*?" I gasp, feeling like I just got doused with cold water.

He furrows his brows. "The Brotherhood knows what you look like, Alexis. Of course we're going to have to alter your appearance. The goal is to hide you in plain sight."

"B–But..." I clutch my hair. It may sound stupid, but my long, thick, curly hair has been my pride and joy. People would stop me all the time to remark on my ringlets. It's the one thing Emma was jealous of as she had pin straight hair that couldn't hold a curl.

It's almost like my security blanket. I'll feel naked without it.

"Do you want to get caught or not?" Damian asks me. "This is the only way, Alexis."

"I can't believe I'm doing this," I mumble, staring at the box of hair dye on the bathroom counter. I've never dyed my hair before as I've always liked the chestnut brown color I was born with.

"Don't chicken out now," came Damian's voice from the doorway. He leans against the doorway, wearing a pair of black joggers and a gray T-shirt. His white bandages peek out from underneath the shirt collar. "This is for the best. Besides, don't all girls want to cut and dye their hair? Isn't it cathartic or some shit?"

I feel my cheeks flush as I meet his gaze in the mirror. "Maybe for some girls, but not for me. I've always liked my hair."

"It'll still be your hair," he points out. "Just a different color and length."

God, men are *clueless*.

My hands shake as I tear open the box, ripping the smiling black-haired model's face in half. I take a deep breath before looking back at Damian. "Are you going to help me?"

There's a predatory gleam in his eyes as he pushes away from the door, chuckling. The sound sends a shiver down my spine. "As you wish."

He steps up behind me, his warm presence surrounding me as he deftly plucks the bottle of dye from my trembling fingers. My breath catches in my throat as his fingers graze my own.

"Turn around," he murmurs, already working the applicator brush through the thick black cream.

I obey, my heart thundering as Damian carefully brushes the first streak of color through my brown hair. His other hand cradles the back of my head, holding me in place as he methodically paints my hair with broad, confident strokes.

The dye is cool against my scalp, but I barely notice. My entire body is burning up from Damian's proximity. His sandalwood cologne clouds my senses, surrounding me until all I can focus on is the scorching path of his hand as it brushes against my neck, my shoulders, the sloping curve of my collarbone...

A soft moan escapes from my lips before I can stop it. Damian freezes, his heavy-lidded gaze locking with mine in the mirror. The corner of his mouth twitches up in a smirk.

"You okay there?" he murmurs, his voice a deep, liquid velvet.

I manage a shaky nod, feeling like I'm ready to faint. Damian's smirk deepens for a moment before he continues painting strokes of black dye through my hair.

"You know your way around a dye brush," I say breathlessly.

"I've helped Nat dye her hair a fair few times," he says, his voice still low and gravelly.

By the time he finishes, I'm seconds away from combusting. Damian pulls his hands away with reluctance, his scorching stare roving over my newly dyed hair.

"That's better." He winks at me. "Now, follow me. Nat's hairdresser is here."

In a daze, I follow Damian out and sit in a salon chair. I'm soon introduced to Richard, who promises to give me the best haircut of my life.

Snip. Snip. Snip.

The sound of the scissors slicing through my long hair is both terrifying and exciting. I grip the sides of the salon chair, watching thick strands of hair fall away in the mirror's reflection.

For years, my hair has been a security blanket. Countless hours have been spent carefully tending to my hair, styling it into elegant twists for fancy events. My hair is a part of my identity, or so I thought.

But as I watch Richard's deft hands shear away the remnants of my past life, I feel something shifting in me. With each snip of the scissors, a weight is lifted from my shoulders.

The shadow of my former life—the scared, meek girl who allowed everyone to speak for me—begins to dissipate.

My reflection in the mirror slowly changes until a stranger stares back at me. This woman has a bouncy, shoulder-length bob that frames her face in feathery wisps at her jaw. Her hazel eyes, no longer hidden behind thick curtains of hair, sparkle with reinvention.

A farewell tear slips down my cheek as my fingers toy with my new, shoulder-length style. Remnants of who I used to be flutter to the floor, scattered at my feet.

"Ta-da!" Richard sings, spinning the chair to face the mirror head-on. "What do you think?"

Damian and Nat's faces appear in the mirror along with mine.

"Wow," Nat remarks to Damian. "With this new look, Alexis bears a striking resemblance to our cousin, Maria."

My lips curve into a slow smile as I stare at my appearance. I was really hesitant when Damian insisted I needed to cut my hair, but I'm seeing that this was an excellent idea.

"I love it," I whisper, touching my black, shoulder-length curls. This was more than just a haircut. It was cutting ties with my past so I can brave the great unknown of my future.

10

DAMIAN

I shoulder my way through the thick oak doors, the scents of Cuban cigars and aged whiskey enveloping me. As I enter the study, my men rise to their feet out of respect.

With a curt nod, I wave for them to remain seated and pour myself a drink from the crystal decanter. Taking my customary chair by the fireplace, my mind isn't on family business for once. Instead, my thoughts drift to a certain curly haired woman living in my home.

Alexis. Just her name alone is a dangerous distraction I can't seem to avoid, no matter how much I try. The curly-haired siren intrigues me like no other, but her past remains a mystery to me. Who is she?

I've had my best men discreetly dig into her background. So far, all they've been able to come up with is that she has a deceased mother, was placed in foster care, and worked at Cake My Day bakery. That bit of information surprised me as I love to go there and get their donuts. I wonder if I've ever interacted with her and just didn't know it?

But she has no other family and no friends to speak of. Her guarded nature only raises more questions. She is an enigma—one that increasingly occupies my thoughts. Alexis is as ordinary as they come. So, why is The Brotherhood determined to have her?

I hate this. I am not used to being so utterly in the dark about anything or anyone who steps foot on my property.

A soft clearing of a throat makes me raise my eyes to meet Edo's questioning gaze from across the study. Right, I'm supposed to be focused on business dealings right now.

I force my mind away from Alexis, drowning my fascination with a steadying sip of whiskey. There will be time later to unearth Alexis's secrets.

∼

"You know, if you want to know more about Alexis, you should just ask her."

Whirling around, I spy an amused Nat leaning against a nearby wall, her lips curled up in a smirk.

"Fuck off," I snarl, wondering how much Nat had overheard. I've been making casual inquiries with the staff about Alexis's preferences and routines. So far, I've learned she likes to practice yoga early in the morning, hates bananas, and has a huge sweet tooth.

Nat snorts and pushes away from the wall, walking over to me. "I'm just saying. For a Mafia Don, you're pretty shitty at being inconspicuous."

To my horror, heat creeps up my neck. I fix Nat with a withering look. "Don't you have something more important to do than harassing me?"

"Nope," Nat says casually, popping the 'p', an annoyingly smug grin on her face. "But I gotta say, it's really cute watching you trying to get information about her. By the way, she also likes to paint."

My jaw nearly drops at this new kernel of information. "How did you find that out?"

She shrugs. "I asked her." Nat's laughter is insufferable as she saunters away, humming an Elton John love song.

If I could tie my sister up and dump her into Lake Michigan, I would.

A painter. I wonder what inspires her. Does she paint haunting images or is she more abstract? I'm determined to find out.

A couple of days later, I steer my path to "accidentally" cross with Alexis's in the hallway. Her black hair is clipped back, with a few errant curls dangling enticingly by her ears. Even though cutting and dying her hair was a good idea, I miss her long, gorgeous curls.

"Alexis," I greet her. "I understand you're quite the talented artist."

She blinks owlishly at me, clearly not expecting me to know such a personal detail about her. "I... well, sort of, I suppose. I'm not very good. It's just a hobby, really."

"But you like to paint, right?"

"Yes. Yes, I do. I find it very soothing."

I nod. "I've had paints, canvases, and other materials brought over for your use. They're in the sunroom downstairs. Consider them yours."

Alexis's eyes widen in surprise and delight. "You didn't have to do that, I—"

"I insist," I cut her off firmly, but not unkindly. "If you're going to stay with us, you should be able to do the things you enjoy."

Her grateful smile in that moment sparks something warm and dangerous in my chest that I swiftly stamp down. This is merely a pragmatic gesture. Nothing more.

"Thank you, Damian. This means more than you know," Alexis says sincerely, looking at me with an unsettlingly gentle expression.

"Maybe you could show me how to paint, too?" I ask, my heart thudding traitorously in my chest. "Fair warning, I can barely draw a stick figure."

Alexis laughs, the sound a soothing balm to my soul. "I think it will be the blind leading the blind, but sure. I would be happy to teach you some basic skills."

"How about this weekend?" I ask.

"It's a date—uh, I mean, yes, of course. The weekend works perfectly." Alexis worries her bottom lip as if berating herself for the slip.

I give one last nod of acknowledgment before turning on my heel, fighting to maintain my unaffected façade. I can't help but replay the phrase in my mind, feeling startlingly thrilled at the inadvertent implication.

The weekend can't come soon enough.

∽

THE MANSION FEELS EERILY quiet with my staff, Nat, and Edo dismissed for the rest of the day. Edo had to drag Nat out of the house as she made kissy noises toward me. Sister or not, I'm going to fucking murder her.

I stand in the empty sunroom, the jarring silence only highlighting the thrum of nervous energy coursing through me.

This seemed like an innocuous enough idea when I asked Alexis to show me how to paint, a simple creative reprieve from the weight of my responsibilities. But now, faced with the reality of the situation—just Alexis and me, alone—doubts start creeping in. When was the last time I allowed myself to be so utterly unguarded with someone outside my inner circle?

The sound of approaching footsteps stills my pacing. Alexis appears at the doorway, all loose, dark curls and soft smiles. My breath hitches at the simple vision she makes in leggings and a form-fitting V-necked shirt.

"Hi," she says shyly.

"Hi," I say stupidly, barely managing to maintain my veneer of unshakeable composure. Biscotti trots in after Alexis, racing to me and jumping at my legs.

Alexis smiles widely, my stomach flip-flopping at the sight. "I have to admit, when I ever thought of a Mob Boss owning a dog, I always thought it would be a great, scary dog—like a pit bull or a German shepherd. I really wasn't expecting a wiener dog."

"Dachshund," I correct, lifting Biscotti into my arms to pet her. "Don't let her small size fool you. She's vicious when she wants to be. She's taken a bite out of Edo before."

Alexis smiles softly. "I don't doubt that."

I make a sweeping gesture toward the arranged canvases and brushes on a gleaming table. "Shall we begin while we still have the light?"

She situates herself at the table, deft fingers sorting through paints and tools. My eyes trail appreciatively over her lithe figure. It's dangerous territory to allow myself such an indulgence.

"We should start with the basics, like color theory, brush techniques, that sort of thing," Alexis says as she dips bristles into rich pigments. "But since you claim you can barely draw a stick figure, maybe we should stick with finger painting."

The teasing lilt to her voice, combined with the playful grin she flashes over one shoulder, immediately heats my blood. My thoughts stray to those delicate fingers trailing through more than just oil paints...

Jesus. I already need a cold shower.

I clear my throat harshly. "I'm a quick learner. But we can start wherever you think is best."

Alexis hums agreeably, her focus already absorbed in mixing a particularly vivid shade of pink. I allow myself to step closer, allowing the subtle citrus scent of her shampoo to envelop me.

Fuck. This is going to be *torture*.

"Let's get started," Alexis says, dragging over a stool and perching on it, our knees grazing as she settles in close. "Remember, this is just for fun. No expectations."

I raise an eyebrow. For someone who deals in ultimatums and power plays, having zero expectations is an utterly foreign concept. But her reassuring smile and close proximity make me want to try.

I attempt to lose myself in the ebb and flow of brushstrokes across the canvas, making swirls and slashes. Alexis leans forward, her citrus scent intoxicating, her fingers warm against mine as she adjusts my hold on the paintbrush. "Like this," she murmurs. "Loose but controlled."

Kind of like my resolve right now. But I give her a stiff nod, struggling to focus on her instructions rather than the gentle sweep of her thumb grazing my knuckles.

Dipping my brush into the paint, I attempt to follow her instructions, but my heavy-handedness takes over, resulting in harsh, uneven lines across the canvas. I curse.

"You're overthinking it," Alexis chides gently. "Painting is feeling, not precision. Let the emotions guide your strokes."

I tense at her words. Allowing myself to be governed by passion rather than sheer force of will? The very notion goes against every ingrained element in me.

Yet here in this sunroom, Alexis seems to dismantle my restraints without even realizing. Watching the way her own nimble hands dance across the canvas in bold, expressive movements... it's utterly captivating.

I try again, swiping dark blue across the canvas in one harsh, slashing gesture.

Alexis's lips curve into a mischievous smile. "Angry brushstrokes for our brooding artist, I see."

"Hardly," I scoff, though my ears heat at being so transparently read. "I deal in absolutes."

"Do you? Because your painting tells a different story."

What on earth could the few paint strokes say about me? This I have to hear.

"I see a struggle between control and craving, desperation and restraint," she says softly.

A tremor cascades through me at her perceptive assessment, one that feels a bit too intimate even from an artist's perspective. I lick my suddenly dry lips, painfully aware of each scorching point where our bodies align. She is too close, clouding my senses with her presence.

"Perhaps we need a break," Alexis breathes. "Clear our heads."

The energy crackling between us is palpable, thrumming with a dozen unspoken possibilities. Of its own volition, my free hand drifts to her hip, fingers splaying possessively over the thin cotton as I tug her nearer.

Alexis's eyes briefly flutter shut before opening again, shimmering with a combination of nerves and want. At this moment, I'm acutely aware of how easy it would be to surrender. To discharge the ironclad control I cling to and give in to these incredibly inescapable urges that leave my body thrumming.

She seems to sense the warring factions within me, her generous mouth curving. As one slender finger trails down the plane of my chest, I shudder violently at her sensual exploration. Rational thought is rapidly becoming an effort in futility.

When she rises on her bare tiptoes, her full breasts brushing my torso, my resolve finally shatters. In one fluid motion, I cradle the nape of her neck as I crush our mouths together in a searing, desperate kiss.

11

ALEXIS

Kissing Damian is electrifying.

My whole body is on fire, my lips molding perfectly to his. The kiss starts off soft and exploratory, but it doesn't stay so for long. The unleashed hunger and passion I had been trying to suppress for Damian comes roaring back.

I kiss him harder, desperately, like I might drown if I don't consume every bit of him. My fingers tangle in his hair, pulling him even closer until there is no more space left between us. Damian matches my fervor, one arm snaking around my waist to pin my body to his.

He feels so powerful, so unrestrained, and yet his other hand strokes my cheek with the utmost delicacy. He is clearly the one in control, and honestly, that only makes me want him even more.

Mark's kisses never made me feel this way, this dizzying loss of control mixed with a sense of utter safety and security. Mark's kisses were hard and unyielding. He never took my feelings and wishes into account.

Damian's kiss alone is enough to upend my entire world while also grounding me. All I know at this moment is the white-hot desire searing through every fiber of my being.

The hand that is on my hip slides down to grip my ass, pulling me even tighter against the unmistakable bulge in his pants. A high-pitched whimper escapes my throat as I shamelessly grind myself against him, unleashing the building desperation between my legs.

"Damian…" I moan breathlessly against his searing kiss. His name on my lips only seems to spur him on further. One hand buries itself in my hair, angling my mouth for even deeper exploration. His other hand moves up from my ass to palm my breast. I gasp at the white-hot pleasure sparking through me.

This is really happening.

I want him more than I ever could have imagined, consequences be damned. I don't care that he's the Don of the Iacopelli Family. I don't care that he won't let me leave his house without his express permission. He's doing it for my own safety.

Wrapping my arms around his neck, I match his fervor with equal desperation, pouring every last bit of desire into this kiss.

When we finally break apart, I am utterly disheveled and panting harshly, our painting exercise completely forgotten. Damian's dark eyes smolder with undisguised lust as he takes in my flushed, wanting form.

I lean woozily against him. "Yes," I whisper.

"Yes?" he asks.

I nod. "I want you. Take me."

Damian's eyes burn with desire as I boldly confess my want for him. A low, guttural growl rumbles from his chest as he swiftly sweeps me up in his powerful arms, cradling me against his rock-solid frame.

"You have no idea what you do to me," he rasps huskily against my parted lips before claiming them in a scorching, possessive kiss.

I melt into his embrace, whimpering softly as his skilled tongue strokes against my own. The world seems to fall away, my senses utterly overwhelmed by the taste, scent, and feel of this commanding man.

We make it only a few steps before Damian pins me against the nearest wall, his toned body aligned with mine from chest to hip. I gasp at the sudden impact but then sigh wantonly as his mouth begins trailing molten kisses along my jaw and neck.

"Damian…" I breathe against his neck like a prayer, tangling my fingers into his thick locks to hold him impossibly closer.

He responds by sucking at the sensitive juncture between my neck and shoulder, coaxing a trembling moan from my lips. I can feel his arousal straining against me, sending a fresh surge of dizzying desire searing through my veins.

Just as I think I might pass out from the tension, Damian abruptly lifts me again and carries me up the sweeping staircase to his bedroom. He alternates between searing kisses and whispering filthy praises against my flushed skin that have me squirming shamelessly in his arms.

By the time we reach his bedroom door, I feel utterly delirious with longing. Damian captures my mouth once more in a molten, languid kiss that has me whimpering and arching against his frame. When we finally part, his eyes smolder with undisguised hunger.

"I'm going to make you mine in every way possible," he vows in a rugged tone that resonates straight to my core. "Every beautiful inch of you."

When he lays me on his bed, the reality of the situation finally sets in. I feel a sudden wave of nerves wash over me. This will be my first time, while Damian is clearly experienced and has probably been with countless women before.

Sensing my apprehension, Damian cups my face, forcing me to look into his piercing gaze. "What's wrong?"

I avert my eyes. "It's just... I'm new to this. What if I'm terrible?" I chew my bottom lip nervously, fighting back tears.

Damian lets out a low chuckle and shakes his head. He places a trail of featherlight kisses along my sensitive skin. "Don't even think like that."

He tips my chin up again to meet his smoldering stare. "This isn't about comparing you to others. With you, everything is new, exciting..." His voice drops even lower. "Utterly consuming me in a way I've never experienced before."

I feel my fears slowly ebb away as Damian's words and scorching caresses surround me. He cradles my face, leaning in to rest his forehead against mine. "I want to worship every inch of you, Alexis. Savor this moment and make it ours."

I gaze up at him, giving myself over to the tenderness simmering beneath his passionate intensity. He's right—this is *our* experience, unlike anything we've ever known before.

With a soft smile, I reach up to pull him into a kiss, ready to fully surrender myself to this man.

His hands slowly trace the curve of my body as our kisses deepen and intensify. My breath comes in shaky pants, desire swirling within me. Mark had *never* seen me this undressed, let alone touched me so intimately. The most I had ever let him do is touch a breast over my bra.

Sensing my trepidation, Damian pulls back just enough to catch my gaze. "Just breathe, Alexis," he murmurs huskily. "We'll go at your pace."

He presses a searing trail of kisses along my jawline and neck, fingers lightly tracing the hem of my shirt. "May I?" The gravelly request vibrates against my flushed skin, pulling a shuddering inhale from my lips.

Giving the smallest of nods, I lift my arms to allow Damian to undress me. He slides the shirt up tantalizingly slowly, caressing every new inch of exposed skin. I can't help the moan that escapes as his gaze rakes over my bare torso.

Any lingering shyness evaporates beneath the heated intensity of Damian's eyes. This is a man thoroughly worshiping and savoring every detail of my body as if I am the most precious work of art.

"Perfection," he rasps in a tone thick with want before claiming my lips once more.

Emboldened, I allow my hands to roam the hard planes of his chest, feeling the taut muscles quivering beneath my touch. I tug insistently at the fabric separating us until he pulls back just long enough to tear it off in one heated motion.

My breath catches in my throat as Damian's chiseled torso is finally revealed to me. He is undeniably the most strikingly handsome man I have ever laid eyes on. His physique is sculpted to perfection—toned and powerful.

However, as my gaze rakes over his bronzed skin, I notice the faint lines of scars marring his otherwise flawless form. Some are thin and faded with age, while others look more recent and jagged. They crisscross his abdomen and chest, reminders of the dangerous world he inhabits.

The dangerous world *I* now inhabit.

He presses our bodies flush together, searing skin against searing skin. The new, intimate contact draws matching gasps of pleasure from our lips. His skilled fingers quickly unclasp my bra with ease as he pauses, a hungry smile on his face.

Damian lowers his head, taking my nipple into his mouth, his tongue lavishing the puckered bud.

"God, you're beautiful," he murmurs, kissing at the fullness of my breast before returning to my nipple.

My hands bury in his thick hair as my back arches, loving the feeling of his mouth on me. His other hand freely plays with my other breast, massaging and flicking the nipple before returning his attention to it with his mouth.

After a few moments, he pulls away and a cold chill runs through me as the air hits my wet, lonely buds. His hands slide down my waist, thumbs hooking on the waistband of my leggings and underwear before pulling them down in one quick, smooth motion.

"Fucking beautiful," he mutters, pressing his lips to my stomach before trailing down my torso to my hips, then my thighs.

He leaves kisses everywhere, and I can't catch my breath.

My brain no longer works as his lips dance around the sensitive skin of my inner thighs, moving closer and closer to my heated core. A hard gasp falls from my mouth as his tongue separates my folds, caressing the engorged, sensitive nub hidden between them.

I can't believe this is happening. Not because it's my first time, but because of how much I want Damian. It feels incredible. Amazing.

I am full of nerves, but not in the self-conscious way I anticipated. I want him, but I can't quite understand the heaviness of my desire. He's gentle but still in control, and I love it.

My grip tightens on his hair as he continues to lick and suck, pushing me closer and closer to the edge.

"Damian!" I pant, closing my eyes and lifting my hips.

He wraps my legs around his head, gripping my thighs as he continues his assault on me. A deep, low moan rolls in my throat and pours out my mouth as my body begins to tremble and shake, just mere seconds away from climax.

But then he stops.

I gasp at the sudden cool breeze hitting me. My eyes fly open as I make a weak, pitiful moan.

"Not yet," he says simply.

I watch as he loosens his belt, undoing the button of his pants and pulling his massive, thick cock out.

My eyes widen at its size, and I hesitate, unsure whether all of it will even fit. As if reading my mind, he chuckles.

"It will fit perfectly fine. Don't you worry."

He leans over me, pressing his cock against the inside of my thigh as he pushes two fingers into my dripping core.

I let out a gasp as a sharp pain courses through me.

His fingers still. "Are you okay?"

I nod, the sharp pain slowly going away. "Yeah, just—a little slower, please."

He acquiesces, pumping his fingers in and out, hooking them upward to stroke my G-spot.

I struggle to take in deeper breaths and hold on to his shoulders as he steadily pumps in and out of me. My nails dig into his shoulders as he pumps harder, faster. His thumb swirls and caresses my clit.

"Oh! Fuck! Damian!"

I moan and lift my hips up, allowing him to go deeper, begging him to go faster. Another moan rolls from my lips, and he growls in response.

"Goddamn it," he mutters, pulling his fingers out. But before I can even make any sort of noise of complaint, I feel his head push into my entrance.

We both cry out as he pushes further into me. The slickness of my pussy makes the act a lot easier.

He grips the mattress as he finally bottoms out, and I lift my hips, biting my lip at the slight pain of his stretching me.

Damian begins at a slow pace. His hands pull my legs around his waist, allowing him to lean further and deeper into me before gripping the mattress again. A low, sensual groan escapes him as he picks up pace. My head slams against the bed with each powerful thrust.

"Ah, fuck!" he groans as he grips the mattress tighter.

I close my eyes, letting out a small scream as his thumb finds its way back to my clit.

He brings my legs up suddenly, pushing them closer to me as he pushes in deeper.

"FUCK YES! DAMIAN!"

The steady sounds of smacking, panting, groans, and moans fill the room.

He splits my legs to lean down, burying his face momentarily in the crook of my neck.

"That's it. Fuck, that's it," he moans against me. "Fuck, you feel so good."

I dig my nails into his back as Damian plants soft, tender kisses along my throat and cheek. That, along with the hard and heavy thrusts into me, feels so good.

Our lips latch together, our tongues tangling and fighting for dominance. His pace grows more erratic the closer he gets. The knot that's been growing in my stomach tightens with each and every thrust until finally, my walls clench tightly around him.

He is pushing me toward a cliff, and as I approach the expanse, I jump, exploding in an ecstasy that ripples through my entire body. When I cry out his name, my voice sounds different. Invigorated. Powerful.

And I love every moment of it.

His pace grows unsteady. The bed groans in protest of his grip. "God! Fuck!" he moans and pulls out quickly, stroking himself hard and fast, until finally, he comes on my stomach as he throws his head back and moans. His hand pumps his cock slowly.

He leans over me, panting. Our exhales intermingle with one another. He rests his sweaty forehead against mine, causing our lips to be inches apart.

My hands reach up to grab his face, pulling him down for another kiss that he allows, and for the first time in a long time, I feel *wanted*.

My thoughts are swirling in the aftermath of my first sexual experience. The rush of emotions is overwhelming. I can't believe it. I *finally* had sex, and it was even more amazing than I had ever dared to imagine.

The sensations, the connection, the sheer *ecstasy* of the moment surpassed all of my expectations. I'm grateful I waited and didn't have sex with Mark. I find I'm grateful Damian was my first.

Despite my initial apprehension and the lingering sense of fear I feel toward Damian, I can't deny the undeniable truth. He made the experience incredibly pleasurable. The intensity of his presence, the passion in his touch, and the way he guided me through every moment leaves me breathless in the best possible way.

I snuggle up close to Damian, resting my head on his chest, wanting to revel in post-sex cuddles. Suddenly, Damian goes rigid beside me.

With a jerk, he abruptly breaks my embrace and swings his legs over the side of the bed. I lay there, stunned by his reaction.

"Damian?" I ask meekly as he stands, not looking at me, and grabs his clothes. He doesn't respond, roughly pulling on his pants and slipping on his shirt. I watch his movements, filled with confusion. Have I done something wrong? Did I overstep some unspoken boundary?

"I have business to attend to," Damian states flatly, still not meeting my eyes. He marches toward the bedroom door.

"But I... I thought..." I stammer, rejection swirling within me. This man, the powerful Iacopelli Don who strikes fear into rivals, is pulling away from my simple attempt at intimacy.

Damian pauses at the door, his hand on the knob, and half-turns toward me. For just a moment, I see a fleeting glimpse of vulnerability behind his steel gaze before the wall goes back up.

"Not tonight," he says, his voice low but firm. "Close the door after you get dressed." Then he's gone, leaving me alone in the rumpled sheets.

As the door clicks shut, I'm left struggling to understand what just happened. Why had a simple cuddle been so unwelcome? Tears well up in my eyes, and I bring my knees to my chest, wrapping my arms around them as sobs start to rack my body.

"What's wrong with me?" I whisper to no one. No matter how much I bend and mold myself to be acceptable, it's never enough.

Except for my mother, the one person in my life who loved me unconditionally—flaws and all—until she was taken from me. My mother's warmth and acceptance kept me from feeling unlovable.

As my body shakes with sobs, I feel an aching loneliness fill my very core. With no family, no true love, I am adrift with the resounding belief that some inherent flaw lying deep within me prevents anyone from ever fully loving me.

In that darkness, the spark of self-worth my mother had kindled feels like it is calling out its last feeble, flickering gasp. Each emotional abandonment presses in, leaving me feeling more unlovable than ever before.

12

DAMIAN

I sit hunched over my desk, the stacks of documents and files completely forgotten. My mind is elsewhere, replaying the events from a few weeks ago, over and over again.

The memory of Alexis's bare skin against mine, the softness of her lips, the way she had trembled with desire in my arms—it is all seared into my brain. I can still smell the faint traces of her perfume that seems to linger in my office.

And then I remember the cold, harsh reality of what I had done. How I had abruptly pulled away from her warmth with a bullshit excuse about needing to attend to business. The confused and hurt look on her beautiful face as I retreated.

Guilt twists in my gut. I had let my own cowardice and fear of vulnerability take over in that moment. Now, Alexis is shutting me out, refusing to speak to me, and she avoids me completely. Not that I could blame her after the way I treated her.

I wearily scrub a hand over my face. As a powerful Don, I am accustomed to always being in control, never allowing emotions to rule me. But Alexis has a way of getting under my skin, stripping away every calculated layer of bravado I show the world.

I have to make this right. I have to find a way to explain myself without the usual lies and deception. If I don't, I know I'll lose her, and that makes me feel hollower than ever.

The door to my office swings open, interrupting my brooding thoughts. I look up to see Uncle Vinny striding in, a gruff but warm smile spreading across his weathered face.

"There's my boy," Uncle Vinny booms, his voice rasping slightly from too many years of cigarette smoke. He pulls me up from my chair and envelopes me in a tight embrace.

Despite his burly frame and imposing demeanor, I feel a surge of affection for my uncle. After my parents and little sister were brutally murdered years ago, Uncle Vinny has been the closest thing to a father, despite the little hiccup of his trying to take over as the head of the Iacopelli Family. He's the last tie to my father, a man I idolized like no other.

As Uncle Vinny releases me, I manage a ghost of a smile. "To what do I owe the pleasure, Uncle?"

Uncle Vinny's expression turns more serious as he takes the seat across from my desk. "Any leads on the Hartley girl's whereabouts?"

A knot forms in my stomach at the mention of Alexis. Right, I'm supposed to be hunting her down. I wonder what color Uncle Vinny's face would turn if he knew Alexis Hartley is only a floor above us?

Normally, I would have told Uncle Vinny that we have her, but since Vinny brought Mario to me and has been encouraging me to help in the search, it's best that Uncle Vinny knows *nothing*.

"No updates to report, I'm afraid," I lie smoothly, keeping my face an inscrutable mask. "My guys are combing every inch of the city, but she's proving a slippery one so far."

Uncle Vinny scowls, an ugly look coming over his face. "Goddammit. It's crucial that we get our hands on Alexis Hartley soon, Damian," he growls, his expression hardening. "Mario is breathing down my neck about it."

I raise an eyebrow. "I don't understand the significance, Uncle. Why is this one girl so damn important? Seems like we could find another target to sell. There's no shortage of options prowling the streets after dark."

I regret the words as soon as they leave my lips. Uncle Vinny's eyes flash with a rare burst of anger and he slams a meaty fist on my desk, making everything rattle. "Don't question it, boy!" Vinny snaps, his gravelly voice rising in volume. "We need Alexis Hartley specifically. No substitutions. Mario's orders."

I recoil slightly at my uncle's vehement reaction. It's unlike the normally even-keeled Vinny to lose his cool like this. Clearly, there are larger machinations at play that I'm not privy to.

Does that piss me off? Sure. But I know when it's appropriate to ask questions and when to keep my mouth shut, and this is one of those times.

Holding my hands up in a placating gesture, I slowly nod. "You're right, Uncle. I'm sorry, I shouldn't have asked. We'll redouble our efforts to locate her immediately."

My mind races over this new revelation. What makes Alexis Hartley so goddamn special? And who is she to The Brotherhood that Mario himself has such a vested interest?

This clearly goes far deeper than any of us know. And my self-imposed personal conflicts are only going to keep getting more and more tangled in the wider web.

The door bursts open again as Nat comes storming into my office, her face twisted into a scowl the moment she spots Uncle Vinny.

"What's that miserable bastard doing here?" she spits, refusing to even look in Uncle Vinny's direction.

Uncle Vinny scowls right back. "Nice to see you too, Natalia."

Nat's eyes flash at the usage of her full name and I sense a rising war. I hold up a calming hand. "Easy, you two. Uncle Vinny is just leaving."

Uncle Vinny stands, understanding the dismissal. "Remember to find her, Damian. As soon as possible."

I incline my head. "Understood, Uncle."

With one last withering glare at Nat, Vinny shakes his head in disgust and turns on his heel, grumbling under his breath as he exits.

As soon as the door closes behind him, Nat rounds on me, her eyes blazing with fury and distrust. "You need to stop letting that fucking snake in here."

I sigh, mentally bracing myself. "Nat, come on..."

"I'm serious!" Nat insists, slamming her palms on my desk. "I don't trust Vinny as far as I can throw his fat ass. He's been sketchy ever since I can remember."

"You don't trust anyone, Nat," I counter, unable to hide the weariness in my voice. "Besides, Uncle Vinny has looked out for me. We're family."

Nat laughs viciously. "Oh, yeah? Then explain why he's so desperate to find Alexis, huh? You've been acting like a world-class dick to that poor girl."

My jaw clenches at the mention of Alexis. Alexis had better not have told Nat anything about how we had sex. I can't keep the defensive edge out of my voice. "Don't bring her into this."

"Like hell I won't!" Nat shoots back fiercely. "In case you've forgotten, *I'm* the one who's been with Alexis while you've had your head shoved up your ass!"

"Oh, so now you're a fan of Alexis? What were your original words when I said we should keep her here? 'Ditch the bitch', right?"

Nat pierces me with an accusing glare. "I've gotten to know her these last few weeks. She's a good kid who doesn't deserve to get tangled up in our nasty shit. But you've been tossing her around like a goddamn ragdoll."

I swallow hard, Nat's words cutting deep. As if I didn't already know I was being an ass to Alexis. The constant warring between my priorities and my emotions has been torture.

Nat opens her mouth to argue more, but I cut her off. "Look, we can debate Uncle Vinny's ethics and my supposed asshole tendencies another time. Right now, we need to get to The Underground. We have a meeting there soon."

Nat scowls at me but thankfully drops the subject. "Fine. Let's go, then."

As we head for the door, I can't help but think about Nat's vehement mistrust of our uncle. I know she has her reasons, her natural skepticism and disinclination to let anyone get too close. But Vinny has been like a father to me. Doesn't that count for something?

My thoughts continue to gnaw me over the true nature of Uncle Vinny's involvement with The Brotherhood. I know I'll eventually need real answers—no matter where they come from or whom they implicate.

∼

THE CLUB IS HOPPING as always, the pulsing beat of music and flashing lights providing a hypnotic backdrop. Nat and I weave our way through the raucous crowd, exchanging terse nods with the security stationed at every entrance.

Once we reach the VIP lounge and sit down, a small entourage appears—three bulky bodyguards leading the way for a statuesque woman with flowing red hair and ice blue eyes. Even from a distance, her aura of coldness and disdain is palpable.

My whole body tenses as I recognize the woman. Goddammit. Here comes Scarlett Rafa.

"Well, well," Scarlett purrs as she approaches, a cruel smile playing across her crimson lips. "If it isn't Damian and his raging Chihuahua, Natalia."

Nat instantly bristles, her body tensing like a loaded spring. "Why don't you slither back into whatever sewer you crawled out of, Scarlett?"

Edo quickly moves to place a restraining hand on Nat's arm as she looks ready to launch herself at Scarlett. The two women engage in a heated glare-off, the air practically crackling with animosity.

I step forward, my voice cutting through the tension. "What do you want, Scarlett? I know you didn't come all this way here to catch up with old friends."

She turns her icy eyes on me, giving an airy shrug off her bare, freckled shoulders. "Can't a girl stop by to say hello to her ex-fiancé without getting the third degree?"

Uh, no. When Scarlett visits, she wants something or has something up her sleeve. And it's never good.

When I simply stare her down, Scarlett rolls her eyes. "Oh, alright, keep your pants on. I only came to offer a... polite invitation."

"We don't deal with scum like you," Nat spits before I can respond. "So you can take your 'invitation' and shove it up your ass."

Rather than getting riled up, Scarlett just tuts lightly. "Such nasty manners, as always, Natalia. I was simply going to suggest a little... business partnership, of sorts."

She turns to me and sits down on the couch, crossing her legs so her short skirt slides up even more. "You know, Damian, we could do so much more together than apart," she murmurs, idly tracing a finger on the back of the couch. "Merge our operations, become a real powerhouse."

Scarlett fixes me with an expectant look. "The Iacopellis and The Brotherhood, ruling Chicago's underworld as partners. Has a nice ring, don't you think?"

I scowl, immediately recognizing where this is going. "Save your breath, Scarlett. We're not merging shit. That flew out the window the moment our engagement ended."

"Oh, come now, don't be so hasty." Scarlett tsks lightly, her blue eyes remaining flinty shards of ice. "That's ancient history, dear. I was simply a silly, naive girl back then. But I've grown... and my ambitions have expanded. I'm offering you an opportunity here, one I'd think you'd be stupid to pass up."

Her eyes glint with veiled menace. "Especially since those Invicta pains in the ass have been breathing down my neck lately. Could use some... *reinforcements* to put them back in their place."

So that's her play—she wants to absorb the Iacopelli family's muscle and resources to bolster her own position against their rivals. I'm not surprised in the least that her motivations are as transparently self-serving as ever.

"Need I remind you, Scarlett, that you are *not* the head of The Brotherhood. If your father, Mario, wants to initiate a discussion, then I'd be open to listening. But you?" I give a mirthless chuckle. "You've got no sway here, sweetheart. Keep dreaming of your little fantasy merger."

For a long beat, fury blazes behind Scarlett's icy eyes. A terrifying smile slowly spreads across her ruby red lips. It is a smile completely devoid of any warmth or humor—cold, cruel, utterly devoid of humanity. The smile of someone not just unhinged, but unbound from any semblance of morality or empathy.

"We'll see about that, Damian, dear," she purrs, her tone laced with soft menace that raises the hairs on the back of my neck. "One way or another, you'll come around to my way of thinking."

With that chilling promise, she gets up and sashays away, her bodyguards falling into step behind her like shadows. I can't tear my eyes away from the sway of her hips, my heart pounding with a sense of sickening dread.

"*Mio Dio*, I hate that bitch," Edo murmurs. "There's a black hole where her soul should be."

I can't help but agree. Scarlett's last words were no idle threat. The last look in her eyes, that paradoxically warm yet utterly cold smile—it bored straight through me, stripping me down to the bone.

This won't be the last I see of Scarlett Rafa.

13

DAMIAN

I whirl around toward Nat and Edo, a thunderous look on my face. Scarlett's last words hang heavily in the air.

I hate to admit it, but I'm unnerved by her smug remark. Scarlett's ambition and ruthless pursuit of power are legendary, and they threaten my own family's territory.

"Fucking bitch," I bite out, looking down at the ground, my hands clenching into fists. God, I want to fucking *punch* something right now.

Edo nods grimly. "There's also the matter of Alexis."

My head snaps up. "What about Alexis?"

"Mario's been looking for her," Edo says. "Do you think Mario shared that information with Scarlett? You said he didn't want Scarlett involved in the search."

"Scarlett most likely already knows Alexis's name. We can't assume she's completely in the dark," I say, raking a hand through my hair. Scarlett is Mario's only child and the heir to The Brotherhood. He's been including her in every decision and execution since we were preteens.

Edo frowns. "Do you think she knows what Alexis looks like? Mario did show you the picture, so it's obvious he's been showing it to the entire Family so they can hunt her down."

I shake my head. "No." I can picture Scarlett's dismissive scoff at being asked to actually look at a photograph. Her arrogance and vanity are legendary. "This is beneath her. She wouldn't want to look at a picture of a woman who is more attractive than her."

Nat laughs harshly. "Vain cunt. But this works to our advantage, especially since Alexis has cut and dyed her hair. But she needs to start straightening her hair. The curls are too distinct. Too risky."

My jaw clenches at the remark. Alexis's curls are one of my favorite things about her. I've watched them bounce up and down her shoulders as she walks down the hall. Her curls were one of the first things I ever noticed about her.

"Absolutely not," I say, a bit too forcefully. "Her hair stays as it is."

Nat arches an eyebrow at my vehement tone. Even Edo looks somewhat surprised by my uncharacteristic emotion.

"Have you lost your mind?" Nat demands. "Leaving such an identifiable trait could expose her if The Brotherhood gets a glimpse."

"Then we'll ensure they don't get that chance," I say in a clipped tone. I've already asked Alexis to cut and dye her hair. I can't ask her to change something else about herself.

Nat glares at me. Her dark eyes—so similar to our father's—bore into mine. "Can you think with your head instead of your dick?" she snaps. "Just because Scarlett probably doesn't know what Alexis looks like, doesn't mean she won't eventually. We all know Scarlett will keep up with the human trafficking aspect once she takes over. Why won't you protect Alexis from that fucking psycho?"

Edo clears his throat, sensing a rising tension between us. "Why don't you ask Alexis before you make a decision for her?" he asks me. "If she doesn't want to straighten her hair, then maybe a wig or head covering could be a compromise. Just if she's somehow off the mansion grounds."

"And even *on* mansion grounds," Nat remarks. "Especially if Damian keeps allowing Vincente to prowl around."

I force myself to breathe evenly before I rip Nat apart. "Very well," I say through clenched teeth. "I'll ask Alexis myself and let her make the decision."

∼

I'M STILL TOO RATTLED by Edo and Nat's comments about Alexis as I'm driven through the gates of the mansion.

We can't be certain that Scarlett *doesn't* know about Alexis, and the last thing I want is for Scarlett to take an interest in hunting her down. Once Scarlett has made up her mind, *nothing* will change it.

Scarlett, with her beguiling charm and calculating smile, once held sway over my heart. But now, as I reflect on our history, I can't help but wonder what I had ever seen in her.

Our relationship had been a façade, a carefully constructed illusion born out of obligation rather than genuine affection. Pushed together by our respective fathers, we played our parts, pretending to be the perfect Mafia couple while concealing our true selves from each other and the world.

But it was only after my father died that Scarlett's mask slipped, revealing the darkness lurking beneath her façade. Her psychotic and sadistic tendencies emerged with a vengeance, leaving me reeling in disbelief and betrayal.

Stupidly, I thought I had been in love with her, blinded by her sweet veneer. But now, as I look back on our relationship, I realize I never did love her. I loved that I was doing what my father wanted me to do.

Scarlett never loved me either, not truly. She used me as a means to an end, manipulating me to further her own ambitions without a second thought. I didn't realize it until she asked me to shoot up the playground.

And now, with her reappearance, I can't help but feel a sense of dread. I know she's dangerous, capable of anything to get what she wants. But more than that, I worry what she will do if she finds out I'm hiding Alexis.

Striding through the mansion doors, I immediately seek out the head of security. "Status report?"

"It's been quiet, sir," the guard responds promptly. "All entrances and exits are secured per your orders. No threats have been detected."

I give a curt nod, some of the tension easing knowing not only that Alexis is safe, but that she hasn't tried to do a fucking stupid thing and leave again. I've had guards patrolling every entry and exit point, ensuring she cannot escape. She's allowed to roam the house and go outside in the gardens, but she is *not* to leave the premises.

Stringent protection is essential until I can figure out why The Brotherhood and Uncle Vinny want her so badly.

Uncle Vinny. That's another thought.

"Has Vincente Iacopelli arrived unannounced again today?"

"No sir. Not since he left earlier today."

I nod again, relief pouring through me. "Vincente is not allowed to enter this house unless he is expressly allowed," I tell the guard. "You must get verbal permission *from me*. Is that understood?"

"Yes, sir," the guard says. "I will let the others know."

Satisfied that Alexis will be safe from my uncle's unannounced antics, I turn and head toward the sunroom. I know she keeps a pretty strict daily schedule, and from what the guards have indicated, she always spends a lot of time painting in the sunroom.

It's empty.

Frowning, I peek outside to see if she decided to practice some mid-afternoon yoga.

Nothing.

I rush back to the foyer, my heart pounding. "Where is she?" I demand of the guards stationed there.

They exchange confused looks. "Miss Alexis? We're not certain, sir. She has not come down this way."

Fear grips my chest as I realize she can be anywhere on the sprawling mansion grounds. What if something happened? What if someone took her? My security protocols are supposed to ensure her complete fucking safety!

I take the stairs two at a time, throwing open doors as I go. "Alexis?" I call out, desperation seeping into my tone. Dread mounts with every empty room.

Finally, I reach the gym facilities and shove the doors open, my eyes scanning the space frantically. There Alexis is, jogging steadily on the treadmill, her earbuds in, completely oblivious to my frantic search.

"Alexis!" My voice is sharp with relief and anger as I approach her, my heart still racing.

She doesn't hear me, concentrating as her feet slap rhythmically against the treadmill. I can faintly hear the sounds of a hip hop song.

My initial fury melts away as I take in the sight of her, safe and sound. I *did* give her permission to roam the entire house. I can't be mad that she's exercising inside. I swallow hard, trying to calm the storm of emotions raging within me.

As I watch Alexis in the dim light of the home gym, clad only in a sports bra and biking shorts, I feel a primal desire stir within me. Her toned muscles flex with each step on the treadmill, her sweat-glistened skin captivating me in a way I can't explain.

Before I know it, I'm moving toward her, driven by an instinctual need to possess her. I close the distance between us in a few swift strides, my hand wrapping around her waist as I pull her against me.

She lets out a surprised squeal, her eyes widening in shock as my hand covers her mouth to stifle any sound. But as I hold her close, I can't ignore the way her body responds to my touch, the heat of her desire matching my own.

For a moment, I'm lost in the raw intensity of the moment, my senses overwhelmed by the heady mix of adrenaline and arousal. But as I feel Alexis's body pressing against mine, I can't shake the nagging question that lingers.

Why do I crave her so much? What *is* it about Alexis that ignites this primal need within me, despite all the dangers and uncertainties that surround us?

With a low growl of desire, I lean in to capture Alexis's lips in a fierce kiss, my hunger for her burning hotter than ever before.

But all too soon, Alexis breaks away from the kiss, her expression clouded with hurt and frustration. She shakes her head.

"No, Damian. No. You can't just kiss me like that after you've been ignoring me for *weeks*."

I know exactly what she's talking about, but I'm not going to give her the satisfaction of letting her know I've been kicking myself for my behavior.

"I don't know what you're talking about," I say coolly.

Alexis's hazel eyes widen before they narrow on me. Ah, it looks like Feisty Alexis is coming out to play. She comes in spurts, but it's always fun when she does emerge.

"You *left* me," she says, her voice barely above a whisper. "You... you treated me like a whore. You couldn't even give me the courtesy of telling me *why* you were leaving. And don't tell me it was for business! You and I both know that's bullshit."

I feel a stab of guilt as I remember how I shrugged off her cuddles, consumed by my own fears and insecurities. But my pride won't allow me to tell her this.

"You can't just use me however you want, Damian," she says, her voice trembling with emotion, her eyes burning with hurt and anger. "I'm not some pawn in your game, some disposable plaything for you to discard when you're done with me."

My jaw clenches with a surge of anger, my own frustrations bubbling to the surface. "I can do whatever I want," I retort, my voice low and dangerous. "I'm the Don of the Iacopellis, Alexis. You're at my disposal, whether you like it or not."

Alexis scowls at me, the expression looking oddly familiar. Where have I seen that before?

"No," she says firmly. "No, I'm *not*."

She tries to push past me, but I grab her arm, pulling her to me again. She struggles against me. "Let me *go*, Damian!"

"No," I growl. "Not until you hear me out."

She stills, and I allow her to move away from me. She crosses her arms against her full chest and taps her foot.

I drag my eyes away from her puckered nipples showing through her sports bra. Fuck me, this is going to *suck*.

"I fucked up," I say softly. "You wanted to cuddle after we had sex and I just... I panicked, okay? I'm not used to anyone showing me that type of emotion. Emotions are a weakness in my world, Alexis. A weakness to exploit."

I run a hand through my hair. "I was frightened, okay? Frightened of what it means to let someone in. I'm so used to being in control, to never allowing emotions to rule me, that I couldn't handle the vulnerability that comes with intimacy."

Alexis shakes her head, tears pooling in her eyes. "I—you were my *first*, Damian. And you tossed me aside like yesterday's trash. Do you know how that made me feel? Unlovable. Unwanted."

I wince. Truly, that wasn't my intention, and now I feel like a gigantic asshole. Alexis has been through so much in her young life, and I just added another pile of shit to her already shitty self-esteem and self-worth.

A-plus fucking job, Damian.

"I'm sorry," I say sincerely. "I've spent so long building walls around myself, shielding myself from any hint of weakness. I've never allowed myself to be so... exposed."

Alexis's expression remains guarded, her arms still crossed tightly across her chest.

"I know I hurt you," I continue, feeling my stomach swirl. "And I do regret that. But I want you to know that I'm trying, that I will do better next time."

If there's a next time. This may have been the one and only time I'll ever taste and feel Alexis Hartley.

Nodding to her treadmill, I stuff my hands in my pockets. This room feels too constricting. I've admitted way too much. I need to get the fuck out of here *now*.

"Enjoy your run," I mutter and turn to leave.

Before I can move, Alexis seizes my arm and yanks me to her.

And her lips cover mine in a hungry kiss.

14

ALEXIS

I stand there, stunned by Damian's words. An apology? From him? I never expected those words to come out of the Don's mouth, *especially* directed at me.

My anger still simmers beneath the surface, but there is something in Damian's tone, in the slight crease of his brow, that makes me believe he is sincere this time. It's not at all like the fake, manipulative half-apologies I endured from the Carters, Emma, or even Mark over the years.

This apology is *real*. And he is going to leave me alone now, just like that. As a Mob Boss, he can do whatever he wants to me. But instead, he's giving me the opportunity to be by myself. I'm not used to having that kind of autonomy. I'm used to others making those decisions for me.

But I saw his face when he grabbed me from the treadmill. He looked —*scared*, like he was worried something happened to me. That realization rattles something inside me. If he went to the trouble of finding me, doesn't that mean he cares about me on some level?

I don't know what comes over me. Maybe it is the longing for someone to finally treat me with true remorse. Maybe it is the realization that even powerful crime lords can have humble moments. Or maybe it's just pure, unbridled emotion bubbling up from somewhere deep inside me.

Whatever the reason, I seize Damian's arm, grab him by the lapels of his expensive suit, and pull him into a searing kiss. My heart pounds with a mix of anger, passion, and something else I can't quite name.

To my horror, Damian pulls back, searching my eyes. "Alexis, what are you doing?"

I immediately feel a flush of embarrassment and panic. My cheeks burn, and I can barely meet his intense gaze. I had acted rashly, boldly kissing him without a second thought. But now reality is crashing down on me. *What was I thinking, throwing myself at Damian like that?*

Tears prick at the corner of my eyes as mortification sets in. Damian's going to reject me, maybe even punish me for my forwardness. As a Mafia Don, he surely has his pick of any woman he wants. Why would he want *me*?

My heart pounds, anger and sadness swirling in my chest. No one wants me. I fight against the lump rising in my throat, blinking rapidly to keep the threatening tears at bay. I barely register Damian's next words as humiliation roars in my ears.

Then his firm tone breaks through my spiraling thoughts. "Don't get me wrong, I want you to continue…"

My head snaps up at that, eyes widening in disbelief. "But I need to make sure you're okay with moving forward here."

I'm stunned. Damian's looking for my consent? I feel a warmth bloom in my chest at Damian's consideration for my feelings.

"I have to be honest, though. For now, at least, I can't do the tender after sex stuff. Cuddling, pillow talk, all that…" He shakes his head. "It's not you, it's me." He winces. "Fuck, that sounds bad. What I'm trying to say is that I'm just not wired that way right now, and I don't want you to get the wrong impression."

To my surprise, I find this blunt admission from the normally uncompromising Don almost… endearing. I reach up and cup his jaw, tracing the stubble with my thumb. "I definitely want this, Damian. All of you, whatever that means right now."

Relief flickers across his handsome features. Then a roguish grin spreads across his lips as he captures my mouth in another heated, hungry kiss. His powerful arms encircle my waist, pulling me flush against his body as the kiss deepens.

His large, calloused hands grip my waist firmly as he walks us backward until my back hits the wall of the home gym. His muscular body presses against mine, the hard planes molding to my soft curves. I can feel his muscles, even through the expensive fabric of his suit.

When his tongue swirls against my lower lip, I eagerly part my lips to let him in. Damian's tongue delves deep, stroking and twisting with mine in a heated duel. The sound of our kissing fills the room, along with my soft whimpers of pleasure.

My entire body feels like it's burning up from the inside out. Liquid heat pools low in my core, an insistent throbbing growing between my thighs. My hands roam feverishly over the hard planes of Damian's body, finally sinking into his thick, dark hair.

Damian growls, the rumbling vibration only stoking the blazing desire coursing through my veins. One of his hands leaves my waist to cup my jaw, holding me in place as he plunders my mouth with his tongue.

I'm drowning in pure sensation, every nerve ending like a live wire. I had never felt so thoroughly consumed by sheer want. My whimpers grow louder and more desperate against Damian's kisses.

Damian pulls back a fraction, much to my displeasure. His piercing gaze bores into mine, lust and hunger burning in those dark depths.

Lust and hunger for *me*.

But there's a question in those dark eyes. He wants me to set the pace.

I can do that.

My mouth falls onto his neck as I suckle and lick the tender skin there. Damian moans and tips his head back, encouraging me further. My hands yank his shirt from the waistband of his suit pants and explore every plane of his hot, muscular chest.

I nip at the sensitive skin where his neck meets his shoulder, and he hisses, digging his fingers almost painfully into my hips. "Fuck, Alexis."

His moan only encourages me as I continue to lavish kisses to his skin, my fingers unbuttoning his shirt until I can push it off his shoulders, sending it pooling to the floor.

I can't help but be struck by the sheer beauty of Damian's body, and his undeniable allure overwhelms my senses. Suddenly, there's an overwhelming need to have Damian *now*.

Running my hand over the bulge in his pants, I laugh softly as he hisses and bucks his hips forward.

"Oh, you like that, don't you?" Damian growls.

I stroke my fingers down the length of his cock again, but this time, Damian captures my mouth in a heated kiss.

I bite his lower lip.

That seems to be his undoing as he grabs me, crushing my body to his. His hands grab my ass as he presses me against his considerable length. I moan into his mouth as I feel his hard cock press against me. My fingers grapple in his hair, tugging the strands as I grind against him.

Hissing, Damian removes me from the wall and pushes me toward an adjustable exercise bench. My back collides with the inclined seat as Damian kneels in front of me. With a wicked grin, he pulls down my biker shorts and underwear until I'm exposed to him.

I want to clamp my legs together and hide, but one look from Damian prevents me from doing so.

"Do you know how hard it is to work when all I think about is my face buried in your pussy?" He growls, and my insides turn liquid at his words. The throbbing between my legs is becoming unbearable.

"Please," I whimper, squirming against the seat, desperate for *any* type of friction.

Damian laughs huskily. "As you wish."

I'm nearly undone when he drags his tongue up my center. I moan at the same time he does, and he licks me again, lingering at the apex of my thighs, sucking and nipping at my clit, before he begins again.

I don't even know what I'm saying as I cry out, arching further into his tongue, but Damian only laughs, denying me what I crave. He slowly licks me again before sliding two fingers inside me.

God, *fuck*. It's just too good. I moan as my hips arch against his hand, thrusting in time with his fingers. Damian's breathing is uneven as he asks me, "How do you want it?"

How can he even expect me to answer him when he's fingering me like this? "Hard," I whimper, only focusing on the exquisite feeling of his fingers pumping in and out of me.

Damian chuckles, a low, sexy sound that makes my toes curl. "Good girl," he purrs.

Then, his fingers are gone and I whimper at the loss of sensation. I'm just about to do the damn job myself when I hear the sounds of his pants unbuckling and unzipping, and then, his mouth is back on my pussy, and I cry out, thrusting against his tongue.

But that wicked mouth of his is moving up, pressing kisses to my stomach, to my covered breasts, and then to my lips where he crushes them in a searing kiss that has my heart thumping even harder than before.

"Damian," I moan against his mouth as he straddles me, his hard cock pressing against my stomach. "Damian, *please*."

He chuckles again, unclasping my sports bra and letting it fall to the ground. My nipples harden as cool air caresses them. "And what would you like me to do, Alexis?"

"Fuck me," I whimper.

Who *am* I? I never expected to beg when it came to sex. But I can't say I hate it.

Damian's tongue caresses the shell of my ear. "As you wish."

His head is at my entrance, and I wiggle desperately, wanting contact. Friction. *Anything*.

Damian smoothly slides in, groaning in satisfaction. "God, Alexis, you're so *tight*."

Breathing escapes me. This already feels so much better than the last time. There's no sharp pain at our joining. I can't think of anything except how deliciously good this feels. Being with Damian just feels so *right*.

We soon settle into a rhythm, his balls slapping against me as he fucks me. He pulls himself nearly out of me before slamming back in. The sensation is so delicious, I cry out, scrabbling to take hold of anything. My brain is complete mush, and I can only focus on the feeling of his body against mine, his breathless pants against my head, and the sounds of our bodies moving together.

I clutch the side of the exercise bench and meet his every thrust, feeling him move deeper inside me. This must be what Nirvana feels like. Every time is better than the last, and I can't get enough of him.

Soon, pressure builds in my lower belly, and I gasp, begging and warning in the same breath. "Damian, I–I'm going to come."

"That's right, baby," Damian snarls, his thrusts becoming deeper and harder. "Fucking come for me."

His words are my undoing, and I unleash myself on him, nearly screaming in ecstasy. He continues to thrust, but the movements are shallower and sloppier.

I know he's close. I twist my hips and push up, meeting his pelvis with mine. I'm not exactly sure what I'm doing, but something about this feels like the right thing to do.

That's exactly what he needs.

Damian barks out a curse as he finishes inside me, shuddering as he finishes before he collapses on top of me, our slick skin sticking together.

Our ragged breaths mingle as we try to control our breathing. I run my hands through his damp hair, my legs shaking as they dangle over the sides of the exercise bench.

Damian slowly pulls out of me, hissing at how sensitive his dick is. He finds his clothes and picks them up, smoothly buttoning up his wrinkled shirt as he looks at me.

"I have work to do," he says shortly. "I'll see you later."

With that, he leaves me, shutting the door behind him with a soft snap.

Even though he told me he doesn't do the after-sex intimacy, I still can't help but be confused.

Will he ever want that with me? Or will I forever be just a booty call?

15

ALEXIS

I toss and turn, the sheets tangling around my restless body. Sleep won't come. My mind is too wired from... well, from Damian. I blush just thinking about his name, heat blooming across my cheeks as flashes of our tryst play through my head.

The way he had taken control, pinning me against the exercise bench as he fucked the living daylights out of me. The delicious friction of our bodies moving together in perfect rhythm. The strangled cries of pleasure torn from my lips as he brought me to the dizzying edge.

I squeeze my thighs together, trying to tamp down the growing ache between my legs. I had never experienced anything so intense, so overwhelming in its eroticism. A part of me is almost... embarrassed by how much I love it, by how badly I crave Damian's touch.

Damian is like a drug I can't get enough of. I've never wanted anyone as much as I want him. The feelings I thought I had for Mark pale in comparison to how I feel about Damian. Did I ever really love Mark, or did I love the idea of someone loving me?

Mark never would have allowed me to set the pace. He never would have asked for consent. He would have just taken me, using me only for his pleasure, my feelings be damned.

Ugh. This won't do. I've been restless for hours.

Shoving aside the rumpled sheets, I decide to head to the kitchen. Maybe a little baking therapy will settle my jittery thoughts. I pad into the large, state-of-the-art kitchen. The sleek stainless steel appliances gleam in the moonlight. I run a hand along the smooth quartz countertops, marveling at how spacious and well-equipped it is. So different from the tiny, cramped kitchen at the Carters' house.

I remember that little room with a grimace. The cracked linoleum floors, the oven that would either burn food or undercook it, the utter lack of counter space to prepare anything more complicated than spaghetti. Yet the Carters expected me to whip up elaborate meals for their family in that pathetic excuse for a kitchen.

The unfairness of it made me clench my jaw so tightly my teeth hurt. I had only been a teenager when I started cooking for them, overwhelmed, trying my best to please the demanding Carters. Emma and Suzanne, in particular, always found something to criticize. I can still see Suzanne's perpetually pursed lips and furrowed brow fixed in a sneer of disdain.

Like I was single-handedly failing as a cook, a human being.

I shake my head, banishing those thoughts like it's all an annoying cobweb. I'm not going to think about the Carters right now. Not now. Not ever.

Opening the baking cabinet, I peruse the ingredients and decide to bake a cake. I had overheard Edo mention that a vanilla cake with chocolate frosting was his favorite, so that's what I'm going to make. As I preheat the oven and gather ingredients, the familiar smells of flour and sugar embrace me like an old friend. I miss working at the bakery—the easy camaraderie with my co-workers, the satisfaction of crafting beautiful pastries.

It had been my safe haven, a place where I was capable and confident.

Not like with Damian, where I constantly second-guess myself, my emotions a tangled, confusing knot. One moment, I am so flustered by him that I can barely breathe. The next, I want to rip his clothes off and have my way with him on the gleaming countertop...

Whoa. I squeeze my eyes shut, feeling a traitorous blush heating my cheeks. I really need to get a grip. Envisioning Damian naked and splayed out amid my baking supplies is *not* going to help my restless mind.

But it's hard *not* to think about him. He confuses me. One moment, he treats me kindly or gazes at me with a scorching intensity, making me melt with desire. The next, he is cool and distant, his walls slamming up without warning. Just like earlier, when he immediately left after sex. I just don't know where I stand with him.

I sigh, pulling out the stand mixer with slightly more force than necessary. Maybe I'm just really bad at sex, and that's why Damian keeps pulling away, using that bullshit reason about not being able to cuddle as an excuse. The thought makes my cheeks burn with embarrassment and shame. Damian had awakened insatiable cravings I don't quite understand, urges that both exhilarate and intimidate me.

As I add the softened butter and sugar to the bowl, I can't help but wonder—is any of this normal? Or am I careening toward something darker, a side of myself I don't fully grasp? Damian confuses me, electrifies me, makes me feel dangerous and powerful and utterly adrift all at once.

I watch the sugar and butter cream into a pale, fluffy mass, cracking eggs and adding them one at a time. I will just have to accept that when it comes to Damian, I don't have any of the answers. All I can do is surrender to the chaos... and pray I don't get consumed by the flames.

"What are you doing up?"

Startling, I whirl around to see a shirtless Damian standing at the doorway of the kitchen, Biscotti at his heels.

My mouth dries at the sight of him and heat floods my cheeks. My gaze rakes over Damian's chiseled torso and powerful arms. Even in just his pajama pants, the man exudes an almost overwhelming aura of rugged masculinity. I have to grip the mixing bowl to keep from melting into a puddle right there and then.

"Alexis?" Damian asks, his voice still rough from sleep. He runs a confused eye over the array of ingredients scattered across the counter.

"I couldn't sleep," I admit, tearing my eyes away from his bare chest with an effort. "So I thought I'd bake something. Burn off some... energy."

I risk a glance at him from beneath my lashes. A slight smirk plays about Damian's lips, making it clear that he knows exactly what kind of "energy" I'm referring to. He saunters closer, that predatory grace of his making my heart race.

"A cake? Didn't peg you as the type," he murmurs, resting a large hand on the small of my back. The simple touch is like a brand, scorching my very soul.

I swallow hard and focus on the mixing process, trying not to get too flustered. "I did most of the cooking and baking while living with the Carters. It's soothing."

Damian frowns at that, a muscle ticking in his powerful jaw. "How old were you when you took over the cooking and baking?" His voice is light, dangerous.

I shrug, adding the vanilla to the pale yellow batter. "Twelve? Thirteen? Middle school, at least."

He scowls. "Those assholes worked you too hard. You were just a kid."

"I managed." I keep my tone light, though the memories still sting.

His grip tightens ever so slightly on my hip. "If I had people like that on my payroll, they'd be at the bottom of the river."

A delicious shiver travels down my spine at his casual threat. I should be horrified. After all, Damian is the head of one of the most dangerous crime families in the city. Instead, hearing the hard edge in his tone just makes my insides liquify with molten want.

As if sensing the effect his words have on me, Damian's smirk deepens. "Need any help with that cake, Alexis?"

He presses himself against my back, his sculpted chest brushing my shoulders. I can feel his hardened dick digging into my backside, stoking the simmering embers of desire banked low in my stomach.

"I–I've got it under control," I manage, silently cursing the way my voice shakes.

"You sure about that?" Damian growls, nuzzling my neck with those sinful lips. "Because you seem a little... flustered to me."

I bite back a moan as he rolls his hips, letting me feel how aroused he is. How effortlessly he can undo me with just a few heated words and touches. I'm so wildly outmatched... and I have never wanted to surrender more.

Giving in, I let my scraper spatula clatter to the counter and lean back against his solid form. "Maybe I could use a little help, after all."

I can feel the ridges of his firm abs, the flexing of his powerful arms as he reaches around to grab the errant tool.

"Told you I'd lend a hand," he rumbles in that sinfully deep voice, his warm breath caressing the sensitive skin below my ear.

I shiver, my body traitorously thrilled by his proximity. "J–just don't mess it up. I'm an expert baker."

Damian chuckles, the vibrations rippling through me. "Yes, I can see your skills are unmatched. I'll try to be a worthy sous chef."

There's an odd lilt to his voice on those last words, something almost... wistful. I glance at him curiously, taking in the faint crease between his brows as he concentrates on blending the wet and dry ingredients.

"My mom used to call me her little sous chef," he says quietly. "We baked all the time when I was a kid—cookies, bread, whatever. Helped her take her mind off..." He trails off, jaw tightening.

I reach over to squeeze his arm, offering silent comfort. I don't know the whole story about his parents, but it's clear they had been killed. Whether it was an accident or by a rival gang is a question I won't ask today.

"My sister Alessandra loved it too," Damian continues in a strained voice. "She was a total mess in the kitchen, flour everywhere, licking batter off the spoon before it was even baked. She used to drive my mom fucking crazy." A sad sort of smile ghosts across his lips at the memory.

Alessandra. The name sounds familiar.

Then it hits me. He had used that name against Nat the night he had been shot. The look on Nat's face now makes sense.

"You had another sister," I say gently.

He nods. "She was home sick from school. Wrong place at the wrong time."

My heart aches for him, aches for the past trauma and loss he and Nat have endured. How similar our lives are, each with our own suffering. "Damian, I'm so sorry."

He avoids my gaze for a moment before those dark eyes meet mine. "She was only twelve. She was just a child."

"Oh, Damian." I stroke his stubbled cheek, wishing I can erase that haunted look from his face.

Seeming to shake off the melancholy, Damian gives me a lopsided grin, covering my hand with his much larger one. "But we can't all be depressing fuck-ups tonight, Alexis. Do you have any good baking stories? Anything with your parents?"

"No," I admit. I barely remember life with my mother. She died when I was so young that sometimes, I'm not sure what's truly a memory and what's something my brain has made up.

"My mom died when I was six. And I barely knew my dad."

"How'd she die?" Damian asks the question gently, but my throat still tightens.

"I… I'm not sure, exactly." I have flashes of memory—my mom and I in a closet, but then I'm all alone and the closet door opens. "I was so young. All I remember is the police finding me and taking me away."

"And your dad?" Damian prompts. "He never tried to claim you?"

I shrug. "If he did, he didn't try very hard. I don't even remember what he looks like. I just remember the smell of his cologne and cigars." I shake my head. "It's all pretty fuzzy. No one bothered to tell me anything, and I used to get in trouble with my foster family if I asked about my mother, so I stopped asking."

Damian frowns, drawing me into the protective circle of his arms. I go willingly, resting my head on his chest and taking comfort in his solid strength.

"For what it's worth," he murmurs against my hair, "I think you turned out pretty great, despite it all."

A lump forms in my throat at the simple words of praise. I blink back the faint sting of tears, focusing instead of the steady thump of his heart under my ear. *This* is the side of Damian I want to see more of. I know the Mafia Don façade is just a veneer for a softer, caring Damian who knows just what to say to make me feel better.

He makes me feel like I matter in a way I haven't truly felt in far too long.

Standing on my tiptoes, I brush my lips against the curve of his neck, needing to be closer still. "Baking's more fun with a partner."

Damian rumbles out a laugh, smoothing a hand down my back. "Then let's get to it, chef. I'll try not to lick the batter this time."

Heat shoots straight to my core at those words, remembering how he feasted on me and licked me like I was his piece of candy. I clear my throat and push away from him. "See that you don't. We don't want to contaminate the cake."

Damian chuckles, clearly seeing how much he's affected me, but he returns to his work, pouring the pale yellow cake batter into two pans, making sure to scrape every last bit of batter before neatly sliding the pans into the oven.

While he does that, I work on making the chocolate frosting. My hands shake as I add the butter, cocoa, and confectioners sugar to the mixing bowl and turn it on high. God, what is *wrong* with me? Baking is supposed to be my therapy, but it's making me more turned on than ever.

And I have a certain shirtless Mafia Don to thank for that.

I squeal in surprise as a dollop of frosting lands on my neck. Goddammit, I had the mixer too high. That will teach me to be distracted while baking.

Before I can wipe it away, Damian is there, backing me up against the counter with a heated look in his eyes.

"Allow me," he growls in that sinfully rough voice that never fails to make my toes curl.

Then his mouth is on me, lips blazing a molten trail along the sensitive column of my throat. I gasp as his tongue laps at the sweet frosting, the intimate rasp sending liquid fire licking through my veins.

"D–Damian..." I manage, hands coming up to fist in his dark, tousled hair.

He hums against my racing pulse point, removing the sticky-sweet frosting from my flushed skin with broad, unashamed strokes of his tongue. I arch helplessly into his sculpted form, chasing the heat of his mouth with shameless abandon.

When he thoroughly cleans the frosting from my neck, Damian continues his sensual assault. His lips trail up the slope of my jaw, his teeth grazing my racing pulse point in a way that has me shuddering violently. Then he's kissing me, deep and filthy and all-consuming, licking my lips and devouring my breathy moans.

I clutch him closer, parting my lips to allow the slick velvet glide of his tongue. I taste sugar and heat and dark, masculine spice—an explosive, intoxicating combination. Damian plunders my mouth with hungry fervor, stoking the whip of desire into a storm of molten need in my core.

His large hands roam with possessive reverence, caressing the soft curves he has already mapped and worshipped before. Yet his touch is still somehow a brand, setting off liquid tremors wherever his callused palms and fingers stroke. I arch wantonly against him, craving that delicious friction.

Finally, the need for oxygen becomes too great to ignore. Damian tears his mouth from mine with a groan, panting harshly against my damp, swollen lips. I cling to him, equally breathless and undone, my heavy-lidded gaze drinking in the lust-darkened expression blazing in his eyes.

"Fuck, Alexis," he growls, resting his forehead against mine. "You taste so sweet."

He punctuates the words with a sharp grind of his hips, letting me feel the ridge of his arousal. An obscene whimper slips free at the raw promise in that simple thrust.

"Maybe we should take this upstairs." I manage in a throaty whisper. "Before I end up debauched on this counter."

Damian's wolfish grin is all the answer I need. Hooking one arm around my waist, he hoists me up and onto the counter in one smooth motion, pinning me beneath his body. His kiss swallows my shocked gasp, melting away any protest I might have—not that I'd been protesting in the slightest.

As his hands shove up my nightgown and his skilled mouth blazes an incendiary path down my breasts, I let my eyes fall shut in abandon, let myself be consumed by the wildfire of sensations, by Damian's dizzying touch that liquifies my higher brain function down to a single, rapturous mantra.

More. God, *yes*. More.

Damian pulls me so the lower half of my body is nearly dangling off the counter. He flashes me a wicked grin before he slowly pulls down my panties, stuffing them into the pocket of his pajama pants.

I've never been so turned on in my entire life.

"You tasted so good with that frosting on your neck," Damian murmurs, kneeling in front of me so he's directly in front of my sex. "Can I have another taste?"

"Yes, *please*," I practically cry, unable to take my eyes off him as he smirks, pressing tender kisses from my knee to my thigh before he eventually reaches that little bundle of nerves where I need him most.

I bite my lip to prevent me from crying out, lest I wake the entire household. Damian's hot tongue drags through my folds to envelope my hypersensitive bud, and I writhe against the counter, thrusting my hips into his willing mouth.

Damian pins my hips down with one hand as he feasts on me, using his other hand to slip two fingers into me. My eyes nearly roll into the back of my head as I revel in the sensations. My thighs begin to shake, and I know I'm getting close. Damian seems to know it too because he presses his tongue deeper and rubs my swollen nub.

"Oh, *Damian*!" I gasp. "I–I'm going to come."

He doesn't say a word, only working my oversensitive clit even more. I explode, biting down on my hand as I come, writhing and bucking against him as I come down from my high.

Damian's lips are shiny as he emerges from between my legs, a triumphant smirk on his face. Oh, I'm going to eat him alive.

A low growl echoes through the kitchen. We freeze, panting heavily, turning to see Biscotti eyeing us with clear impatience.

I flush bright red, hurriedly tugging my nightgown back into place. Damian runs a hand through his tousled hair with a rueful chuckle.

"Looks like someone needs to go out," he murmurs, voice still husky with unfulfilled desire. Pressing one last kiss to my lips, he stands up and grabs Biscotti's leash.

As he heads to the back door, I sag against the counter, trying to calm my breath and racing pulse. I can still taste him, feel the echoes of his caresses burning through me.

I splash some cold water on my flushed face, wondering what the hell I'm doing. I can't believe I allowed him to go down on me in the kitchen! On the counter! Where anyone could see!

But there's something about Damian that bypasses all my usual defenses, rendering me helpless against the relentless pull of temptation he represents. The way he touches me, kisses me... it unlocks a deep, primal part of myself I hadn't even known existed until him.

And if I'm being truly honest, the intense physical chemistry is only part of my growing fixation. There are glimpses of tenderness, of protectiveness, of searing vulnerability that make me ache to know him more deeply, to break through the walls he has erected.

Once Damian returns, I quickly get the cake layers out of the oven and let them cool on the counter. Frosting them can wait until tomorrow. There's no way I can handle that right now.

An awkward pause stretches between us, rife with lingering heat and unspoken questions. Damian clears his throat. "We should, uh, probably get some sleep."

"Right, yes. Sleep." I hate how strangled my voice sounds.

We part ways in the hallway, sneaking sidelong glances at each other. Alone in my room, I sink onto the bed with a shuddering sigh. I can still smell him all around me, can still feel his tongue on my skin.

Arousal still thrums hotly through my veins, my body aching with unquenched craving. But it's more than that—there's a different kind of yearning blooming in my chest, one that terrifies me even as it draws me even deeper under Damian's spell.

Restless shadows dance across the ceiling as I turn on my side, emotions churning.

I'm in so much trouble. And I have no idea how to free myself from this exquisite torture.

16

ALEXIS

A few weeks later, Damian informs me that I will be accompanying him, Na, and Edo to a funeral down in Carbondale, Illinois. My eyes go wide as Nat and Edo immediately object.

"You can't be serious, Damian! Bringing an outsider to one of our funerals is a huge breach of protocol," Nat protests.

Edo shakes his head vigorously. "She doesn't know how to move in our circles. One wrong look or comment could raise suspicions." He winces as he finishes his sentence, flashing me an apologetic look. Ever since I made him his favorite cake, Edo has warmed toward me considerably.

Damian waves a dismissive hand. "It'll be fine. Carmine was just a low-level soldier. None of the heavy hitters will be there except maybe a few capos from the DeAngelo family as a courtesy. The Brotherhood certainly won't be there. And Uncle Vinny never attends these things, especially if they're low-ranked soldiers."

"That's not the point," Nat insists, looking ready to pull out her hair. "Even a nothing funeral is no place for civilians."

"She'll be in disguise as our cousin Maria, and Edo can keep her safe. It's an easy in and out to pay respects to Carmine."

The trio continue to argue heatedly for several more minutes. I stay silent, feeling a knot of anxiety twisting in my stomach. Finally, Nat and Edo seem to give in, though obviously still against the idea.

"When is the funeral?" I finally ask.

Nat and Damian whirl toward me, as if finally remembering I'm in the same room as them. "It's tomorrow," Damian remarks, looking at his watch. "Nat will help you find appropriate attire and give you the backstory on our cousin."

Nat gapes at Damian. "*What?*"

But Damian's already walking out of the room, cell phone to his ear as he answers a call. Edo shakes his head. "You're on your own with this one, Nat," he says before he also leaves, leaving Nat and me alone.

Nat takes several steadying breaths before grabbing my hand and pulling me out of the room. She drags me to her room and into her walk-in closet. I'm immediately struck by the sheer extravagance of the space. It's unlike anything I had ever seen before, a testament to Nat's lavish lifestyle and her status within the Mob.

"Wow," I whisper, looking around in awe. Towering mirrors reflect every angle of the opulent display of designer clothes and accessories. Meticulously organized shelves are filled with luxurious garments that speak volumes about Nat's impeccable taste.

"This is bigger than both bedrooms at the Carters' house," I finish, placing my hand on a gleaming marble countertop in the center of the closet.

But Nat doesn't hear me—or she ignores me—as she rifles through a shelf full of black dresses. "We need something conservative but understated," I hear her mutter before she emerges triumphantly, holding up a black knee-length dress with three-quarter-length sleeves.

She throws it at me, and I catch it, fingering the luxurious material. I've never worn anything so nice in my life.

"Put this on. It'll do."

I slip the dress over my head, smoothing it down. It is a little big but otherwise fits me well. Nat nods in approval before she disappears into the back of her closet, pulling out a wide-brimmed black hat. She tosses it at me like a frisbee, and I catch it.

"Pull your hair back in a bun tomorrow and wear the hat. It'll help disguise you a bit more if anyone tries to take a closer look."

I nod fervently, my throat too dry to speak.

"Now, about your backstory..." Nat sits on the counter and gives me the rundown on Cousin Maria.

"You're my second cousin on my mom's side. You live out on the East Coast with your parents and brother, Joey. You're visiting us because you're hoping to find work in Chicago because the job market in New York sucks. Your dad is a minor capo for the Genovese Family."

My head spins trying to absorb all the details of this elaborate backstory. Nat can sense my overwhelm and grips my shoulders firmly.

"Just let me and Edo do the talking unless someone addresses you directly. Then give short, simple answers. If you get stuck on a detail, just say you don't like to discuss 'Family business'."

Nat fixes me with an intense look. "This is really important, Alexis. One misstep, one slip up, and there'll be consequences. You gotta sell this Cousin Maria identity one hundred percent. Do you understand?"

I nod jerkily, my heart pounding. I have no choice but to pull this off. My life may depend on it.

∼

As we pull up to Carmine's family home for the viewing, I can't help but gape at the beautiful home before us. Edo notices my surprise and chuckles.

"What, you were expecting a shack?" he asks dryly. "Carmine may have been a low-ranked soldier, but he was a crafty motherfucker and good with his money."

I shake my head slowly, taking in the perfectly manicured grounds and brick exterior. Edo tugs on my arm to get me moving.

"C'mon, Maria. Let me give you the lay of the land before we go in." He discreetly points out the different clusters of well-dressed mourners.

"See those older guys in the expensive suits with the fat ruby rings? They're the capos from the DeAngelo Family. Don't even think about making eye contact."

I gulp nervously and adjust the brim of my black hat so it covers most of my eyes. My head hurts from how tightly Nat pulled my hair back in a severe bun.

Edo goes on to identify members of the Kansas City and Milwaukee Families who had made the trip to pay respects. My head is spinning trying to keep it all straight. Edo leans in close and discreetly points out another group of well-dressed mourners.

"See those guys over there? That's the Santiago Family from Milwaukee," he murmurs. "They're the biggest crew in the Midwest these days outside of the Chicago area. Made their fortune in gambling and union rackets."

I nod, trying to keep the various Families and territories straight in my head. Edo continues in a hushed tone.

"The older guy in the middle, that's Alfonso Santiago himself. Used to be the underboss before the last regime change. Now, he's the king of Milwaukee. And you see the younger dude next to him? That's his nephew, Carlos. Word is, he's being groomed to take over one day."

I study the two men Edo indicates. Alfonso has an imperious air about him, surveying the room like a lord overseeing his court. Carlos stands slightly behind, clean-cut and attentive. Despite his relatively youthful appearance, I can see a simmering intensity just below the surface.

An impeccably dressed woman speaks to Carmine's wife—a pale-faced woman who looks to be in her mid-forties. The woman has her hand on Carmine's wife's shoulder, speaking to her in a hushed tone.

"That's Louisa, Carlos's wife. The Santiagos are here paying respects because Carmine was married to Alfonso's niece," Edo explains. "*Famiglia* comes before everything in this life."

I give a small nod of acknowledgment, not daring to ask any follow-up questions. Edo's grip on my arm tightens slightly.

"Just stay quiet and don't gawk at anyone too long," he warns under his breath. "This is neutral territory for now, but you never know what might set one of these hot-heads off."

I swallow hard and unconsciously shrink a little closer to Edo's side, grateful for his protective presence. One misstep and I could inadvertently insult the wrong person. The consequences didn't bear thinking about.

Edo and I enter another room, and I spot Nat and Damian working the room. I'm struck by how confident and assured they both appear—especially Damian. He moves with an easy grace, embracing people and offering condolences like a benevolent lord holding court.

In his impeccably tailored suit, he looks every inch the powerful boss, born for this life of wealth and status.

I can't help but notice how exceptionally handsome he looks as well. An undeniable air of command and intensity radiates from him. This is a man used to having things go his way. Yet, I know there is another side to Damian that only I get to see—a more vulnerable, almost gentle side that he keeps carefully hidden away from this world.

As I watch him work the crowd, I wonder if he relishes inhabiting this powerful "boss" persona or if he finds it stifling at times. Does he ever tire of wearing that unflappable mask?

I don't think he even knows. That mask is probably second nature to him at this point.

When our eyes meet across the crowd, he gives me the slightest wink and nod, letting me know I'm doing well so far. My cheeks warm, and I force a tight smile in return, my stomach churning with nerves despite the awe I feel at witnessing Damian operate in his natural element.

My musings are interrupted as a couple of older men approach Edo and me. Edo deftly steers the conversation, giving short replies that don't invite any questions directly to me. I keep my head down, trying to fade into the background.

Eventually—to my horror—Edo is pulled away, leaving me alone by the ornate French doors that open onto the back patio area. I press myself against the wall, hoping to remain unseen and inconspicuous. This world terrifies me and I have no desire to draw any attention.

This shadowy Mob world that Damian and his family inhabits is so far removed from anything I've ever known. The opulence, power, and underlying threat of violence are utterly terrifying to an outsider like me.

Can I ever truly be part of this life? Over the past few weeks, Damian has let me see glimpses of his softer, more vulnerable side outside of the family business. The kind, thoughtful, even tender man he can be when we are alone together. That is the Damian I am slowly but surely developing deeper feelings for.

But here, at Carmine's funeral viewing, I see the other side of him on full display. The powerful, imposing boss radiating a cold, ruthless intensity. An untouchable prince holding court over his criminal empire. This side of Damian terrifies me, if I'm honest. Can I ever become accustomed to his harsh, uncompromising edges, the constant perceived threats and need for a protective mask?

Could a relationship between us ever truly work? Even if Damian somehow returns my feelings, being with him means being permanently entangled in the dangerous underworld he presides over. Do I have the courage for that kind of life? I was trying to escape Mark and the Carters when I somehow got ensnared with Damian. Do I want a life of always watching my back, never feeling safe?

I know I care for Damian. I can see myself loving him, too. But loving him means loving *all* of him—including the sinister, brutal side of his existence. Can I reconcile those two warring realities? I couldn't for Mark.

Damian isn't Mark, though. Damian has saved me from a fate worse than death. He cares about my feelings, unlike Mark and the Carters.

But even through all that, I still have no answers. Perhaps some sacrifices are too great, no matter how strong the feelings.

I turn toward the open French doors, hoping that a little fresh air will help me compose myself. That's when I spot an unattended toddler—no more than two years old—in a tiny suit, wobbling his way toward the large swimming pool just beyond the doors.

I look around frantically, but none of the adults seem to notice or are watching him. For a moment, I freeze, wondering whether I should try to intervene and find his parents.

Then with a sickening plunge of my heart, I see the boy's foot catch on a loose patio stone. He topples forward, arms pinwheeling, a scream escaping his mouth, and disappears under the dark waters of the pool with a small splash.

Before I realize what I'm doing, I kick off my heels and run forward, throwing myself into the pool after the child.

17

DAMIAN

A piercing scream slices through the somber gathering like a knife.

My head whips toward the sound, eyes widening as I exchange a look with Edo and Nat. It hits me that Alexis is nowhere to be found.

We aren't the only ones startled—the entire viewing erupts into chaos. Guests surge forward from the sitting room, suits and black dresses swirling. Flashes of silver pistols emerge from suit coats. Panicked shouts and the clack of high heels on marble fill the air as the crowd rushes toward the patio doors.

I shove through the throng, bursting out the doors to the chaos outside. What I see makes my heart nearly stop.

A waterlogged Alexis is treading water in the pool, a thrashing toddler clutched against her chest. The child's earsplitting wails slice through the air as he flails in Alexis's arms.

"Emilio!" A woman's scream, laced with primal terror, cuts through the panic.

I'm going to have a fucking heart attack.

It's Louisa Santiago—wife to the heir to the Santiago crime family. Her husband and heir to the Santiagos, Carlos, is hot on her heels, his face drained of color.

The gathered crowd parts like the Red Sea as the couple barrels toward the pool. Carlos and Louisa reach the water's edge just as Alexis hefts the soaked child up with a grunt.

Louisa seizes her son, pulling him into a fierce embrace as great, racking sobs shake her entire frame. Carlos wraps his arms tightly around them both, lips pressed to his wife and child's brows in fervent thanks.

There's a beat of heavy silence from the assembled onlookers before the questions start.

"What happened?"

"Is the boy okay?"

"Who's that woman?"

I grab a towel and toss it to Alexis as she hauls herself out of the pool, dripping wet. She deftly catches it, wrapping it around her trembling form.

"What the *fuck* just happened?" My low growl cuts through the clamor. She was *supposed* to stay undetected, and now she's the fucking center of attention.

She shoots me a withering look, shoving her sodden hair out of her face. "I just saved a child's life," she hisses.

The words had no sooner left her mouth than Louisa Santiago is upon us, Carlos right behind her. Louisa's face is streaked with tears, but her eyes shine with profound gratitude as she looks at Alexis.

"Thank you," she breathes, clutching the toddler tightly to her chest, not caring about the rapidly growing wet spot on her expensive gown.

"*Thank you* for saving my baby." She steps forward and throws her arms around Alexis, holding her close for a lingering moment before pulling back.

Carlos places a hand on Louisa's back, his eyes finding Alexis's. "What's your name?"

I hold my breath, hoping against hope that Alexis sticks to her cover. For the love of fucking *God*, do this goddamn right.

There's the slightest pause before Alexis replies, her voice admirably steady. "Maria. I'm Don Iacopelli's cousin."

I could fucking collapse right now, and from the looks on Nat and Edo's faces, they are two seconds away from doing the same.

Carlos extends a hand, taking Alexis's in his and pressing his lips to her knuckles in an old-world gesture.

"Maria, we owe you a debt that can never be repaid." His voice is thick with emotion. "You saved my son's life. Anything you need, it's yours."

I can barely believe what's unfolding before me. The Santiagos—the most powerful fucking crime family in Milwaukee and the goddamn Midwest—have rebuffed my attempts at an alliance for *years*.

And now, because of Alexis's quick thinking, that's changed. Carlos Santiago is known for getting his uncle to change his mind on decisions.

I stare at Alexis with a newfound admiration as Carlos and Louisa continue lavishing praise upon her. I quickly usher her away before any of the other guests can approach with prying questions about the mysterious "Maria".

As we retreat inside, I spy Nat deep in conversation with Alfonso Santiago, the current Don of the family. I wonder what's being said, but my focus remains squarely on a shivering, coughing Alexis.

Steering her to a side room, I drape a fresh towel over her shoulders as her teeth chatter. I begin to gently towel off her dripping hair, pins falling to the floor, my movements almost tender.

Moments later, Nat enters the room with Edo in tow. There's an expression of shock on Nat's face.

"Alfonso just told me…" she begins, then trails off with a disbelieving shake of her head. "After 'Maria' rescued little Emilio, he says anything we want—within reason—will be granted by his Family, *including* an alliance."

I still, the towel slipping from my fingers as the weight of Nat's words sinks in.

"He wants to meet with you soon," she continues, a smile spreading across her face. "To hash things out properly."

A slow grin spreads across my face. I turn to Alexis, giving her shoulders an affectionate squeeze as elation blooms in my chest.

"You hear that?" I ask, my voice slightly awed. "You just handed us the keys to the kingdom on a silver fucking platter."

∼

THE PLANE RIDE BACK to Chicago is a silent one, but my thoughts are anything but quiet. My mind keeps drifting back to Alexis—the way her soaked dress had clung to her curves as she emerged from the pool, the fierce determination blazing in her eyes as she hissed that she'd saved a child's life.

She'll be a tremendous asset, I muse. *If only I can fucking figure out a way to get The Brotherhood off her trail for good.*

As soon as we arrive home and settle back in, I seek Alexis out. Pushing open her door, I stop short when I see her in a bathrobe, toweling off her damp hair. The sight sends an unexpected jolt through me.

I clear my throat, and Alexis jumps, her eyes growing wide as she turns to face me, a hand on her heart.

"Jesus, Damian," she whispers as she relaxes. "You scared the shit out of me."

I wink at her. "Best to keep you on your toes that way." I clear my throat again. Goddamn, why am I so *nervous*?

"How would you feel about going on a date with me tonight?"

Her entire face seems to brighten at my words, and I pointedly ignore how my heart stutters in my chest.

"I'd love that," she replies with a smile.

"Great. Get ready, then," I toss over my shoulder, already turning on my heel to leave. I have plans to make.

"You sure that's wise?" an exasperated voice says as I shut the door.

I whirl around, hand already reaching in my suit jacket for my gun, but I relax slightly when I see Edo standing in front of me, arms crossed against his burly chest.

"Goddamn, Edo," I snarl, my heart beating a staccato. "Don't sneak up on me. I nearly shot you."

Edo rolls his eyes. "You're a terrible shooter anyway, Damian." His face turns serious, though. "Are you seriously taking Alexis out of this house to a restaurant *in this city*? There's a manhunt going on for her."

I shoot Edo a quelling look, irritated that he's questioning my decision. "Mind your fucking business, Edo."

He opens his mouth like he wants to argue further, then seems to think better of it. I don't stick around to find out. I have a reservation to make.

A few hours later, I'm holding the door open to the car for Alexis as she slides inside. She looks stunning in a deep green dress that brings out the golden flecks in her eyes.

"Where are we going?" she asks. The smell of her perfume is intoxicating.

"Basil and Olive," I reply, unable to resist stealing glances at her out of the corner of my eye. She's a vision in that dress, her hair slightly pulled back as one curl tumbles over her collar bone.

When we arrive at the restaurant, I inhale deeply as we enter its doors. Alexis, on my arm, gasps as we enter the main dining room. Basil and Olive has an atmosphere of nostalgia and timeless elegance. The dimly lit interior casts a warm glow over the polished mahogany tables draped with crisp white tablecloths, creating an intimate ambiance that seems to harken back to a bygone era.

The walls are adorned with black-and-white photographs of Italian landscapes, vintage posters, and framed newspaper clippings, hinting at the restaurant's rich history and storied past. Soft jazz music plays softly in the background, adding to the allure of the place.

"I've always wanted to go here," Alexis muses as she sits down in her seat, her face alight with joy. "I've heard it's so good."

"The best," I confirm, already telling the waiter to bring a bottle of wine. "I come here often. Their lasagna is to die for."

Alexis's smile gets even wider as she reviews the menu, tucking a piece of hair behind her ear.

The meal is a jovial affair, filled with laughter and effortless conversation. I've never been able to connect with someone this way before.

As the evening wears on, I find myself letting my guard down in a way I rarely ever do.

"You know, this life..." I say at one point, toying with my wine glass. "It's not an easy one. The blood, the fear, the constant looking over your shoulder. But I'd be lying if I said I didn't love it, too. The power, the respect, the adrenaline rush."

I meet her gaze steadily. "It's in my veins, Alexis. And I wouldn't have it any other way."

"No?" Alexis's brow furrows at my words, clear disturbance flashing across her pretty features. "You'd never consider leaving this life behind?"

I scoff dismissively. The thought has never crossed my mind. "Of course not. I was born into this world, and I'll die in it. It's in my blood."

Alexis worries her lower lip between her teeth, and I arch an eyebrow. Something's bothering her about what I just said. "What is it? What's on your mind?"

For a long moment, she's silent, clearly weighing her words carefully. "I just… this life, Damian. The violence, the fear, the constant threat of death. Can you really stomach bringing someone else into that permanently?" Her gaze is earnest, almost pleading. "Isn't there a part of you that dreams of something… more?"

Her questions make me pause, my mind immediately spinning to dark places. I've only ever dreamed of becoming Don of the Iacopellis, nothing more. Even Nat has never dreamed for more, or if she has, she's never told me. We know our place in this life, and we belong to the Family.

But we grew up in this world and know it intimately. Could Alexis truly handle the visceral realities of being with me, of being part of the Iacopelli family? She's proven to be tough, but there's still an air of naivete about her, a lightness that this bloody life so often snuffs out.

Am I really willing to risk that for my own selfish desires? Could I ask a woman only used to violence to willingly spend the rest of her life in more violence?

I manage a tight smile, quickly steering the conversation into safer waters before Alexis can notice the direction of my thoughts. Thankfully, our entrees arrive at that moment and the waiter sets down a steaming plate of lasagna in front of her.

She takes a bite and her eyes flutter close in pure bliss. "Oh, my God, Damian," she murmurs once she'd swallowed. "This is the best lasagna I've ever had in my life."

A smug grin tugs at the corner of my mouth. "I know," I reply, leaning back in my seat confidently. "It's one of the reasons I love this place so much. When it comes to culinary tastes, I'm never wrong."

She lets out an audible scoff, though her eyes are sparkling with amusement. "But maturity lies in knowing when to let a moron be wrong."

That teasing remark startles a laugh out of me, reverberating through my entire frame. If anyone else would have said that to me, I would have ended them. But Alexis's delivery was just too perfect.

Her face splits in a wide, beaming smile at the noise, bright enough to figuratively stop my heart in my chest.

Goddamn, she has the most beautiful smile, I think somewhat dumbly. It transforms her entire face, brings a radiant warmth to her eyes that I can easily see myself getting lost in.

I clear my throat, forcing myself to regain my composure as warmth blooms in my cheeks. "What can I say?" I admit wryly. "I am, after all, a man of exceptional taste."

Alexis smiles again and bends her head to take another bite of her food. As she does, my gaze lands on a familiar figure standing in the dining room entrance, her hair cascading down her back in red waves.

Scarlett Rafa.

I feel my stomach plummet as our eyes lock across the distance, and a wicked smile settles over Scarlett's mouth.

Fuck.

18

DAMIAN

Fuck.

My heart sinks as I see Scarlett making a beeline toward us, her eyes narrowed and a saccharine smile plastered across her face. I mentally kick myself for not listening to Edo's advice. He warned me that it wouldn't be a good idea.

Fuck.

"Damian, *darling*, what a lovely surprise!" Scarlett coos as she approaches, leaning in to air kiss my cheeks. Her eyes flicker over to Alexis, who shifts uncomfortably under Scarlett's overtly hostile gaze. "And who is this?"

Fuck.

I swallow hard. "This is Maria. She's a cousin visiting from out of town."

Scarlett's brow furrows as she looks Alexis up and down appraisingly. "You've never mentioned having cousins before."

"Well, you never asked," I reply with a tight smile, trying to keep my tone light.

Scarlett's eyes glint dangerously. "I suppose I didn't. How... interesting." She steps closer to Alexis, who unconsciously leans back. "It's so nice to meet family. We simply *must* get together for dinner soon, Maria. You, me, and the Chihuahua, Natalia."

The thinly veiled threat in Scarlett's sugary words makes my stomach twist into knots. I should have listened to Edo—bringing Alexis around my unhinged ex-fiancée is a huge fucking mistake. Now we're both caught in Scarlett's viper-like glare, and I have no idea how to extract us.

My heart pounds as Scarlett turns her full attention to Alexis, studying her intently. "You know, you look awfully familiar," Scarlett muses, tilting her head, studying Alexis like a predator would its prey.

Alexis opens her mouth, no doubt with a million curious questions about who this unhinged woman is. But thankfully, seeming to sense the tension, she stays silent.

Cold dread grips my chest. What if Scarlett actually looked at the picture Mario has of Alexis? If Scarlett recognizes Alexis...

I'm ready to have a damn heart attack right here. This had been an incredibly foolish risk to take.

Alexis appears to try to defuse the situation, extending her hand for Scarlett to shake. "It's nice to meet you..."

Scarlett lifts her hand, and I see the glow of a knife in her fist before Alexis does.

Before Scarlett can even move toward Alexis, I jump out of my chair and yank Scarlett's arm, twisting her wrist back. Alexis screams and throws herself backward, knocking her chair over.

The waitstaff gasps, and a handful of men jump up from their booths.

Scarlett spins around, moving faster than me, and lifts the knife so it is pressed against my carotid artery.

Multiple men raise their weapons, half pointing guns on me, half pointing them at Scarlett. There is a moment of tension, and then Scarlett and I smile at each other.

I ignore Alexis's confused look as I lean down and kiss Scarlett's hand that's holding the knife. "You're still faster than me at that, I see."

"Always, baby," Scarlett croons, retracting the knife. "You know how much I love knife play."

Yeah, don't I fucking know it. It used to freak me the fuck out how Scarlett wanted to be tied up and nipped with the tips of knives. I like kinky shit too, but Scarlett's idea of foreplay was beyond the pale.

We need to get the fuck out of here.

But before I can make a move, Scarlett drags over a chair and plops herself down at our table. "Well, since we're all here, we might as well have dinner!" she announces brightly, though her eyes glitter with malice.

I want to groan. This is going to be a nightmare.

True to form, Scarlett proceeds to mostly ignore Alexis, instead monopolizing the conversation by reminiscing with me about old times.

"Remember that weekend in Cabo, Damian? When we danced until dawn and made love on the beach?" She reaches across and puts a possessive hand on my arm. I stiffen, shooting an apologetic look at Alexis, who is bright red and staring down at her plate, her lasagna barely touched.

"Or that time in the Dominican when we went skinny dipping in the moonlight?" She traces a finger along my arm. "Those were such magical nights."

Goddammit.

A muscle twitches in my jaw, but I keep my expression impassive. I have to be the picture of the unflappable Mob Boss.

"Those were different times," I state coolly, gently shrugging off Scarlett's wandering hand.

Scarlett waves a dismissive hand. "Oh, don't be such a stick in the mud in front of your cousin." Scarlett shoots Alexis a scathing look, her blue eyes icy. "Unless Maria here is some uptight little church bitch?"

Alexis's blush deepens, but she remains silent, shoulders tense. My eyes narrow infinitesimally at the insult, but my voice remains even. "My cousin is a lady who deserves respect. Watch yourself, Scarlett."

A flash of irritation crosses Scarlett's face before her saccharine smile returns. "Of course, of course. We're just having a little fun reminiscing, aren't we?"

Before I can respond, she launches into a graphic story about our past debauchery in Venice, making sure to throw in every sordid detail.

I keep my face an inscrutable mask even as Alexis squirms uncomfortably beside her. I will *not* give Scarlett the satisfaction of seeing how repulsed I am by her.

"Such romance and passion we had!" Scarlett gushes with a wistful sigh, oblivious to Alexis's deepening mortification. "Don't you miss that, baby?"

My voice is steel. "Those days are gone, Scarlett. Best we stay in the present, don't you think?"

My eyes bore into hers with an intensity that finally, *finally* gives her pause. For a beat, Scarlett looks chastised and slightly unnerved by my unruffled demeanor. But she quickly recovers with a bitter laugh. "You're no fun anymore, Damian."

As she launches into another R-rated tale from our past, I fight to keep my expression bland and unbothered. I'm the picture of cool indifference, not letting Scarlett see how deeply she's twisting the knife.

Alexis grimaces at Scarlett's tale from my past, clearly trying and failing to keep her composure. Her hand shakes, clumsily knocking into her water glass and nearly sending it toppling.

"Everything okay over there, Maria?" I ask evenly, even though I'm concerned.

She nods quickly, flashing me a tight smile that doesn't reach her eyes. It's painfully obvious that she's deeply uncomfortable, despite her attempts to hide it.

Scarlett watches the exchange with a sickly sweet look of faux sympathy. "Aw, are we making poor little Maria blush with our grown-up talk?" She flutters her lashes in mock innocence. "I forgot what a delicate flower you are."

The jab hit its mark and Alexis's cheeks burn crimson. My jaw ticks, but otherwise, my expression remains unreadable. Inwardly, I'm seething at Scarlett's bullshit.

For her part, Scarlett looks utterly delighted at having rattled Alexis so thoroughly. She aims another barb her way, no doubt hoping for an angrier reaction to feed on.

But Alexis stays mute, eyes downcast as she shrinks into herself. After a moment, Scarlett's grin fades into a petulant pout at being denied the show she wants.

"Ugh, you're no fun," she spits before she turns to me, her blue eyes like ice chips. "You know, I don't care whether she's your cousin or not. Get rid of the third wheel."

I tense, caught between wanting to protect Alexis from Scarlett's jealous rages and not blow Alexis's cover. Even though Scarlett thinks she is just my cousin, her irrational jealousy is flaring up dangerously.

I have to get Alexis out of here, away from Scarlett's increasingly unhinged behavior. Keeping my expression neutral, I pull out my phone and send a discreet coded text to my driver to come around the back entrance immediately.

When I look back up at Alexis, the hurt and confusion are plain on her face. She searches my eyes, clearly wanting an explanation for why I'm seemingly discarding her. Steeling myself, I slip into my Mob Boss persona—cold and aloof.

"Maria," I say coldly. "It's time for you to leave. My driver will escort you out."

Scarlett looks delighted at my brisk dismissal, smirking victoriously.

Moments later, my driver appears at Alexis's side, giving a subtle nod. Scarlett waves a mocking goodbye as the driver leads a bewildered Alexis away.

But as she leaves, Alexis turns back, and the hurt, confused look on her face is like a punch to my gut. I force myself to remain stoic, but it takes every ounce of restraint.

The second she disappears from view, my icy mask cracks. My chest feels hollow with self-loathing. I had just so convincingly written off and dismissed Alexis to appease my psychotic ex.

But it's all for her safety. If Scarlett figures out that "Maria" is actually Alexis Hartley, there's no telling how far her jealous rage would take her. If she realizes I'm harboring their target right under their noses, she would turn Alexis over to her father in a heartbeat.

The consequences don't bear thinking about. If The Brotherhood got their hands on Alexis, she would disappear forever, lost in a trafficking underground, never to be seen again. I can't allow that to happen, no matter how much it kills me to push her away.

Scarlett slides her chair up closer, her smile saccharine sweet. "There, that's better with the dead weight gone."

I barely hear her words over the wave of nausea. This evening, meant to be romantic, has become an utter failure thanks to my inability to keep Alexis safe.

The betrayal in Alexis's eyes haunts me.

19

ALEXIS

I lean against the buttery soft leather seat of the car, arms wrapped tightly around myself as I struggle to breathe deeply. Tears sting my eyes as I replay the events of the night over and over in my mind.

It had started out so promising—my date with Damian at Basil and Olive. He had been so utterly *charming*, regaling me with stories and jokes that made me laugh until my cheeks hurt. When he smiled at me, I felt a spark like never before.

I was on cloud nine. It felt so natural, *so right* to be at that dinner with Damian.

It felt like I meant something to him. Why else would he have asked me out on a date?

Then that woman Scarlett appeared, seemingly out of nowhere, like a venomous snake, slithering up to our table uninvited. I shiver when I recall her cold eyes glinting with sadistic delight as they raked over me in disdain.

I honestly felt like I needed to shower right then and there.

Words were exchanged, and I remember my heart thumping rapidly when Scarlett remarked that I looked familiar to her. Where would I have met her before? How would she have known me?

But then before I knew what was happening, Scarlett brought out a knife, intending to attack me. I had been bewildered, scared, looking to Damian for support and protection.

But the way he responded—or rather didn't—felt like a searing betrayal. Damian didn't lift a finger to defend me. In fact, he pressed a kiss to her hand and his tone became light, friendly even, as if exchanging pleasantries with an old pal.

He didn't even bother telling me that Basil and Olive was clearly a Mob restaurant. I had to figure that out myself when half the restaurant turned guns on us, scaring me half to death.

Scarlett proceeded to dominate the conversation, regaling us with stories and anecdotes from her apparently long relationship with Damian. All the while, her eyes frequently raked over me with undisguised derision and mockery.

Paralyzed with bewilderment and growing dread, I desperately looked to Damian for assistance, for clarification on this bizarre situation. But his expression remained infuriatingly impassive, betraying no hint that something was amiss.

Hot tears spill down my cheeks. How could he? After the wonderful night we shared, the connection I thought we had? Yet he simply cast me aside, sending me home alone in a daze of hurt and confusion.

As questions and doubt swirl in my mind, one ugly possibility takes root—has it all been an act on Damian's part? Some kind of twisted game? The thought makes my chest constrict painfully. I had seen a side of him that seemed so genuine.

Or had I?

And I gave him my virginity.

Oh, God, how could I have done that?

Cradling my face in my hands, sobs rack my body. My heart lays shattered, and I don't know if it can ever be pieced back together.

When I get back to the house, I rush through the front door, tears streaming down my face. I just want to get into my room so I can cry in peace.

Unfortunately for me, I nearly collide with Nat who is walking down the hall, looking at her phone.

"Jesus, Alexis, be careful!" Nat yelps, snatching her phone before it falls to the ground. She takes a closer look at me, brow furrowing when she notices my distraught expression. "Where's Damian? What happened?"

Those questions are my undoing. Sobs rack my body, and I bury my face in my hands, shoulders heaving.

Nat looks around before dragging me into another room and guiding me to a chair.

"Sit," she demands, sitting next to me. "Tell me what happened."

Between gasps, I recount the disastrous date—how Damian and I were having a great time, how Scarlett showed up, how she almost stabbed me, and then how Damian didn't defend me and dismissed me.

Nat scowls when I mention Scarlett's name. "That fucking bitch," she seethes, her face turning red with anger.

"Who *is* she?" I choke out. "She and Damian have a history—she did a great job making that *very* clear by telling me every sordid detail."

"Scarlett Rafa," Nat explains, "is Damian's ex-fiancée."

I feel like the wind has been knocked out of me. *Fiancée*? Damian never mentioned being that serious with someone before. But then again, why would he? I clearly mean nothing to Damian—just another passing fling he didn't need to share details about his past with.

This revelation stings deeply. Damian has so many secrets, so many layers I know nothing about. I am just a bit player in his life, easily dismissed when his ex shows up out of the blue. Fresh tears spring to my eyes as the stark reality sinks in.

"Scarlett is Mario Rafa's daughter," Nat continues, oblivious to my internal pain. "She's a fucking crazy bitch, Alexis. I'm sure Damian was just trying to protect you from her by trying to seem disinterested. The last thing we need is for her to figure out who you actually are and tell her father. Or come here herself and get you."

I shudder at the thought. I haven't even considered the potential danger if Scarlett realized I wasn't really "Maria", cousin to the Iacopellis. No wonder he pushed me away so abruptly.

But the sting of his deception still burns. He could have simply told me the truth instead of hurting me like this. Doesn't he trust me at all? Haven't I proved over the last few months that I'm loyal, that I wouldn't do anything to harm him?

Another wave of tears threaten me as I realize how insignificant I must be to Damian—easily brushed aside without a second thought when faced with his ex's reappearance.

"Rafa," I repeat, tasting the word on my tongue. Why does that last name sound so familiar? A faint sense of deja vu tingles at the back of my mind. Where have I heard that name before? Perhaps on the news? No, that doesn't feel quite right.

Frustration simmers within me as I rack my brain, trying to grasp the elusive memory. It dances just out of my reach. The more I try to recall, the more it slips away, leaving me feeling agitated and unsettled.

"How did they break up?" I whisper, sniffling.

Nat frowns, her face darkening. "She wanted Damian to shoot up a playground because she was pissed that some guy flipped her off on the road." She locks her gaze on mine. "Damian said no, so she broke up with him and then had the driver's son killed. She's fucked up."

I freeze, horrified. She asked him to commit an unspeakable crime. She should be *blacklisted*. But instead, Damian rejected me.

"Damian's over Scarlett," Nat explains. "You don't have to worry about that. She's literally psychotic."

I'm not sure I believe her. My heart aches with jealousy over Scarlett's connection to Damian. The rejection dredges up all the insecurity from my past—the Carters who hated me, Mark who never loved me. I really thought Damian was different.

Nat pats my shoulder, her matter-of-fact demeanor unable to recognize or soothe my churning emotional turmoil. "Don't worry, I'll kick his ass for this," she says before getting up and leaving.

I wish Nat could have done more to comfort me instead. But I recognize that my relationship with Nat is surface level at best. We aren't truly friends. She's Damian's sister. Her loyalty lies to him and the Family.

Nat's brusque reaction highlights how alone I really am. The Iacopelli crime Family is Nat's entire life, same as Damian's. They are able to compartmentalize emotions in a way I could never fathom.

My hurt and heartbreak burn raw, with no one to confide in or find solace with.

With tears streaking down my cheeks, I retreat to my room and lock the door, curling up on my bed as sobs continue to rack my body. I feel so stupid thinking I could ever really matter to Damian or find a place in this world.

I must have drifted off to sleep because I'm awoken later by the sounds of my doorknob rattling.

"Alexis, open the door."

Damian.

His pounding on the bedroom door rattles the walls. "Alexis! Open this door right now!"

I flinch at the fury in his voice but remain steadfast, curled up on the bed clutching a pillow. I have nothing more to say to him—not until he's willing to bare his soul completely without lies or omissions. Enough with the secrets and half-truths and mind games.

"Alexis! Open the fucking door! We need to talk!"

"Leave her be, man," Edo's low murmur comes through the door. "Give her some space."

"Fuck off, Edo!" Damian's responding snarl sends a chill down my spine. "Alexis, I want to talk to you. Open this damn door!"

His demands are met with stony silence. Furious banging resumes, the doorknob rattling like it might rip free any second.

"Would you get your shit together?" It's Nat's irritated tone now, coming closer. "You're scaring her half to death. Fucking back off!"

"She doesn't understand! She *has* to talk to me!"

"Like you gave her that courtesy earlier?" Nat's biting retort hangs in the air. I hold my breath.

A tense pause, then, "C'mon, Bro. Walk away."

More silence, then grudging footsteps storming away from the door. Nat's parting words drift back, tinged with irritation. "I'll deal with your dumb ass later."

I lie awake, staring at the ceiling through puffy eyes. This heartbreak is the final straw. I can't allow Damian to keep me trapped here any longer. I'm not some pawn in his twisted fucking game.

Enough is enough.

Only once I'm sure they're gone, I scramble out of bed, rummaging for a pen and paper on the desk near the window. Part of me can't believe I'm really going through with this, but Damian has left me no choice.

Not after today's brutal revelation about his past with Scarlett.

I'm just another one of his secrets, another player to be manipulated as he sees fit without a second thought for my feelings. The cold, hard truth pierces my heart.

I'm done being a pawn in Damian's games.

With a steadying breath, I begin to write.

Damian,

I deserve better than being just another one of your twisted games. You won't be able to stop me. Don't try to find me, because I'll disappear for good. I'm done. Done with you and this Mafia insanity.

I don't care if The Brotherhood is after me. Let them try.

-Alexis

I leave the note atop my dresser, easily visible, before stripping the bed and ransacking the ensuite bathroom for towels again. My hands move of their own volition, weaving the bedsheets and towels into a makeshift rope ladder. Just like the last time.

Except this time, I'm actually going to escape.

After tying it to the four-poster bed, I open the window, the cold night air stinging my face. But I feel numb inside. Numb from Damian's cavalier cruelty in shutting me out and numb from the finality of my decision.

With one last glance around the room, I toss the makeshift ladder out the window and slowly climb down.

My escape is finally complete. There is nothing left for me here but painful memories and shattered illusions about a man I can never fully know.

I disappear into the night, leaving Damian's secrets behind for good.

20

DAMIAN

The night's stillness is shattered by a frantic pounding on my door. I startle awake, my heart pounding as I glance at the clock—six a.m.

"What the fuck?" I growl, throwing off the covers, snatching the gun that always sits on my nightstand and stumbling to my door, my eyelids still heavy. There had better be a goddamn good reason I'm being woken up so goddamn early. I had barely gotten to sleep before this.

The door bursts open before I even have a chance to open it and Edo rushes in, white as a sheet, his whole body trembling with shock.

My mouth suddenly dries. The last time I saw Edo this rattled, it was when my parents and sister were murdered. "What the fuck is going on, Edo?" I demand, my heart racing.

"It's Alexis," he gasps, his eyes wide. "She's gone."

Those words snap me fully awake. "What do you mean, she's gone, Edoardo?" I ask, my voice rising in pitch.

Before Edo has a chance to respond, I'm pushing past him and racing down the hallway. I slam against the door, growling as I remember she locked it. Fuck this shit. I should have done this last night when she refused to talk to me.

I kick down the door, and it breaks, falling down with an almighty crash. Stepping into the cold room, my worst fears are confirmed. The window is open, a rope ladder swaying in the cool morning breeze. On the dresser sits a folded note, a pen acting as a paperweight.

With trembling hands, I snatch up the note and unfold it, my eyes rapidly scanning the words.

A torrent of emotions surges through me—devastation, fury, and fear for her safety. I crumple the note in my fist, my jaw clenched.

"Edo, get everyone up!" I bark. "I want a full manhunt for Alexis. She's to be brought back immediately, no questions asked."

Edo roars out orders and the house springs into action. Nat storms into the room, her eyes blazing.

"This is your fucking fault," she spits, getting in my face. "If you had been fucking honest with her from the beginning and hadn't allowed that fucking bitch to nearly kill her, she wouldn't have felt the need to escape!"

The crumpled note falls from my trembling fist as the full weight of Alexis's disappearance crashes over me. My chest heaves with ragged breaths, a vein pulsing at my temple as white-hot fury courses through my veins.

I don't fucking need a lecture from my sister.

"Shut the *fuck* up, Nat!" I roar, whirling on her. My hands clench into white-knuckled fists, aching to lash out and destroy something. "You think I wanted this? You think I didn't do everything to keep her safe?"

Nat stands her ground, eyes blazing with righteous anger. "Safe?" she spits. "You call taking her out—when Edo TOLD YOU NOT TO—and running into Scarlett, who fucking tries to attack her, and then you do *nothing* to protect her, safe? No wonder she ran!"

"I *was* protecting her!" My voice cracks with raw emotion. I rake my hands through my disheveled hair, my heart pounding a frantic staccato in my chest. Images of Alexis alone, cold, frightened, assail my mind, each one more terrifying than the last. My breath catches as another image of Alexis being captured by The Brotherhood and sold to an unnamed pervert runs through my mind.

I want to vomit.

Nat's derisive snort snaps my focus back. "From what? Your obsessive need to control her? You're so fucking selfish, thinking only about yourself and not what's best for the woman who is being fucking hunted down by The Brotherhood to be sold. You're no better than her fucking foster parents."

I lunge forward, hands outstretched as if to wrap around her throat. But Edo quickly steps between us, his bulky arms straining to hold me back.

"Damian, this isn't fucking helping! We need to focus on finding Alexis. Stop fucking fighting with Nat!"

The ringing of my phone cuts through the tension like a knife. I wrench free of Edo's grasp, breathing heavily while glaring at my sister, and snatch it up, my uncle's name flashing on the screen.

What the *fuck* does Uncle Vinny want so early in the goddamn morning?

"What?" I snarl, clenching the phone so tightly my knuckles turn white.

"Is that how you talk to your uncle?" Uncle Vinny's gruff voice filters through the phone. "Mario's getting antsy. Wants to know how the search for Alexis Hartley is going."

A muscle ticks in my jaw as I fight to keep my tone even. This is what he goddamn called for? A fucking text would have sufficed.

"I've got more important things to deal with right now than trying to find a fucking ghost."

There's a pause on the other end before Uncle Vinny speaks again. "That's interesting because Scarlett said she had dinner with you and your cousin, Maria, last night."

My heart plummets into my stomach. Oh, God. I never should have taken Alexis out. I swallow hard. "Maria's a cousin."

"Is that so?" Uncle Vinny's tone makes it clear he doesn't believe a word I'm saying. "Funny, I don't recall any Marias in the Iacopelli family fitting that description. Scarlett said she has short black hair, a real ugly thing."

Irritation courses through me at Scarlett's description of Alexis. Of course the vain bitch would play down Alexis's looks just to make herself look better.

"She's a cousin on my mother's side," I remark coolly, ignoring Nat and Edo's wide-eyed stares.

The line crackles with irritation as Uncle Vinny's voice takes on a sharper edge. "You listen to me, Damian. I don't give a shit about your wop cousin, Maria, or whatever game you're running here."

I bristle at my uncle's dismissive tone, anger flaring hot in my chest. I open my mouth to protest, but Vinny bulldozes on, his words laced with venom.

"Mario's been riding my ass about this Alexis Hartley situation for weeks now. He wants updates, he wants results, and frankly, I'm running outta excuses to give him." My uncle's gravelly timbre descends into a threatening growl. "You get your head out of your ass and find that girl before this whole clusterfuck blows up in our faces. *Capisce*?"

The line goes dead, leaving me staring at my phone in bewildered fury. I look up at Nat and Edo's questioning stares, my brow furrowed in consternation.

"Seriously, what is his fucking deal with Alexis?" I mutter, mostly to myself. "Since when does Vinny take orders from Mario Rafa? And how the hell does he know so much about what's going on here?"

Running a frustrated hand through my hair, I pace the room in agitation. "I don't give a flying *fuck* what Mario wants right now. Alexis is my priority." I wheel on Nat and Edo, eyes blazing with renewed determination. "We find her and bring her back. Then we deal with Uncle Vinny and Mario."

An uneasy silence falls over the room as we try to process the situation and figure out Alexis's potential whereabouts. I rake my hands through my hair again, frustrated.

"She couldn't have gone far," I mutter, mostly to myself. "Not on foot, at least. Edo, do you know what time she left?"

"Cameras show four thirty a.m.," Edo responds.

Anger courses through me. Where the *fuck* were the guards who were supposed to be patrolling that area?

"So she has a one and a half hour head start," I say.

Edo nods slowly. "You think she'd risk going back to the Carters' place, though? After everything?"

Nat fixes Edo with a withering glare as she opens up drawers. "Of course she would. Where else would she go?" She throws up her hands in exasperation. "You two are so dense sometimes. Look around—everything is exactly as she left it. She didn't pack a goddamn thing."

Realization dawns on me and I curse under my breath. Nat's right—Alexis's room shows no signs of a planned escape. Just a spur of the moment decision to flee.

With that goddamn rope ladder again. When I get her back, she's not going to be allowed any bed sheets or towels. She can freeze for all I care.

"She's still in Chicago, then," Edo says thoughtfully. "Probably trying to get her bearings before making a move."

"No thanks to this asshole," Nat sneers, rounding on Damian. "You've been so awful, so monstrous to her. Can you really blame her for wanting to get away? To go *back* to the fucking Carters instead of enduring one more day with you?"

The accusation pierces my heart like a white-hot blade. I recoil as if struck, Nat's words rendering me speechless. A part of me wishes she had simply punched me instead. Physical pain I can endure, but this?

This cuts deeper than any fist ever could.

"You have no idea what you've done to her," Nat continues, her eyes full of disgust. "You weren't there to see her crying over you, wondering why you didn't get rid of Scarlett. You *fucking* asshole. If The Brotherhood gets her, I'm personally coming after you."

I already loathe myself for this nightmare. I don't need Nat driving the knife deeper into my gut. Swallowing hard, I give a sharp nod.

"Let's go. We hit the Carters' place first. If she's not there, we widen the search."

We scramble into action, a towering sense of dreading hanging over me. *Please let her be okay*, I pray silently. *I'll never forgive myself if anything happens to her.*

The car eats up the miles as we race across Chicago, Edo quickly confirming the Carter residence address. An uneasy silence hangs in the air, tensions high. We're encroaching on Invicta territory now.

Everyone knows the risks of having a soldier lurking around every corner.

Especially since an Invicta soldier tried to kidnap Alexis the first time.

As we turn down the rundown street, Nat scoffs under her breath. "*This* is where she lived?"

The neighborhood looks distinctly depressed, the houses weathered and dilapidated. My jaw clenches as my knuckles turn white on the steering wheel. How could anyone let Alexis suffer in conditions like these? How could her social worker allow her to stay here for all these years? This isn't any place for a child to grow up.

The street seems deserted as we pull up in front of the Carter house, the only movement a few stray pieces of litter skittering across the cracked pavement. I kill the engine and we quickly pile out, eyes roving the area for any signs of trouble as the sun struggles to come up over the horizon.

"Stick close and keep your eyes peeled," I mutter, checking the Beretta tucked into my waistband. "You know the drill if any Invicta guys show up."

We approach the sagging porch cautiously. My mind is already racing ahead. I'd make a beeline for the basement first. If Alexis is here, that's likely where she'll be after her initial escape from that hellhole.

My hand settles on the door handle when a piercing scream splits the air, coming from inside the house.

"NO!"

That scream is achingly familiar. My blood turns to ice in my veins.

Alexis.

The unmistakable sound of gunshots immediately follows, echoing like thunderclaps down the empty street.

21

ALEXIS

I stand on the sidewalk, staring up at the Cape Cod style home, my heart pounding in my chest. I can't believe I'm back here, standing on the sidewalk of the very place I never thought I would return to.

Yet somehow, when I got off the train, my feet led me right back to the house of my former foster parents—the ones who had betrayed me.

A shiver runs down my spine as the memories come rushing back. This place had never been a haven for me, only a prison and a living hell. The Carters made my life a nightmare, abusing me emotionally and sometimes, physically. It's a miracle I was able to escape. I don't want to imagine where I'd be if I hadn't.

I'd probably be someone's slave, and the Carters would sleep soundly at night, probably never thinking about me again. They were willing to sell me to The Brotherhood for their own greed.

The Brotherhood—the organization currently hunting me down. I know I'm putting myself in grave danger just by being here. Every instinct is telling me to turn around and run as far away as possible.

And yet... something deep inside me had compelled me to come back. Maybe it's a need for closure, a desire to confront the demons of my past.

Or maybe I'm just a glutton for punishment.

Whatever the reason, I find myself unable to tear my gaze away from the old familiar house.

Clenching my fists, I swallow hard. I wasn't going to go inside—that would be so fucking stupid. But standing here on the sidewalk feels like a way to reclaim a piece of my own history, to say a final goodbye to the place that had once held me captive.

I don't know where I'm going to go, but I need to get out of Chicago—and fast. This city holds nothing but painful memories and danger for me now.

Turning to walk away, I rack my brain, trying to figure out where I can go. I still have a few of my old coworkers' phone numbers. Maybe one of them would be willing to let me crash on their couch while I figure out my next move.

Which would involve getting new identification.

I curse myself for not grabbing more of my belongings when I fled the Iacopelli mansion. But my exit had been so hasty, driven by pure survival instinct. I hadn't even thought to pack a bag. All I have are the clothes on my back and a few meager possessions in my pockets, including my phone.

Damian's face flashes through my mind, and I feel a sharp pain in my chest. I push the thought of him away, unwilling to dwell on the pain of his betrayal. He's part of the life I'm trying to escape—a life that has become far too dangerous.

Picking up the pace, I scan the streets. There's a train station not too far from here. I need to put as much distance between me and

Chicago as possible. This city is no longer safe for me, not with the Brotherhood breathing down my neck.

As I walk, my mind races with a thousand questions and uncertainties. Where would I go? What could I do? Can I ever truly outrun my past?

But for now, the only thing that matters is getting away—even if it means starting over with nothing. I've done it before and I'll do it again.

Suddenly, a hand grabs me by the hair, yanking my head back sharply. I let out a panicked gasp as the cold, hard metal of a gun presses against my temple.

"Well, well, well, look who decided to come back," a sickeningly familiar voice hisses in my ear. My blood runs cold as I recognize Mark's gruff tones.

His grip tightens and he gives my head another harsh yank. "You have no idea how happy I am to see you, sweetheart," he growls. "This makes my job a whole lot easier."

My mind races as I realize the trap I had stumbled into. I never should have come back here. Mark is going to call The Brotherhood, and they will come and take me, just like I feared.

This is what Damian had been trying to protect me from.

"Please," I beg, my voice shaking. "Mark, just let me go. I won't tell anyone, I swear."

But Mark just laughs, the sound cold and cruel. "Oh, I don't think so, darling." He strikes me hard across the face, making my vision blur. I cry out as pain rockets across my cheeks and mouth.

"The Brotherhood wants you badly, and I'm going to make sure they get you. Oh, what a pretty penny you'll get me."

I whimper in pain as Mark drags me toward the Carter house, the gun still pressed against my temple. Terror lashes through me at the thought of going through those doors. I know once I cross that threshold, I'm a goner. The thought of seeing Dennis, Suzanne, and Emma's smug faces is too much to bear.

My survival instincts kick in, and I begin to frantically struggle against his hold. I claw at his arms, trying to pry his hand off my hair, but Mark's grip is like iron.

"Let me go, you bastard!" I cry, desperation fueling my actions. I rake my nails across his face, drawing blood, but it only seems to enrage him further. With a growl, he slams me against the side of the house, dazing me.

"Quit fighting, you stupid bitch!" he snarls, tightening his grip on my hair.

My vision swims and my head throbs, but I refuse to give up. I lash out with my fists, striking any part of him I can reach. But Mark is simply too strong, overpowering me with ease.

As we approach the front door, I notice with a sinking feeling that the house is eerily silent and dark—no sign of the Carters anywhere.

"The Carters skipped town after you left," Mark sneers. "Because of the danger *you* put them in. But don't worry, sweetheart. The Brotherhood is more than happy to keep you company. In fact, I know they have a list a mile long of prospective masters who will *gladly* keep you company for the rest of your miserable fucking life."

Tears of terror burn in my eyes as Mark opens the door and shoves me inside. I've been a stupid, naive idiot. And now I'm trapped with no way out.

My nose is assaulted by the familiar scents of the Carter house as Mark drags me into the kitchen. The musty, stale odor of neglect mingles with the faint, lingering traces of cooking spices—scents that had once been so comforting to me but now turn my stomach.

I shudder involuntarily, memories flooding back. This kitchen had been my domain, a place where the Carters wouldn't touch me because it would taint their food. I had spent hours not only slaving over food, but tinkering with recipes and creating new and more delicious meals.

If I whipped up something especially delicious, I would receive a rare smile from Dennis and Suzanne. Those smiles used to make my entire day. I thought if I made enough good food, the Carters would finally love me.

But those memories are tainted now, overshadowed by the abuse and manipulation that had occurred within these walls.

As Mark forces me into a chair and begins binding my wrists, I can almost feel the weight of those past traumas pressing down on me. The scrape of the rope against my skin, the hard, unyielding wood of the chair—it's all too familiar, too visceral. I have to fight the urge to scream, to beg him to stop.

Despite my terror, a small part of my mind registers the sloppy knots—a stark contrast to the intricate bindings my old Navy friend had taught me years ago.

"There, that should keep you from trying anything stupid," Mark sneers, giving the ropes a final tug.

I fight to keep my hands from trembling, memories of my friend's lessons flooding my mind. He had been so insistent that I learn these skills, warning me that I might never know when they might come in handy. At the time, I had thought it was just an odd quirk.

But now, I'm thanking my lucky stars.

I force myself to focus, to push past the fear and the nausea and the memories, and slowly, methodically, I begin to work at the knots. The ropes chafe and burn, but I ignore the pain, my sole focus on freeing myself.

As Mark fishes his phone out of his pocket to make a call, my heart races, adrenaline fueling my efforts. I can't let myself be taken by The Brotherhood. I have to get out of here, no matter what.

"Hey, babe, guess who I've got?" Mark drawls, a grin spreading across his face. "That's right, the prodigal daughter herself!"

Although I can't hear exactly what the other person is saying, I can hear their voice. And it's a voice I recognize.

It's Emma.

Mark paces the room, engrossed in his conversation. He's too busy to notice me inching my hands back and forth, slowly working the knots free.

"Yeah, I've got her all trussed up and ready for pickup," Mark says smugly. "The Brotherhood will be thrilled to have their little collateral back." He pauses, listening to Emma's response. "Sounds good. Yes, go ahead and call them." He turns his back to me. "This is gonna be sweet, babe. We're finally gonna get what we deserve."

Fury and indignation burn through me as Mark's conversation with Emma becomes more heated. How *dare* they treat me like this.

Nat's voice floats through my head as I work at the last few knots. *"You're a wolf in sheep's clothing, Alexis. Fucking embrace it."*

At the time, I hadn't fully understood what Nat was trying to tell me. But now, in this moment of sheer desperation, the meaning becomes crystal clear.

I have always seen myself as the victim, the sheep trapped among the wolves. But Nat had recognized something more in me—a strength, a resilience, a capacity for darkness that I had been too afraid to acknowledge.

As the last of the ropes fall away, my fingers close around the cool metal of the gun on the table. Stupid Mark. If it's one thing I've learned while living with the Iacopelli family, it's to *never* leave a gun unattended.

A surge of primal power courses through my veins, a feral instinct to survive at all costs.

Embrace it.

With a steely glint in my eye, I turn the weapon on Mark's unsuspecting back. "You son of a bitch," I growl, my voice steady and unwavering. "I'm *nobody's* collateral."

At that moment, I know what I have to do. I'm no longer the sheep. I'm the wolf, ready to bare my teeth and fight for my freedom. And I will do whatever it takes to escape this nightmare, once and for all.

My words cause Mark to turn around. His eyes widen in shock at the sight of me freed from my bonds and wielding the weapon. "You bitch!" he snarls, lunging forward.

The situation quickly spirals out of control. A fierce struggle ensues as we grapple for the gun. My fingers slip on the smooth metal, and Mark manages to knock it from my grasp, sending it clattering to the floor.

In an instant, he has me pinned to the ground, his hands wrapped around my throat, squeezing mercilessly. I claw at his hands, gasping for breath, panic setting in. This can't be how I go out. Not after everything I've been through. Mark's screaming at me, spittle flying from his mouth, but I can't hear a word he's saying.

Desperate, I blindly reach out, my fingers finally grasping the fallen gun. With a primal scream, I swing the weapon upward, smashing it against the side of Mark's head.

He howls in pain, his grip momentarily loosening. I suck in a ragged breath, precious air rushing into my lungs, and shove him off, scrambling to my feet.

But Mark is relentless, surging forward and tackling me once more.

"You fucking bitch," he spits, his eyes glittering with malice. "I hope whoever owns you makes you *suffer*."

We wrestle violently, the gun slipping and sliding between us as we fight for control. My finger tightens on the trigger, but Mark wrenches the weapon away, his eyes wild.

"NO!" I scream in a last-ditch effort, summoning every ounce of my strength. And as Mark lunges toward me, I manage to get the gun back, leveling it at his chest.

Time seems to slow as I stare into his eyes, my finger trembling on the trigger. Then, with a deafening crack, I fire.

Mark's body jerks, his expression frozen in shock before his lifeless body collapses on top of me, the weight of him crushing the air from my lungs. I struggle to push him off, gasping for breath, when suddenly, the sound of the front door bursting open makes my head snap up.

Standing in the doorway, their expressions a mixture of shock and horror, are Damian, Nat, and Edo.

22

ALEXIS

I cry out as Mark's body falls heavily on top of me, his warm blood soaking into my clothes. I struggle to push him off, my hands slipping in the crimson pool that surrounds us. Panic seizes me as the reality of what I have done crashes over me, and I feel myself disconnect from the present moment.

Suddenly, I find myself back in the familiar closet, crouched beside my mother. I can hear the faint sounds of footsteps outside, my heart pounding in my ears. The comforting scent of my mother's perfume envelopes me, a stark contrast to the metallic tang of blood that still fills my nostrils.

My mother's voice is barely a whisper as she instructs me to be perfectly still and silent. "If you're very quiet, you'll win," she whispers, her eyes wide with fear. I nod obediently, not understanding the danger we are in, focused only on the prospect of victory.

The cramped quarters of the closet surround me, the musty scent and the familiar perfume grounding me in that distant memory even as the horror of the present day threatens to overwhelm me.

For a brief moment, I'm a child again, unaware of the violence and trauma that will one day shape my life. I simply wait, anticipating the prize my mother promises if I play the game well.

In the present, I'm yanked upright by Damian, his arms pulling me into his chest. "Come on, we have to get out of here," he urges, his voice laced with concern.

I feel the warmth of his body, the fabric of his shirt rough against my skin, but it is as if I'm disconnected from it all. The blood that smears onto him doesn't register in my mind.

Damian ushers me out of the house, but before we leave, I see Edo quickly moving Mark's body, arranging it in a chair and tying him up. "This will make it look like a robbery gone wrong," Edo mutters, casting a wary glance in my direction.

Damian says something else, but I'm trapped in my own thoughts, my consciousness keeping me in that closet. Faint footsteps outside the closet grow louder, and my mother trembles.

"If you're very quiet, you'll win," she breathes again, gathering me into her arms and holding me close.

In the car, I hear Nat's worried voice, but her words sound distant and muffled, as if I'm underwater. Damian's arms tighten around me, his touch barely registering. I'm trapped, my mind lost in the past, oblivious to everything around me.

When we arrive back at the mansion, Damian scoops me up and carries me upstairs to my room. I'm still trapped in the memory of the closet, my mother's terrified breathing echoing in my mind.

I can feel Damian gently stripping me of my blood-stained clothes. I hope he burns them. As he cleans the remnants of violence from my body, the closet door suddenly opens and my mother's agonized screams fill my ears. I panic, my body thrashing as I cry out.

"Mommy! Mommy, no!" I scream, my voice raw with terror.

"Alexis! Alexis, it's okay. You're safe," Damian says, his strong hands gripping my shoulders, trying to ground me in the present. But the memories are too vivid, the pain too real.

I can see my mother's face twisted in fear as she shields me from the unseen danger. The acrid smell of smoke and the metallic tang of blood fill my senses, transporting me back to that fateful day.

I thrash against Damian's hold, desperate to reach my mother, to save her. Tears stream down my face as I beg, "Please, help her! Don't let them hurt her!" The anguish in my voice is palpable, a raw reminder of the trauma that has shaped me.

Damian pulls me into his chest, enveloping me in a fierce embrace. Then, in a soft, soothing voice, he begins to sing a gentle Italian lullaby, the familiar melody washing over me.

"*Dormi, dormi, bel bambino,*

Dormi, dormi senza affanni.

La tua mamma è qui vicino,

Veglia i tuoi tranquilli sonni."

The comforting words and the gentle cadence of his voice slowly coax me back from the brink of despair. Damian's warmth and the steady rhythm of his heartbeat anchor me in the present, chasing away the ghosts of my past.

I cling to him, my body trembling as the adrenaline begins to subside. "Stay with me, please," I beg, my voice small and trembling. I can't bear the thought of being alone, not when the horrors of my past are so vividly alive in my mind.

Damian nods and settles on the bed beside me. The familiar scent of his cologne and the comfort of his embrace finally allow me to let go, the tension draining my muscles as exhaustion takes over.

He carefully tucks me into bed, never once leaving my side. I feel safe, secure in the knowledge that I'm no longer alone. As I drift off to sleep, lulled by the soothing melody of his lullaby, I know that—for now—the ghosts of my past will not haunt me.

∼

As I slowly open my eyes, the first thing I notice is Damian sleeping peacefully beside me. His face looks so much younger in repose, the harsh lines and tension smoothed away. I find myself studying his features, wondering how I ended up back in this house.

But then the memories come rushing back—Mark finding me outside the Carter house, the gunshot, the way Mark's warm blood had soaked into my clothes, how his limp body felt on top of mine as I struggled to get him off.

Bile rises in my throat, and I scramble out of bed, stumbling toward the bathroom as the nausea overwhelms me.

Damian is instantly by my side, holding my hair back as I retch violently into the toilet. "You're okay, Alexis. The first kill is always the hardest," he murmurs, his voice low and soothing as he gently rubs circles on my back.

I can't stop the sobs that rack my body, the anguish and revulsion pouring out of me. "I–I can still feel it, Damian. His blood, all over me..." I choke out between heaves. The visceral memory of that moment is seared into my mind, the metallic scent and the warmth of the crimson fluid haunting me.

Damian pulls me into his arms, holding me tightly. "I know, I know. But you're safe now. You're going to be okay," he whispers.

I cling to him, desperate for the comfort and security he offers.

As my sobs slowly subside, I can't help but wonder how he found me.

Pulling back slightly, I look up at him, my eyes still glistening with tears.

"How did you know where to find me?" I ask, my voice small and uncertain.

He offers me a half-smile. "It was the most obvious answer, Alexis. The Carter home is the only place you've ever known as home. Of course you would go back there."

Damian's expression then grows serious. "But why the hell did you leave in the first place? Why didn't you talk to me?"

I feel a twinge of embarrassment wash over me. In the aftermath of the Carter house incident, my little "temper tantrum" feels utterly unwarranted. Averting my gaze, I confess, "I... I felt pushed aside when you chose Scarlett over me. Especially after she tried to *stab* me."

He lets out a heavy sigh. "Alexis, Scarlett means *nothing* to me. I was trying to protect you. She's unstable and dangerous. My priority was getting you to safety, making sure she didn't uncover who you really are."

I blink up at him, the weight of his words sinking in. Nat was right.

"You were trying to protect me?" I whisper, suddenly feeling foolish.

"What do you think I've been trying to do this entire time?" Damian asks, exasperation clear in his voice. "I've not been putting my ass at risk for no good reason."

I don't know what to say to that, but I now feel the weight of the day's events still hanging heavily on my shoulders. "I need to shower," I murmur, my voice barely above a whisper. "I still feel so... *disgusting*."

Damian nods in understanding, helping me to my feet. "I know the feeling. It took me weeks to feel clean again after my first kill." His gaze grows distant, as if he can still feel the phantom trace of blood on his hands.

"How old were you?" I ask, unsure whether I really want to know the answer.

Damian studies me for a long moment, his dark eyes probing. "Twelve," he says quietly.

Twelve. The realization hits me like a punch to the gut, my horror palpable. To think he had taken a life at such a young age…

Damian senses my distress, shrugging, "It's a weight no child should have to bear. But this life… it demands sacrifices."

In that moment, I feel impossibly small, my own trauma paling in comparison to the scars Damian must bear.

As I step into the shower, the image of Mark's shocked expression flashes in my mind, the sound of the gunshot still ringing in my ears. I can *feel* the gun recoil in my hand, the warm spray of blood against my skin.

I let the scalding water cascade over me, but no matter how hard I scrub, I can't wash away the remnants of what I had done. The sobs come anew, my body shaking as I claw at my flesh, desperate to shed the taint of violence.

Suddenly, Damian is there, pulling me into his embrace, his own body slick with water. I lean against him, craving the comfort and security he offers. Without a word, I reach up, my lips finding his in a desperate, searing kiss.

I need to forget, to lose myself in the sensation of his touch, to drown out the echoes of that fateful moment. Damian responds eagerly, his hands roaming over my curves as he pulls me impossibly closer.

In his arms, I feel a glimpse of peace, a fleeting respite from the horrors that haunt me. For now, I can simply *be*, without the weight of the world crushing down upon me. Damian is my anchor, my salvation in the midst of the storm.

As our kiss deepens, I pour every ounce of my anguish and longing into it, silently begging him to take it all away.

Damian's wet hands curl under my ass, and he lifts me up in one fell swoop, pressing me against the wall. I moan as Damian's mouth finds my neck and he thrusts roughly against me, his hard dick rubbing against my pussy in the most delicious way.

"Fuck, Damian!" I gasp, clutching onto his hair.

Damian chuckles and enters me, both of us moaning as he fills me. I wrap my legs tighter around his waist, trying to bring him as close to me as possible.

As our lips meet again in a languid kiss, the world narrows to just the two of us—a private sanctuary amid the chaos. Hands roam reverently, relearning the curves and planes we have committed to memory, rediscovering the nuances of each other's body.

There's an unhurried cadence to our movements, a gentle ebb and flow as we surrender to the pull of desire. I completely forget what has happened in the last twenty-four hours as I give in to just *feeling*. The feel of Damian's cock thrusting in and out of me is all I can focus on, the sounds of his ragged breathing filling my ear and the feel of the hot water spraying on me keeping me grounded.

"Fuck, Alexis," Damian rasps out. "I'm going to come."

I tighten my legs around him in response and move my hips in time with his, wanting to get him to jump off that cliff.

Damian groans loudly, his thrusts becoming shallower and sloppier as he speeds toward his release, emptying his seed inside me. I can feel my own orgasm building, and I cry out, feeling that delicious pressure rise, rise, *rise* before it crests and I feel euphoric, riding a wave of bliss and pleasure.

As Damian helps me get down, my legs trembling from the force of my orgasm, I think I detect a faint murmur from him—a whispered confession of love. However, the rush of sound in my ears from the water and the intensity of the moment make me unsure whether I had truly heard the words.

Damian's dark eyes search my face, a tender vulnerability flickering across his expression. He seems to be gauging my reaction.

I gaze up at him, my own heart pounding with a mixture of hope and uncertainty. Had he really said those three little words?

Or is it simply my own desperate desire to hear them manifesting in my mind?

23

ALEXIS

Over the next few weeks, I can't stop thinking about what happened at the Carter house. How could I have been so stupid as to go back there?

I cringe as I remember the terror I had felt when Mark grabbed me and dragged me into the house. But the part that weighs heaviest on my heart is the memory of pulling that trigger, of taking a life, even if it was Mark's.

I'm not sorry that Mark is gone. He had been a vile, abusive man who had been planning to sell me to The Brotherhood. At that moment, I knew I had no choice. It was either kill him or he would kill me.

And yet, the guilt still gnaws at me. I had never taken a life before, not even in self-defense. The weight of that responsibility is crushing. I know that taking a life—even a wretched one like Mark's—will change me forever. I wonder if I'll ever be able to forgive myself.

Damian had found me trapped under Mark's body, terrified but alive. He held me and soothed me, trying to tell me that the first kill is always the hardest.

Like he expects me to do it again.

I can't shake the feeling that I had crossed some invisible line, that I lost a piece of my own humanity.

As much as I know my actions had been justified, I can't silence the voice in my head that keeps asking, *what kind of person am I now?* The thought of having to take a life again, to defend myself or the people I love, fills me with a deep, unsettling dread.

I need to learn how to protect myself, to be strong and capable. That moment in the Carter house where I became the wolf feels like a fluke, like it was just a survival instinct.

But the price of that power now feels far too high. With a heavy heart, I resolve to find another way, one that doesn't require me to become a killer.

I seek out Damian first. Since that night, I feel like our relationship has changed. He seeks me out more, and I've started spending some nights in his room. My cheeks turn red as I recall how many times Damian and I have had sex since then, too. He's insatiable, but I also can't get enough of him.

"I need you to teach me how to defend myself," I tell Damian in his office.

He looks up at me, an eyebrow raised. To my dismay, he flatly refuses. "Absolutely not. I'm not letting you out of my sight ever again. You're staying right here where it's safe."

I bristle at his patronizing tone. "That's not a good enough reason! I was able to defend myself against Mark—"

"That was *luck*, Alexis," Damian says sharply, setting down his pen. "Not skill."

"I'm not a child, Damian! I need to be able to take care of myself. I can't just rely on you to protect me all the time."

But Damian's unmovable.

Gritting my teeth, I storm out of the office and run into Nat. Thankfully, once Nat hears my request, she immediately acquiesces.

"Of course you should learn how to shoot a gun! You can't just rely on the men to save you, especially my idiot brother."

Nat wastes no time in roping Edo into helping teach me some self-defense moves. "Edo's the best person I know when it comes to this stuff," Nat says confidently. "He's going to show you some killer techniques."

We meet in the home gym, and Edo gestures for me to stand facing him. "Okay, let's start with some basic strikes. The key is using your whole body, not just your arm." He demonstrates a sharp jab, pivoting his hips to generate power. "You try it."

I mimic the movement, my fist snapping forward.

"Good, but really put your weight into it. Use your legs to drive the strike." He repeats the motion, his powerful muscles contracting. He nods approvingly as I repeat the punch, my eyes narrowing in concentration.

Next, Edo shows me how to block an incoming strike. "When someone comes at you, don't just try to stop their hand. Redirect the force." He has me practice parrying his own strikes, guiding them safely aside.

"Now let's work on escapes. You've had way too many fucking people grab you recently. If someone grabs you—" Edo suddenly lunges forward, his hand closing around my upper arms. In one fluid motion, I pivot, pulling free and striking the side of Edo's neck with the heel of my hand.

"Nicely done!" Edo praises, a wide smile on his handsome face. "You really got the movement down. Remember, the key is using their momentum against them."

We continue drilling various self-defense techniques, Edo offering constant feedback and encouragement. My movements grow sharper, more confident as I commit the motions to muscle memory.

Doing this makes me feel like I'm reclaiming my power. Like I'm not weak anymore.

After a while, Nat grows bored watching Edo drill me on self-defense techniques.

"Alright, that's enough of the martial arts stuff," she declares, grabbing my arm. "Time to work on some *real* firepower."

She drags me down to the lavish indoor shooting range hidden in the basement of the mansion. "This is where the real action happens." Nat grins, gesturing around the state-of-the-art facility.

I feel a flutter of unease in the pit of my stomach as Nat begins thoroughly explaining gun safety and handling. The memory of squeezing the trigger to end Mark's life flashes vividly through my mind, making my breath catch in my throat.

Nat pauses her speech, seeing my growing distress. "Hey, you okay?" Nat asks gently, placing a hand on my shoulder. "We can stop if you're not ready for this."

I shake my head rapidly, swallowing hard. "No, I need to do this," I say, my voice trembling slightly. "That's exactly why I need to learn—so I'm never that helpless, that unprepared, ever again."

Nat and Edo share a glance before Nat shrugs. "Suit yourself."

Nat demonstrates a proper stance and fires the gun. To my surprise, Nat proves to be an incredible shot, hitting the targets with impressive accuracy. She makes it look so *easy*.

The shock and awe in my face must be apparent because Edo chuckles, amusement clear in his eyes. "Yeah, Nat's a better shot than even Damian. Don't tell him I said that, though. You know how he loves to be the best at everything."

Nat preens, clearly pleased with the comparison. "What can I say? I'm a natural. Alright, Alexis, let's see what you got."

They watch me apprehensively as I grasp the handgun Nat handed me. My fingers are shaking slightly, but my grip is firm. Taking a deep breath, I raise the weapon, sighting down the barrel.

The memory of that night floods my senses—the tang of gunpowder, the deafening crack of the shot, the awful, final thud as Mark's lifeless body fell on top of me, his blood surrounding me. I feel bile rise in my throat, my chest constricting painfully.

But then, something shifts. The terror and revulsion give way to a steely resolve. I steady my stance, exhaling slowly. I will not let that moment define me. I will take back the power that had been stolen from me.

With renewed determination, I squeeze the trigger, the gun bucking in my hands.

The bullet strikes the target dead center.

"Holy fuck," Edo breathes while Nat stares at me with something like admiration in her eyes. I lower the weapon, my eyes shining with a newfound strength.

"Let's do that again," I say, my voice unwavering. I'm done being a victim. From now on, I will be the master of my own fate.

I spend the next few hours diligently practicing my shooting, determined to gain proficiency. Nat offers helpful tips and suggestions, occasionally barking at me when I hold the gun wrong. But as time goes on, I begin to feel increasingly fatigued and nauseous.

Chalking it up to the stress and shock of recent events, I finally call it a day, my arms trembling from not only Edo's self-defense lessons but from holding a gun for hours.

"Keep practicing," Nat tells me as we head upstairs. "And there are cameras everywhere in that gun range. If I see you with an improper stance, I will fight you."

Somehow, I don't doubt that Nat would.

After a long, hot shower, I sink into my plush bed, Biscotti immediately curling up beside me. Biscotti's approval of me was the subject of much amusement from Edo and Damian and consternation from Nat.

As I lie there, idly petting Biscotti's fur, a nagging thought suddenly occurs to me.

When was my last period?

With everything that had happened, the trauma and upheaval, I hadn't even been keeping track. Closing my eyes, I mentally try to retrace the calendar in my mind.

Suddenly, I bolt upright, my heart pounding. Seizing my phone, I frantically scroll through my period tracking app, my eyes widening as the data confirms my suspicions.

It has been eight weeks since my last cycle. Right before I escaped the Carter house and found myself tangled in Damian's web.

Panic grips me as I contemplate the implications. Damian, Nat, and Edo have been vigilantly watching over me, not allowing me to leave their sight. How am I going to get the test I need to confirm my fears?

Swallowing hard, I make my way to the door, peering out cautiously. One of Damian's guards is stationed nearby. Steeling my nerves, I approach him.

"Excuse me, I need to go to the store. It's... an emergency," I say, my cheeks flushing.

The guard eyes me skeptically. "I can't let you leave the mansion. Boss's orders."

"Please, I really need to go," I plead. "I need to get... feminine products."

The guard's expression immediately shifts, a look of discomfort washing over his face. "O–oh, I see. Well, in that case, let me escort you to the nearest convenience store."

I breathe a sigh of relief, grateful that the guard hadn't questioned me further or asked why I don't borrow items from Nat.

As we make our way out of the mansion, I silently pray that the test will confirm my suspicions are wrong.

The security guard waits in the car as I rush inside the convenience store, snatching a pregnancy test and making a beeline for the bathroom.

I'm just not feeling well, I tell myself as I set the test on the counter, setting a timer on my phone for three minutes. *I'm probably getting sick.*

This is going to be the longest three minutes of my life.

I pace back and forth in the cramped bathroom, my heart racing. This can't be happening, it just can't. There's no way I can be pregnant, not after everything I had endured.

I try to rationalize it in my mind—the stress of finding out the Carters and Mark wanted to sell me to The Brotherhood, the upheaval of being brought into Damian's world, the trauma of killing Mark. Surely, that's enough to throw my menstrual cycle off track, to make my period skip a month or two.

It happens to women all the time, right?

Clasping my hands together, I close my eyes and take a shaky breath. I have to stay calm, stay positive. When I look at the test, it'll be negative.

It has to be. I can't handle the alternative, the terrifying implications of a positive test.

Slowly, I turn my attention to the test stick sitting on the edge of the sink. The wait is agonizing, each second feeling like an eternity.

My phone's timer suddenly goes off, indicating the three minutes are up.

Feeling like I'm going to my doom, I peer at the test, my heart pounding in my ears.

"No, no, no…" I whisper, staring at the test in disbelief. This can't be happening. Not now. Not after everything I have been through.

Two pink lines.

I'm pregnant.

24

DAMIAN

The pulsing beat of the music reverberates through The Underground, the rhythmic vibrations matching the frenetic pace of my thoughts.

As I survey the crowded dance floor from the VIP lounge, brandy glass in hand, where bodies writhe and twist in a display of unbridled hedonism, my mind keeps returning to the one person I'm deliberately keeping away from this world—Alexis.

An ache settles deep within my chest as I think of her, safe and sound at home, removed from the dangers that lurk within the shadows. The Brotherhood is a constant threat, and I would sooner die than allow them to harm the woman who has managed to breach the fortress around my heart.

My jaw tightens as I consider the impossible dilemma I face. I want nothing more than to lose myself in Alexis, find solace in her company and forget—even if for a moment—the burdens I bear. But the fate of my parents and sister loom large, a painful reminder of the price paid by those I dared to hold dear.

If Alexis were to become truly mine, she too would be marked, a target for those who seek to eliminate me. My fingers clench into fists as I contemplate the endless ways in which my enemies could use her against me.

The mere thought of her being harmed sends a surge of protective rage through my veins. No one will harm her. *No one.*

With a deep exhale, I force myself to turn my attention to the business at hand. The latest shipment will be arriving soon, and I need to ensure everything is in order. But Alexis remains at the forefront of my mind, a constant source of both longing and trepidation.

My gaze lifts from the dance floor as the door to the VIP lounge swings open and Nat strides in.

Even after all these years, the sight of her still manages to steal my breath away—not because of her beauty, though there is no denying she's a striking woman, but because of the uncanny resemblance she bears to our parents.

In Nat's features, I can see the delicate, refined beauty of our mother, the same high cheekbones and smile that have captivated so many. Yet, it's the way she carries herself—the confident swagger, the unwavering determination in her every step—that's a mirror image of our father, the man who built this empire with an iron fist.

A pang of nostalgia and regret tugs at my heart as I watch Nat approach. Though she's my second-in-command, a part of me still sees the little girl who had once looked up to me with such adoration.

Now, her gaze is hardened, honed by years of navigating the treacherous waters of our Family's enterprise.

"The shipment's here," Nat announces without preamble, her voice clipped and efficient. "I've already handled the logistics. Everything's been weighed, bagged, and sorted, ready to be distributed as planned."

I nod, my expression betraying none of the turbulent emotions stirring within me. "Good work," I say, my eyes briefly flickering with a barely perceptible hint of pride.

In moments like this, I'm reminded of just how capable and invaluable my sister is to the family business—a stark contrast to the vulnerable child she had once been.

The door to the VIP lounge swings open once more and Edo steps inside. His intense gaze sweeps over the room before locking onto me.

"We've got some funny business going on out there on the main floor," Edo says, his voice low and tinged with a hint of urgency. "Thought you might want to take a look."

My brow furrows, my grip tightening momentarily on the glass I hold. "What kind of 'funny business'?" I ask in a clipped tone.

Edo's eyes narrow. "Not sure, exactly, but it's got my hackles up. Might be worth checking out personally, you know?"

I glance over at Nat, who has been standing silently, her expression unreadable. A silent understanding passes between us, and I give a curt nod.

"Alright," I say, setting down my glass and straightening my suit jacket. "Lead the way, Edo."

We make our way down the staircase, my sharp gaze scanning the dance floor as we descend. The pulsing music and writhing bodies do little to distract me from the underlying tension that now permeates the air.

As we near the main bar, I catch sight of a commotion brewing near the back entrance. My jaw tightens, and I quicken my pace, Nat and Edo flanking me like twin shadows.

"Let's see what's going on," I murmur, my voice low. Whatever is unfolding, I'm determined to nip it in the bud before it can threaten the delicate balance I have worked so hard to maintain.

The last thing I need is for the cops to raid this place. I'm already on thin ice with them.

Suddenly, the doors burst open, and a flood of armed Invicta members spills into The Underground. Chaos erupts as screams of terror pierce the pulsing music as patrons scramble to flee the sudden onslaught.

Fuck!

My eyes narrow, my body tensing like a coiled spring as I recognize the rival gang's insignia emblazoned on their tactical gear.

Without a moment's hesitation, I bark orders to my soldiers, who immediately spring into action, drawing their concealed weapons and forming a protective barrier around me and Nat.

Nat's expression is grim, her fingers curled around the grip of her handgun as she scans the chaotic scene, her tactical training kicking into high gear. "Edo, secure the VIP lounge!" she commands, her voice cutting through the pandemonium. "We need to hold that position at all costs!"

Edo nods sharply, his own weapon raised as he leads a contingent of Iacopelli men toward the staircase, engaging the Invicta forces in a brutal exchange of gunfire.

My gaze sweeps over the emptied dance floor, my mind racing as I formulate a plan of action. The Invicta members are clearly attempting to storm the club, no doubt seeking to disrupt my operations and send a message.

But I have no intention of yielding an inch to these fuckers.

This club is *mine*.

With a nod to my remaining soldiers, I surge forward, my weapon raised and my finger poised on the trigger. The sound of gunshots echoes through the cavernous space as we clash in a violent struggle for dominance.

We fight to repel the Invicta onslaught, the air crackling with the staccato of gunfire. My eyes narrow, my focus honed with the intensity of a seasoned predator as I methodically pick off one Invicta soldier after another.

Nat's commanding voice cuts through the chaos, her orders barked with the precision of a seasoned military tactician. Edo mirrors her movements, his weapon steady as he and his team hold the line at the VIP lounge staircase, determined to protect our stronghold.

Suddenly, I feel a searing pain in my shoulder, and I glance down to see a crimson stain blossoming on my tailored suit jacket. A hiss of frustration escapes my lips, but I refuse to let the injury slow me down.

This is my goddamn turf, *my* domain, and I'll be damned if I let these fuckers desecrate it.

As the smoke and sounds of battle fill the air, my mind races, trying to piece together how Invicta managed to pull off this brazen assault. Undoubtedly, this will make national news, and the police will soon be swarming the club, their badges and questions a nuisance I can't afford.

Bobby Shields's fingerprints are all over this.

My jaw tightens, my grip on my weapon unwavering despite the searing pain in my shoulder. That bastard Shields had taken everything from me once before, and I'll be damned if I let him do it again.

With renewed vigor, I surge forward, my soldiers flanking me as we systematically eliminate the Invicta forces. The clash of our gangs is a grim, unforgiving dance, each side fighting with the desperation of those who have lost far too much.

As the battle rages on, my eyes narrow, a cold resolve hardening my expression. I will not be cowed—not by Shields's petty vendetta, not by the looming threat of police intervention.

This is *my* world, built on the foundations of blood, sweat, and an unyielding determination to succeed.

The fallout from this clash will make national headlines, dragging my family's name into the spotlight once more. But in this moment, as the acrid scent of gunpowder fills the room, all that matters is ensuring the Iacopelli clan emerges victorious.

I will not rest until Shields and his Invicta fucks are purged from my territory, no matter the cost.

The Invicta soldiers are shouting something and my eyes narrow.

They're demanding to know the whereabouts of one Alexis Hartley.

A flicker of alarm crosses my features—how the hell do they know about her?

"Now they've got fucking Invicta after her?" I growl, my grip tightening on my weapon. "Who the fuck *is* this girl?"

If The Brotherhood has teamed up with Invicta, we're fucked.

The realization that my enemies have somehow discovered Alexis's connection to me only fuels the burning rage within me. She doesn't deserve any of this, and the thought of her being targeted makes my blood boil.

We fight with a renewed ferocity, determined to eliminate the Invicta threat and protect the woman I'm so fiercely drawn to, despite my efforts to keep her at arm's length.

My men fight with the aggression of those defending their home turf, while the Invicta soldiers, sensing their precarious position, grow increasingly desperate.

In the end, we emerge victorious, eliminating the majority of Invicta soldiers. Nat manages to capture one lone Invicta soldier, and I plan to *personally* interrogate him myself. I'm not leaving until I get some goddamn answers.

My jaw tightens as I survey the carnage that mars the once vibrant atmosphere of The Underground.

This attack had been a direct challenge to my authority, a brazen attempt by Shields to strike at the heart of my empire. But I'm no stranger to such threats, and I'm determined to ensure that Alexis and all that she represents remain out of the crosshairs.

With a nod to my soldiers, I turn my attention to the task of securing my territory and ensuring that the fallout from this clash will not jeopardize the delicate balance I have spent years cultivating.

The battle may have been won, but the war against Shields and Invicta is far from over.

I stride over to where Nat and Edo are standing, my shoulder still throbbing from the gunshot wound.

"Did you get anything out of that Invicta piece of shit before he bit down on the cyanide?" I growl, pinning them with a piercing gaze.

Nat shakes her head, her expression one of barely contained fury. "The fucker took the coward's way out," she spits. "Bit down on a hidden cyanide capsule before we could stop him. Didn't say a goddamn word."

"FUCK!" I roar, my knuckles whitening as I clench my fist. "Fucking figures."

There goes any opportunity to find out what the *fuck* Shields is playing at.

Edo steps forward, his blood-stained brow furrowed. "Speaking of which, how the hell did Invicta know about Alexis? Why are they looking for her?"

My eyes narrow, a grim realization dawning on me. "It's obvious, isn't it?" I say, my heart hammering as all the pieces come together. "The Brotherhood and Invicta are teaming up. They must have shared information about her."

Edo's eyes widen, the implication of this revelation clear. "But why?" he presses, his voice tinged with confusion. "What the fuck is so special about this Alexis Hartley that two of our biggest rivals are after her?"

I shake my head, my brow furrowed in deep thought. "I don't know," I admit, my frustration evident. "But we're going to find out."

Before any of us can say another word, our phones simultaneously chime with new messages. I feel a chill run down my spine as I read the contents, my expression darkening. Nat swears violently.

"Mario Rafa is dead," I announce, my voice low and grave. "And Scarlett is now the head of The Brotherhood."

Edo curses in Italian, the gravity of this news weighing heavily on us all. My grip on my phone tightens, my mind racing with the implications of this change of power.

"Shit," Edo mutters, the word barely audible over the cacophony of sirens in the distance. "This just got a whole lot more complicated."

"The bitch killed Mario," Nat whispers, still staring at her phone. "She finally did it."

I nod, my gaze hardening with a renewed determination. "We need to find out what the hell is going on," I say, my voice laced with a sense of urgency. "And we need to protect Alexis, no matter the cost."

25

ALEXIS

I hurry out of the bathroom, the positive pregnancy test wrapped in toilet paper and buried deep in the depths of my purse. My heart is pounding, my mind racing as I replay the last few minutes over and over again.

How could Damian and I have been so *stupid*?

I've never had to worry about birth control in the past. It just never crossed my mind since I wasn't having sex with Mark, and I figured that when we got married, I wouldn't need birth control.

And truthfully, I never thought to ask Damian whether he was being responsible. He probably thought I was on birth control.

Holy *fuck*. The consequences of our inability to communicate are staring me right in the face.

I hurriedly grab some tampons—although I won't need *these* for the next nine months—and quickly make my purchase, my hands shaking. I have to at least make it believable to the guard that I came in here for period products.

Nausea roils in my stomach, but I can't tell whether it's from the shock of the positive pregnancy test or the beginnings of morning sickness. I want to throw up, purge my body of this sudden, unwanted development. But I can't, not here in the middle of this dingy convenience store.

Cold air blasts me in the face as I leave the store and slide into the backseat of the car.

"Did you get everything you needed?" the security guard asks, his face red as he eyes my bag, the blue and green tampon box clearly visible against the plastic grocery bag.

I nod, pasting a weak smile on my face. "All good. Thank you."

As we drive off, my mind is still racing. What am I going to do? Part of me wants to keep this baby. This child will be the first real family I've had in almost two decades. I finally wouldn't be alone anymore.

But the thought of bringing a child into this world, where they could potentially grow up to be as fucked up as Damian and Nat, fills me with dread.

The idea of getting an abortion, though, makes me feel sick to my stomach. This is *my* child, a part of me. How could I just get rid of it?

But can I really be a good mother?

My own memories of my mother are so faint, and my experiences with foster mothers have been nothing short of awful. What if I end up just like them, incapable of providing the love and nurturing that a child needs?

Panic seizes me as I think about having to tell Damian. What if he's furious with me? What if he accuses me of trying to baby trap him? The very thought makes me feel sick to my stomach.

An even more horrible thought hits me then. What if Damian tries to take this baby away from me? He has unlimited funds, connections, and power as a Don. He's probably paid off numerous judges to get his own criminal convictions thrown out.

Who's to say he wouldn't do the same to take my child from me?

I have no home, no job, and a target on my back. Damian, on the other hand, has all the resources in the world. He could bury me in legal battles, use his influence to turn the system against me. I'd never stand a chance.

I'd lose my baby, the only family I've ever had.

Tears sting my eyes as the horrific reality of my situation sets in. I can't breathe, can't think straight. All I know is I have to protect this child, no matter what. Even if it means facing Damian's wrath. Even if it means going on the run, disappearing completely.

I'll do whatever it takes to keep my baby safe.

I consider making a run for it, just disappearing before Damian ever finds out about the pregnancy. I wouldn't be stupid this time and head to the Carters' house.

But I know that would be futile. He has the resources and connections to hunt me down, no matter where I try to hide. He's a Mafia Don with seemingly unlimited funds and influence. He could mobilize an entire army to search for me.

And even if I manage to evade him for a time, what kind of life would that be, constantly looking over my shoulder, terrified that he'll find me and take my baby away?

No, I can't run. I have to face this head-on, as terrifying as the thought is.

But I can't tell Damian. Not yet.

As the panic over telling Damian subsides, at least temporarily, my body is overcome with an overwhelming urge to eat something—*anything*—to settle my roiling stomach.

Once we get back to the house, I decide a few plain crackers or a piece of dry toast might be just what I need, so I head toward the kitchen.

But as I round the corner, I come face to face with a man I've never seen before. He's tall and imposing, with salt-and-pepper hair that gives him an air of authority. His brow is heavy, conveying a sense of perpetual scrutiny, and his nose is slightly crooked, as if it had been broken at some time. The lines that frame his mouth and eyes speak of a lifetime of hardship and struggle.

But despite his advancing age, there's an undeniable strength and vitality that radiates from him. His jawline remains sharp and defined, and the muscles in his neck stand out subtly beneath the fabric of his expensive, tailored suit.

But something about him sets my teeth on edge, my entire body instinctively telling me to get as far away from this man as possible.

"Can I help you?" he asks, his voice smooth and measured.

"I'm... I'm sorry, I was just looking for something to eat," I stammer, suddenly feeling very small and vulnerable.

"And who might you be?" the man inquires, his gaze piercing right through me. His face exudes an aura of danger and mystery. "I don't believe we've met before."

I put on my most convincing smile. "I'm Maria, Damian and Nat's cousin." I repeat the cover story that Nat and Damian had drilled into me, hoping my nerves don't betray the lie.

"Maria," the man says, his expression unreadable. "I'm Vincente Iacopelli, Damian and Natalia's *uncle*. I don't believe I've had the pleasure of meeting you before. What brings you here?"

"Oh, you know, just visiting family," I reply, hoping my voice sounds casual enough. "And what about you? What brings you here?"

Vincente's gaze narrows slightly. "I'm here looking for Damian. Haven't you heard the news? Mario Rafa is dead, and his daughter Scarlett is now the Donna of The Brotherhood."

My blood runs cold at his words and my stomach heaves. Mario Rafa is... dead? And Scarlett has taken over? I'm not sure whether it's just pregnancy-related nausea or that the sheer gravity of the situation is overwhelming me. Either way, I can feel the color draining from my face.

This is the last thing I needed to hear.

If Vincente is looking for Damian, it can't be for any good reason.

"No, I'm afraid I hadn't heard that," I say, trying to sound more surprised than concerned. "That's quite a development."

Vincente's eyes narrow as he scrutinizes me from head to toe, his gaze almost predatory. The look makes me feel incredibly uncomfortable, as if he can see right through my "Maria" façade.

It's almost as if he *knows* who I really am.

"Are you alright, my dear?" Vincente asks, his voice infuriatingly patronizing. "You look a bit... pale."

I swallow hard, desperately trying to maintain my composure. "I'm fine, just a bit under the weather, that's all," I lie, cursing the quaver in my voice.

Vincente hums noncommittally, his eyes still piercing into me. "I see. Well, I do hope you recover soon. I'd hate for you to miss any... *important* Family matters."

I want to throw up. The implications in his words are clear, and it sends a chill down my spine. Does Vincente know I'm not who I'm pretending to be?

He's toying with me, sizing me up, and I have no idea how to handle this increasingly precarious situation.

I need to get away from him, to find Damian and warn him about what's happening. But I also can't risk Vincente seeing through my ruse completely. One wrong move will put me and this baby in grave danger.

Just as I'm about to make my escape, a guard suddenly appears, hurrying toward me.

"Miss, you're needed upstairs immediately," he says urgently, his eyes darting nervously between me and Vincente.

I glance back at Vincente, who is watching me with a predatory gleam in his eyes, a chilling smile playing at his lips. The sight sends a shiver down my spine.

"Ah, rushing off already?" Vincente purrs, his gaze never leaving mine. "How unfortunate. I was so looking forward to getting to know you better, *Maria*."

The way he emphasizes my supposed name makes it clear that he sees right through my ruse. Panic rises within me, but I force myself to remain outwardly calm.

"Please excuse me," I say hastily, turning to follow the guard. "I'm needed elsewhere."

As I hurry away, I can't help but look back one last time.

Vincente is still watching me, that unsettling smile still on his face. It takes every ounce of my willpower not to break into a dead sprint.

The guard ushers me up the stairs and down a hallway, away from Vincente's prying eyes. Once we're a safe distance away, he leans in and murmurs, "*Quel uomo è pericoloso.*"

I furrow my brow, not understanding the foreign words. "What does that mean?" I ask, a thread of anxiety in my voice.

The guard glances around cautiously before translating, "That man is dangerous."

My blood runs cold at his words. Dangerous? Why on earth would Damian want me to stay away from his own uncle?

"Why?" I press, my mind racing. "What has Vincente done?"

The guard shakes his head grimly. "I should not have said anything. Just trust that the Boss knows what he's doing."

But I can't simply accept that. Not when my safety—and the safety of the child I'm carrying—could be at stake.

"Please," I plead. "If Vincente is as dangerous as you say, I need to know why. I have a right to understand the risks I'm facing."

The guard hesitates, clearly torn. Finally, he sighs and says, "Mr. Vincente... he is a ruthless man. He has done many unspeakable things. He was the underboss before Mr. Damian's father died. He is close to The Brotherhood."

My heart hammers in my chest as the gravity of the situation sinks in. Vincente isn't just some benign relative—he's a dangerous criminal, someone Damian evidently wants me to avoid at all costs.

And yet, Damian never thought to *tell* me about this. He's kept me in the dark, leaving me vulnerable to Vincente's machinations. The realization fills me with a mix of fear and frustration.

There Damian goes again, with all his *secrets*. How can I trust him to keep me and this baby safe when he's clearly withholding crucial information? My stomach twists with worry and uncertainty.

The guard looks at me anxiously. "You will say nothing about what I've told you, *si*?"

I nod shakily, my mind racing. If Damian has specifically warned his men about Vincente not seeing me, then he must know how dangerous the man is. And the way Vincente was looking at me? It fills me with a sense of dread I can't quite shake.

I can only hope that by putting some distance between Vincente and me, I'll be able to keep myself and my baby safe.

But something tells me this is only the beginning of the nightmare I've found myself in.

26

DAMIAN

I storm through the front door, clenching my jaw in fury. Invicta's attack already left me on edge, and now this news from the head of security only stokes the fire burning within me.

"Sir, there's a situation," my security chief reports with a grave expression. "Your Uncle Vincente was allowed into the house and crossed paths with Ms. Alexis. He was able to speak with her before one of the guards rushed her away."

Fuck. My blood boils at the same time my heart clenches with fear. How the fuck did this happen? I had ordered stringent security protocols specifically to prevent unauthorized access, especially where Alexis is concerned. How the hell did Uncle Vinny manage to bypass those measures?

"I thought I made it clear that Vincente Iacopelli is not to be allowed access without my express permission!" I roar, the familiar scent of a rat in the air. Someone has betrayed my trust, and I'm going to find out who.

I clench my fists, fury coursing through me. "Find the person who allowed my uncle into this house!" I roar at the head of security. "I want to see the footage where he spoke to Alexis."

The security chief nods quickly, scurrying away to retrieve the requested footage. I need to see this footage, to understand exactly what transpired between my uncle and Alexis. This is a direct threat to everything I hold dear.

Moments later, the security chief returns, cuing up the hallway footage on a nearby monitor. I step forward, eyes locked on the screen as the scene unfolds.

I watch the footage intently, my body tense as I see Vinny approach Alexis. The way he speaks, the look in his eyes—it sets off every alarm bell in my head.

"How unfortunate," Uncle Vinny says, his tone dripping with false sincerity. "I was so looking forward to getting to know you better, *Maria*."

The emphasis he places on her supposed name sends a chill down my spine. It's clear he doesn't believe her cover story for a second. My heart races as panic starts to set in.

Edo places a hand on my shoulder, trying to calm me. "Relax, Damian."

Nat chimes in, although she too looks a bit worried. "Alexis knows her story backward and forward. Plus, she really does look like Cousin Maria with the dyed hair. Vincente never paid much attention to Mom's side of the family, anyway."

I whirl around, glaring at them both. "Don't you see?" I hiss. "He *knows*. Uncle Vinny isn't buying her story for a second. This is a direct challenge. He's toying with me, with *us*."

"Even if he doesn't buy her story," Edo says, watching as Alexis is hurried away by a guard, "he has no reason to suspect who Alexis truly is."

Turning back to the screen, I watch as Uncle Vinny's gaze lingers on Alexis, a predatory gleam in his eyes. My fists clench at my sides, knuckles turning white.

This is exactly what I feared, why I did not want my uncle to be allowed to wander my home without my controlling every step.

"We need to get Alexis out of here. *Now*," I growl, already formulating a plan of action. We have other safehouses across the state, and I can stow her there until it's safe to bring her back.

I won't let Uncle Vinny lay a single finger on her, no matter what it takes. He may not know who Alexis really is, but he's suspicious, and a suspicious Vinny is never good.

Edo and Nat exchange a worried glance, clearly sensing the panic and fury radiating off me in waves. But I don't care—all that matters is keeping Alexis safe, no matter the cost.

I waste no time in seeking out Alexis, my mind racing with the implications of Uncle Vinny's visit. As I approach her in her room, I'm surprised to see Biscotti at her side, curled contentedly next to her.

"Alexis," I say, trying to keep my voice even despite the turmoil swirling within me. "We need to talk."

Her voice has a slight edge to it as she responds. "Yes, Damian, we do need to talk."

She sets Biscotti down, the dog letting out a disgruntled whine at the disruption.

"What did my uncle say to you?" I demand, my tone brooking no argument. "And why didn't you stay on the top floor like you normally do?"

Alexis's eyes flash with irritation. "I'm sorry, I thought I was allowed full range of the prison—I mean house."

"Alexis," I growl, but she ignores me.

"I'm so *sick* of your keeping secrets from me, Damian," she bites back. "Why didn't you bother telling me about your uncle and his connections to The Brotherhood?"

My brow furrows. How the fuck does she know that? "Who told you that?" I ask sharply.

She throws her hands up in exasperation. "That's the point I'm trying to make!" she exclaims. "I'm always on a need-to-know basis with you. But this is my *life* that's at stake here. I deserve to know what's going on!"

Alexis steps closer to me, her gaze unwavering. "Stop keeping me in the dark, Damian. My life depends on your being honest with me."

I stand my ground, my expression unwavering. "I understand your concerns, Alexis, but you need to trust that I'm doing what's best to keep you safe. That means staying close and letting me handle things."

Her eyes narrow as she glares at me. "That's exactly the problem, Damian! You're treating me like a child, keeping me in the dark. I'm not some fragile doll you can just lock away."

"This isn't up for debate, Alexis!" I say firmly. "My uncle is dangerous and he wants to hand you over to The Brotherhood. I can't have you wandering around where I can't protect you."

"Protect me?" Alexis scoffs. "Or control me? Because that's what this feels like. You're more concerned with maintaining your grip on the situation than actually keeping me safe."

Irritated, I open my mouth to retort, but she cuts me off. "No, Damian. I'm done with the secrets and demands. If we're going to get through this, we need to be *partners*, not adversaries."

My jaw clenches as I consider her words, the tension palpable in the air. Finally, I let out a long sigh, my shoulders slumping slightly.

"Alright, *fine*. No more secrets, no more demands. We'll figure this out together."

As she stands before me, I can't help but be captivated by her beauty. The way her cheeks flush with a hint of pink, the way her ebony curls bounce as she moves her head—it all serves to stoke the heat building within me.

I find my gaze drawn to the expressive planes of her face, the way her full lips part ever so slightly as she speaks. There's a rawness to her in this moment, a vulnerability that only makes her all the more alluring.

I can feel the familiar stirrings of arousal as I drink in the sight of her. Alexis is a force to be reckoned with, her spirit and strength igniting something primal within me. The way she challenges me, refuses to back down, only serves to make her all the more captivating.

My eyes trace the curve of her neck, the slope of her shoulders. I know I should be focused on the task at hand, on the threat my uncle poses, but at this moment, all I can think about is how badly I want to pull her into my arms and lose myself in her.

The tension crackles between us, a charged energy that seems to hum in the air. I can feel the pull of it, the desire to close the distance and claim her as my own. I know I need to maintain control, to keep a level head, but Alexis makes it increasingly difficult to think about anything other than the way she makes me feel.

My cock hardens painfully, and I feel the need to touch her, to feel her beneath my hands.

The tension builds to a fever pitch as we stand facing each other, the air practically crackling with pent-up desire. My control is slipping, my gaze drawn inexorably to the curves of her body, the way her soft lips part ever so slightly.

Unable to resist any longer, I surge forward, capturing her mouth in a searing kiss. Alexis responds with equal fervor, her fingers tangling in my hair as she presses herself against me.

Somewhere in the periphery, Biscotti lets out a curious yip, but I pay the dog no mind. All that matters in this moment is the feel of Alexis's body against mine, the taste of her on my lips.

Reluctantly, I break the kiss, my breathing ragged. "We can't do this here," I murmur. "I can't have my baby girl watch me have sex, Alexis. That's just wrong."

Without another word, I scoop Biscotti up, depositing the confused dog outside the room and closing the door before pulling Alexis close once more. My mind finds hers in a hungry, desperate kiss as I back her toward the bed, intent on putting as much distance between us and the rest of the world as possible.

She melts into my embrace, her fingers deftly working the buttons of my shirt. I growl low in my throat, my hands roaming her curves as the last vestiges of my control slip away.

The rest of the world fades away as we tumble onto the bed, clothes removed, our bodies tangling together in a frenzy of touch and taste. I know I should be focused on the looming threat of Uncle Vinny, but with Alexis in my arms, all rational thought seems to slip away.

For now, there is only this—the urgent press of our naked bodies, the desperate clash of our lips. Everything else can wait. At this moment, I'm consumed by a single, all-encompassing desire to make Alexis mine, in every sense of the word.

I massage her breasts slowly as we kiss. Alexis arches and reaches a soft hand to touch me. Her grip is tender and smooth and feels so good that I'm nearly immobilized.

As I exhale with pleasure, I mount her to kiss her again. This isn't like our other moments. This is something intense that makes my heart race in a way it hasn't before.

I gaze down at her beautiful body, and Alexis smiles at me, her eyes soft as she strokes my cock nice and slow. She spreads her legs wide for me and fingers her clit twice so I can see how wet I'm making her.

Leaning forward, I set my hands beside her head. Alexis holds onto my wrists and forearms while I position myself to enter her. We both moan as I slide into her, and her grip around my wrists tightens. She bites her bottom lip as we gyrate together.

I move against her with long, controlled thrusts. God, she's so fucking beautiful. I could do this forever.

Alexis slides her hands down from my wrists to my hands, and we lock fingers. My heart is pounding and I feel reborn. Sex has *never* been this good, this pleasurable before.

I pick up the pace of my thrusts, kissing Alexis wildly. Every kiss of hers makes me hungrier for the next. Keeping one hand locked with hers, I guide my other hand down onto her round ass and give it a firm slap.

Alexis moans but then pushes me away, and I slide out of her. She leans up on her elbows, her breasts heaving in tune with her breaths.

I look at her questioningly, my dick throbbing as it screams to keep fucking her, to enter her wet pussy and fill her up.

She smiles at me before rotating her body, planting her face between her elbows and raising her ass into the air.

My lust for her becomes primal.

I force away any thought outside of the beautiful body I've got in front of me and how much I want her.

Grabbing hold of each of her hips, I slip my dick back inside her. We both moan as I thrust quickly, and her knees start to shake.

"Oh, *Damian*," she groans.

Fuck, the way she says my name almost makes me come right then and there. I put one hand over her pussy and rub rapid circles along her clit. Her toes clench and my shoulders tighten. The bed frame creaks as I pound my cock into her.

I explode in an orgasm, filling her to the brim.

Alexis's thighs fold inward, and she brings a pillow in front of her face, screaming in ecstasy. Each inhale and exhale she makes is muffled by the pillow.

Catching my breath, I run a hand through my sweaty hair and roll onto my back. I extend an arm out to Alexis for her to snuggle against, and she does so. I normally don't do this, but after everything that's happened today—from Invicta to Uncle Vinny—I want to be close to her.

We lie tangled in the sheets, our bodies still humming from the intensity of sex. I press a kiss to her hair, breathing her in.

I can't believe how much this woman has come to mean to me in such a short time. As I lie here with Alexis in my arms, I'm overwhelmed by the depth of my feelings for her.

It's terrifying, if I'm being honest.

I've never been one to open my heart, to let anyone get this close. Even Scarlett was never truly able to breach the perimeter of my heart. My world has always been about control, about power and influence.

But Alexis has a way of slipping past my carefully constructed defenses, making me feel things I never thought possible.

The way she looks at me, the way her touch ignites a fire within me—it's intoxicating. She's become an integral part of my life, my very being, in a way no one else ever has.

And the thought of losing her, of something happening to her—it fills me with a fear I can barely comprehend.

I've always prided myself on my ability to remain calm, to think clearly in even the direst of situations. But with Alexis, all of that goes out the window. She has a way of stripping me bare, of rendering me vulnerable in a way that should terrify me.

Yet, somehow, it doesn't. Because when I'm with her, when I'm wrapped up in her warmth, in her gentle caress, I feel more alive than I've ever been. She completes me in a way I never knew I needed.

"Alexis," I say softly, my fingers tracing idle patterns on her bare skin. "There's something I need to tell you."

She turns to face me, her brown eyes searching mine. "What is it?"

I swallow hard, suddenly feeling uncharacteristically vulnerable. "I... I care about you. A lot. More than I ever thought possible."

Her lips curve into a small smile, and she reaches up to gently caress my cheek. "I feel the same, Damian. You've become so important to me."

The words are on the tip of my tongue, those three little words that hold the power to change everything. But I hesitate, suddenly unsure of how she feels, of whether she's ready to hear them. I can't bear the thought of laying my heart bare, only to have it shattered.

But something else is niggling at me, and I can't help but shake the feeling that something else is weighing on Alexis's mind.

Gently, I reach out and brush a stray curl from her face, my fingers lingering on the soft contours of her cheek. "Alexis," I murmur. "Is there something else you want to say?"

Her eyes meet mine, and for a moment, I swear I see a flicker of something unspoken in their depths. But just as quickly, it's gone, replaced by a small, reassuring smile.

"No, it's nothing," she says, shaking her head. "I'm just... happy, that's all."

I nod, but I can't quite shake the nagging suspicion that she's holding something back. There's a guarded quality to her expression, a subtle tension in the set of her shoulders that tells me all is not as simple as she's letting on.

I want to press her, to coax the truth from her lips. But I know Alexis, and I know that forcing the issue will only serve to push her further away. She'll open up to me when she's ready, in her own time.

I just have to be patient.

~

THE NEXT DAY, my phone rings. Glancing down, I see Uncle Vinny's number flash across the screen. Tension grips me as I answer. "Uncle Vinny. What is it?"

"I was hoping you could join me for lunch at Basil and Olive today. I've got something important to discuss with you," my uncle's smooth voice crackles in my ear. "You can always bring Maria if you'd like."

I feel a chill run down my spine at my uncle's words, but I quickly reject the suggestion. "Maria is heading home after spending some quality time with family," I lie. The last thing I want is for Alexis to be anywhere near my uncle, not when I can sense danger radiating from his words.

"What a pity," Uncle Vinny purrs. "I was so looking forward to getting to know her better."

My mind races. I want to refuse, but I can't without raising suspicions. Steeling myself, I agree to a lunch at Basil and Olive, making sure to bring Nat with me as backup.

As Nat and I approach the restaurant, I can feel the weight of my concealed weapons, the reassuring heft of the guns giving me a small measure of comfort. Edo and my best guards have been tasked with keeping a close eye on Alexis in my absence. I'll be damned if my uncle gets his hands on her.

Walking through the doors of Basil and Olive, I immediately spot Uncle Vinny seated at a table, an unfamiliar woman beside him. Squaring my shoulders, I approach, Nat a silent shadow at my back.

"Ah! Damian! Natalia!" Uncle Vinny greets us, a faint smile playing on his lips. "Please meet my friend. This is Emma Carter, Alexis Hartley's foster sister."

27

ALEXIS

I pace the room anxiously, glancing at the clock every few minutes. This meeting has me all twisted up inside, though I can't put my finger on why. There's something unsettling about Vincente Iacopelli. Something that awakens some primal part of me, wanting to flee when I'm in his presence.

"*Quel uomo è pericoloso,*" the guard had whispered to me.

He is a dangerous man.

All I know is that I need Damian back by my side. The distance between us is making me more on edge than usual. And with the secret I'm carrying—that I'm pregnant with Damian's child—my nerves are frayed.

Deciding I need a distraction, I seek out Edo, hoping his calming presence might help soothe my anxiety. I find Damian's consigliere in his study, absorbed in some papers.

"Edo, do you have a minute? I could really use some company right now."

He looks up, pushing away some of his black hair off his face. He meets my gaze with a warm smile. "Sure, Alexis. Come, sit." He gestures to the chair across from him.

I settle into the plush seat, fidgeting with my hands as the unease bubbles up inside me. "It's this meeting with Vincente. I don't know, there's something off about him—something dangerous. And I'm so anxious for Damian to get back."

Edo nods before dropping his gaze back to his paperwork and scrawling a signature across the page—Edoardo Bianchi.

Bianchi, not Iacopelli.

I furrow my brow. It is now hitting me that he doesn't share the same last name as Damian and Nat.

"Your last name isn't Iacopelli," I blurt out.

Edo looks up, raising one eyebrow at me. "No, it's not."

"You aren't related to Damian and Nat?" I ask, unsure how this all works. I thought all crime families were related somehow.

He shakes his head. "No, I'm not related to them. My connection to the Iacopelli family is a bit different."

I lean forward, intrigued. "How did you come to be involved with them, then?"

He runs a hand through his hair, a pensive look on his face. "I'm the son of immigrants, Alexis. I grew up in Cabrini-Green. It's not—it wasn't the safest place to live." He exhales. "When I was in high school, I got into a bit of trouble—nothing too serious, but enough to catch the attention of the local Iacopelli capo."

Edo pauses, his eyes earnest. "Rather than turning me over to the authorities, he saw potential in me and offered me a chance to turn my life around. That's how I ended up here, working for the Family. It's not the life I would have chosen for myself, but it's given me stability and opportunity I never would have had otherwise. And enough money to send to my parents so they can live in a safer area."

"How did you end up meeting Damian?" I ask. "No offense, but you sounded like a low-ranking soldier. How did you cross paths?"

Edo smirks, his dark eyes lighting up with amusement. "In case you haven't noticed, Damian is a bit too full of himself. Damian's father placed him in a position of authority over my division and I… disagreed with Damian's methods. I had to kick the shit out of him a few times when he got too mouthy." He shrugs, looking quite pleased with himself.

"Damian's dad didn't try to kill you for beating up his heir?" I ask breathlessly. If someone beat up *my* baby, there would be hell to pay.

Edo tips his head back and laughs, a warm, rich sound. "*Mio Dio*, no. I think the Boss was pleased that someone actually took Damian to task. We've been friends ever since."

The mental image of a younger Damian getting the shit kicked out of him amuses me. "It's hard to imagine Damian getting his ass handed to him."

Edo grins. "I may be on the quiet side, but I've got a few inches and a lot of muscle on him. Damian's never really liked that I'm bigger and stronger." He shakes his head fondly. "When the Boss… died, it was a no-brainer for him to appoint me as his consigliere. I've been by his side ever since."

I'm amazed at the depth of their friendship. I never would've guessed. "I had no idea you two were so close."

He nods, leaning back so that his shirt strains against his broad chest. "Damian and his family, they gave me a chance when I needed it most. I'll always be grateful for that." His expression grows serious. "And that's why I'm always going to have his back, no matter what."

"Damian's a piece of work," I tell Edo, wanting to be honest since he gave me honesty.

Edo shrugs. "He may be," he says, "but he also uses his position to do a lot of good for the community."

"What do you mean?" I ask, intrigued.

"He donates regularly to the local church, the one where his parents married and all three Iacopelli children were baptized. He's also the reason the low-income public elementary schools in the area have free meals for students."

My eyes widen. "Free meals? How so?"

"He pays off every outstanding balance so those kids can eat," he explains. "He doesn't want a single child to go hungry. He does it in memory of Alessandra."

A swell of admiration rises up in me. For all Damian's flaws, deep down, he's a good person. "That's... actually really impressive. I had no idea he did all that."

Edo nods. "Damian even volunteers at the local UAW hall, making homemade spaghetti and meatballs or lasagna once a month for the workers."

Stunned, I sit back, processing this new information. Damian, the feared Mafia Don, is also a pillar of the community, using his resources to help those in need. It makes me wonder how he will be as a father.

My hand unconsciously drifts to my abdomen, where our child grows. Despite my initial fears, I have decided to keep the baby. Damian's impending return suddenly feels more urgent. I need to tell him the news, to see how he reacts.

"Thank you, Edo," I say sincerely. "Knowing all this about Damian... it means a lot to me."

He smiles warmly, his eyes crinkling at the corners. "I'm glad I could provide some perspective. Damian may be a complicated man, but he has a good heart."

He winks at me slyly. "You know, Damian's really been a different man since you came into his life, Alexis."

I feel my cheeks grow warm at his implication. "Oh? How so?"

Edo chuckles, his eyes gleaming with mirth. "Well, let's just say that Damian regularly getting laid makes him a *lot* more tolerable to be around."

Oh, God. If I could melt into the floor right now, I would. "Edo!" I scold, my face flaming.

He holds up his hands in mock surrender. "What? It's the truth! You've been a very good influence on him, Alexis." His expression softens. "Like I said, he's a good guy, deep down. And I think you've really brought out the best in him."

I feel a surge of affection for both Edo and Damian. "Thank you, Edo. That... means a lot to hear."

At that moment, I make a vow to myself. I will go to the doctor, get the proper prenatal care, and do everything in my power to ensure the health and well-being of our child. My baby's needs have to come before my own fears. Even if Damian wants nothing to do with me or our child, I will face this challenge head on.

Suddenly, a blaring alarm cuts through the air, causing Edo to snap to attention. His entire demeanor shifts as he transitions into his role as Damian's consigliere.

"Alexis, we're under attack," Edo says, his voice urgent. "I need you to go to your room, lock the door, and hide. Understand?"

I feel a surge of fear, my heart pounding. "What's happening?" I ask, my voice trembling.

"No time to explain," he says firmly. "A guard will take you to your room. Stay there until I come get you. Do you hear me?"

Before I can respond, a burly guard appears at my side. "Come with me, Miss," he says, gently but firmly guiding me toward the door.

As I hurry down the hallway, Biscotti comes scurrying after us. Despite the chaos, I can't help but feel a sense of relief at the dog's presence. Somehow, her familiar, stubborn energy makes me feel a little safer.

The guard ushers me to my room, and Biscotti scurries in as well, immediately making herself comfortable on the bed.

"What's going on?" I ask the grim-faced guard as he stands by the door.

"I'm not sure of the details, Miss," he replies. "But Mr. Edo says it's an attack, and we need to keep you safe. Just stay here and don't open the door for anyone but him, understand?"

I nod, my mind racing with questions and fears. The guard shuts the door, and I quickly lock it, my hands shaking. Scanning the room, I try to see if I can shove anything in front of the door. The dresser is too heavy, the antique wood seemingly a thousand pounds.

Sitting on the bed, Biscotti cuddles up next to me. For whatever reason, I can't help but feel a sense of profound gratitude for the loyal, if cantankerous, little dog.

The sounds of gunshots and frenzied shouting echo through the halls, causing my heart to race with terror. I clutch Biscotti tightly to my chest, the little dog's frantic whining only adding to the cacophony of chaos.

"Shh, Biscotti, it's okay," I whisper, my voice trembling. "We're going to be alright."

But deep down, I'm not so sure. I have no idea who is attacking us or what their intentions are. All I know is that Edo and the guards are out there, fighting to protect this place—and me.

I can only hope they will make it through this ordeal safely.

Suddenly, the sound of splintering wood makes me jump. My head snaps toward the door as it bursts open, and I let out a terrified scream.

Biscotti leaps from my arms, her tiny body bristling with defensive fury as she lunges toward the intruder, who kicks her away. I scream as Biscotti sails through the air and hits the ground. My blood runs cold when I see who is standing in the doorway.

A woman with striking red hair and cold eyes stares back at me, her clothes splattered with what I could only assume is blood.

"Hello, *Maria*," Scarlett Rafa says, her red-painted lips twisting in a vicious smile that makes her appear almost inhuman. "Or, should I say, *Alexis?*"

28

DAMIAN

My blood freezes at the mention of Alexis's name, my grip tightening on the concealed weapon beneath my jacket. Something about this situation feels inherently *wrong*. My uncle is up to something, and I have a sinking feeling that it has everything to do with the woman sitting across from him.

I do my best to maintain a bored, unaffected expression, even as my mind races with the implications of my uncle's words. Beside me, I can feel Nat stiffen, the tension radiating off my sister in palpable waves.

"Are you fucking her or something, Uncle Vinny?" I ask, my tone deliberately nonchalant. "Why is she here?"

Uncle Vinny chuckles, a predatory gleam in his eyes. "Straight to the point, as always, Damian. No, I'm not *fucking* her, as you so eloquently put it." He gestures toward Emma, who glares daggers at me, her eyes full of hate. "I've simply grown tired of waiting around for you to fulfill your promise to The Brotherhood. So, I decided to take matters into my own hands."

A chill runs down my spine at my uncle's words, my body screaming at me to run. "What are you talking about?"

"Well, you see," Uncle Vinny begins, leaning back in his chair, "I went to the Carter home to ask some questions. Imagine my surprise when I arrive to find her boyfriend—or was it fiancé—tied up and dead in a chair." He shakes his head, clucking his tongue in mock sympathy. "Poor thing was quite distraught."

My jaw tightens, my fingers itching to reach for the weapon hidden beneath my jacket. "And what, pray tell, does this have to do with me?"

Uncle Vinny's smile widens, a predatory gleam in his eyes. "Ah, well, you see, dear nephew, that's where it gets interesting. It seems our Alexis returned to the house and young Mark captured her. But before he could deliver her to The Brotherhood, it seems Alexis got to him first." He gestures to Emma, who looks ready to pounce. "Miss Carter here overheard everything."

I want to fucking scream. I didn't expect the fucking idiot to actually *call* Emma and brag about snatching Alexis.

But I'm not about to let my uncle or Emma know the truth. I adopt a bored, dismissive expression. "It's obvious Mark was lying about capturing Alexis Hartley. I highly doubt Miss Carter could have understood *everything* over the phone."

Emma's eyes flash with rage, her face twisting into a mask of fury, marring her otherwise pretty features. "Mark would *never* lie about something like that!" she nearly shrieks. "That dirty slut Alexis killed him, I know it!"

I have to resist the urge to lunge across the table and throttle this stupid woman. But Nat's grip on my shoulder is a silent warning, reminding me to keep my cool.

Uncle Vinny's eyes widen, a predatory gleam in his eyes. "Oh, but Damian, that's where you're mistaken. You see, a Brotherhood soldier has been stationed by the Carter house day and night, since Alexis disappeared, keeping an eye on things. And he saw the strangest thing—you, Natalia, and Edoardo coming to the Carter house and escorting a *bloodied* Alexis Hartley out."

I feel the bottom drop out of my stomach. Uncle Vinny has me cornered, and he knows it.

"You've been lying to me, Damian. You've had Alexis Hartley the whole time and you didn't give her up, even after she murdered young Mark in cold blood!"

Cold blood my ass. She was fucking protecting herself from Mark's attempt to sell her.

Uncle Vinny's eyes narrow dangerously as he fixes me with a withering glare. "You've always been too soft, Damian, too distracted by petty concerns to see the bigger picture."

He leans back in his chair, an accusatory sneer on his face. "You don't deserve to be the head of this Family. Not when you're more interested in harboring property of The Brotherhood, playing house with some pretty little piece of ass, than doing what needs to be done."

I bristle at the insult, my hands clenching into fists beneath the table. But before I can retort, Nat speaks up, her voice dripping with anger.

"You fucking asshole," Nat spits, her eyes burning with fury. "This isn't about Alexis, and you know it. You've been gunning for the Don position since Dad was alive. You can't stand knowing that the title passed to Damian over you."

Uncle Vinny's jaw tightens, the muscles in his cheek twitching. "Don't be naive, Natalia. This is about the survival of our Family. Damian's soft heart is a liability we can't afford."

He leans forward, his gaze boring into mine. "The Iacopelli Family needs a strong leader, one who isn't distracted by petty concerns and personal attachments. It's time for a change, Damian. And if you can't make the tough decisions, then you need to step aside."

I let out a harsh laugh. "And you think that's you? You couldn't even get this title when Dad died. What makes you think I would step aside?" I can feel my temper flaring as Uncle Vinny's words sink in. "I've spent the last fifteen years pouring every last bit of myself into this Family, making sure it's the best damn crime syndicate this city has ever seen."

Leaning forward, my voice drops to a low and dangerous tone. "Well, you can forget it, *Vincente*. This family is *mine*, and I'll be damned if I let you or anyone else take it from me."

"You arrogant bastard," Nat snarls, her body tense and ready to pounce. "Damian has done more to strengthen this Family than you ever could. You're just jealous that he has what you never will—the respect and loyalty of those who truly matter."

Uncle Vinny ignores Nat's outburst, casually sipping his wine as he fixes me with a cool, calculating gaze. "You know, after meeting your… *Maria*, I decided to do a little digging. And do you know what I found?"

I feel a weight settle in the pit of my stomach, my jaw tightening in anticipation of my uncle's next words.

"The *real* Maria hasn't been to Chicago in ages," Uncle Vinny continues, a hint of amusement in his voice. "In fact, she hasn't seen or talked to you or Natalia in years."

The implication hangs heavily in the air, and I know at that moment that this meeting was a trap. I exchange a tense glance with Nat, both of us realizing the gravity of our situation.

Nat moves to stand, her expression grim. "I need to make a call," she says, her voice tight.

But Vinny's grin widens, a predatory gleam in his eyes. "I don't think Edo will be able to get to the phone right now, my dear."

My blood runs cold at my uncle's words, my heart beating rapidly. The implication is clear—Edo has been harmed, or worse. Beside me, Nat pulls out her phone, her fingers trembling slightly as she dials Edo's number.

The phone rings, once, twice, three times... but there's no answer. Nat's eyes widen in horror as she meets my gaze, the unspoken fear hanging between us.

Across the table, Vinny begins to laugh, a cruel, mocking sound that sets my teeth on edge. The older man casually picks up his fork, slicing into the veal scallopini that has just been delivered, a contemplative look on his face.

"You might want to run home, Natalia," Vinny says, his voice laced with amusement. "I think you'll find a surprise waiting for you."

The blood drains from my face as the implication sinks in. Something has happened at the house—something that Vinny has orchestrated—and the thought of what we might find there fills me with a bone-deep dread.

Nat is already on her feet, her face a mask of barely contained panic. "Damian, we have to go. *Now*."

But I hold up a hand, my gaze locked onto Vinny's. "No," I say, my voice trembling with the effort to maintain my composure. "We stay. I'm not going to play your game, Vincente. Not this time."

Vinny's brows rise in mock surprise. "Oh? And what do you propose we do instead, Damian? Shall we have a nice, *civilized* discussion over our meal?" He takes another bite of his veal, his expression one of feigned innocence.

My hands clench into fists, my nails biting into the flesh of my palms.

"What have you done, Vincente?" I growl, the words barely audible over the pounding of my heart.

Vinny simply smiles, his eyes gleaming with a dangerous light. "Why don't you go and see for yourself, Damian? I'm sure the answer will be... enlightening."

The tension in the air is palpable, and I know I'm running out of options. Whatever has happened at the house, I can't ignore it. Alexis's safety, and the safety of my people, is on the line.

We rush back to the mansion, a growing sense of dread weighing on us with each passing second. As we approach the property, the scene that greets us is nothing short of horrific. Nat cries out in horror.

Broken glass and debris litter the ground, the once-grand entrance marred by the evidence of a violent confrontation. My stomach twists as I catch the sight of the lifeless bodies of my men scattered across the foyer, blood staining the pristine floors.

Bile rises in my throat as the full weight of what has happened sinks in. This isn't just a random attack by The Brotherhood—it's a calculated, orchestrated strike, one that has Vinny's fingerprints all over it.

The realization hits me like a punch to the gut. Vinny had known from the moment he laid eyes on Alexis that she wasn't "Maria".

Rage boils up in me, a white-hot fury that threatens to consume me. I have to fight the overwhelming urge to march right back to Basil and Olive and put a bullet between Vinny's eyes. This is no longer just about protecting Alexis—it's about making my uncle pay for his callous disregard for human life, for his willingness to sacrifice an innocent woman to further his own twisted agenda.

Pushing past the devastation, we make our way deeper into the house, following the sound of ragged breathing. There, in a side hallway, we find Edo—bloodied and battered, but still clinging to consciousness.

Nat screams and rushes to Edo's side. He's bleeding from a large wound in his stomach, his shirt stained crimson.

"Damian, Nat..." Edo croaks, his voice barely above a whisper. He's pressing a makeshift tourniquet against the thigh of a fallen soldier, desperate to stem the bleeding.

I fall to my knees beside him, my heart pounding in my ears. "Edo, what the hell happened?" I demand, my voice laced with barely concealed panic.

"The Brotherhood," Edo gasps, his eyes wild with a mixture of pain and urgency. "They... they hit us hard, came in firing... We never saw it coming."

I suck in a deep breath, my face draining of color as I grip Edo's shoulder, my eyes narrowing with urgency. "Alexis," I breathe. "Where's Alexis?"

Edo winces, the pain etched into his features. "I don't know, Damian," he admits, his voice strained. "When The Brotherhood attacked, I ordered one of the guards to take Alexis to her room and lock the door. I haven't seen her since."

We waste no time in rushing to Alexis's room, my heart pounding with desperation fueled by equal parts fear and fury.

As Nat and I approach the door, my stomach lurches at the sight—it's nearly off its hinges, the wooden frame splintered and broken. The room beyond is in complete disarray, a testament to the violent struggle that must have taken place.

Biscotti comes bounding out, my usually aloof dog now cowering and trembling in my arms. The sight of my normally bold creature reduced to such a state only serves to heighten my dread.

Nat inhales sharply, her gaze fixed on the door. I follow my sister's line of sight and feel the blood drain from my face. Bile rises in my throat.

There, painted in a sickening crimson, is a giant smiley face. And beneath it, a message that sends a chill down my spine.

"*Got her.*"

29

ALEXIS

I slowly blink my eyes open, my head pounding with a searing ache. As my senses gradually return, I realize with growing dread that I'm no longer in my room, but tied to a chair—much like I had been at the Carter house.

But this time, the knots are tied properly. I won't be able to unknot them. And from the way the rope is digging into my wrists, whoever tied me up did this purposefully to maximize my discomfort.

My heart races as the memories come flooding back—Scarlett bursting through my door, an inhuman grin on her blood-spattered face. A shiver of terror runs down my spine. I have to get out of here.

But how? Not only am I tied up, but this room is stark and barren. The walls are bare, devoid of any decoration or distinguishing features, and there's only one door leading out. There are no windows in this room, which leads me to believe I'm either in an interior room or in the basement.

Just then, Scarlett saunters into the room, a cruel smile playing on her lips. "Well, look who's finally decided to join us," she purrs, her tone dripping with false sweetness.

I open my mouth to speak, but my throat feels raw and parched. Scarlett seems to sense my struggle, and her smile only widens.

"Don't worry, dear," she coos, producing a knife from her pocket and pressing the blade lightly against the soft skin of my neck. "I want you nice and alert for our little chat."

I swallow hard, trying in vain to pull away from the sharp edge. "Where am I?" I rasp, hating the fear that laces my words.

Scarlett clicks her tongue disapprovingly. "Now, now, let's not worry about the details." She leans in closer, her breath hot against my face. "What's important is that I finally have you right where I want you."

My mind races as I desperately search for a way out of this nightmare. But there's no way out. Not with Scarlett standing before me with her menacing blade.

My baby's life depends on my getting out of this alive, but I know Scarlett will never let me go willingly. I have to play this carefully, keep my wits about me.

Be the wolf.

Scarlett clicks her tongue disapprovingly. "Tsk, tsk. And here I thought you'd be happy to see me." She leans in closer, her breath hot against my face. "You've done an excellent job hiding, you know. But you just *had* to go back to the Carter house, didn't you?"

My blood runs cold. "How did you...?"

"Find you?" Scarlett interrupts, a mocking laugh escaping her lips. "Oh, darling, we've had Brotherhood members stationed outside that house since you first slipped out of Mark's grip." She pauses, her eyes glinting with malice. "But that's not what I'm really interested in."

She pulls the knife away, only to trace the sharp edge along my jawline. It takes everything in me to not whimper in fear. "No, what I really want to know is..." Her voice drops to a whisper. "Did you kill Mark?"

I feel my breath catch in my throat as I slowly nod, unable to deny it.

Scarlett's face splits in a wide, terrifying grin. "Good girl. He was so fucking annoying." She leans in even closer, her lips nearly brushing my ear. "But you couldn't have offed your stupid foster sister, too? She's so very mad at you, *Alexis*." Scarlett drags the syllables of my name out.

Fear grips me, but I refuse to let it show on my face. I have to be strong for my baby's sake. Desperately, I try to recall the self-defense lessons Edo had taught me, searching for any weakness I can exploit.

Scarlett's eyes narrow as she studies me, sensing my defiance. Suddenly, her hand shoots out, backhanding me across the face with such force that my head snaps to the side. I cry out in pain.

"You stupid girl," she hisses, gripping my chin painfully, her long nails digging into my skin. "Do you know how *infuriating* it's been knowing you've been with Damian for all these months? Damian is *mine*."

I wince, both from the sting of her blow and the vise-like grip on my jaw. But I refuse to give her the satisfaction of seeing my fear.

Scarlett's lips curl into a cruel smile as she presses the knife against my neck, just hard enough to draw blood. Pain shoots up my neck as I feel a drop slide down my skin, and I have to fight the urge to scream.

"You think you can just waltz in and take what's rightfully mine?" she spits, her blue eyes devoid of any emotion. It's like looking into a black hole. "Well, I've got news for you, *Alexis*. This ends *today*."

I steel myself, determined not to beg or plead. Instead, I force myself to meet her gaze, silently daring her to do her worst. If I'm going to die here, I will do it with dignity, for my baby's sake.

Be the wolf.

Scarlett's cold eyes gleam with malice as she presses the knife harder against my neck, the bead of blood turning into a rivulet.

"You know, I've been just *itching* to slice open your pretty little neck, just like I did with my dear old dad," she muses, her voice dripping with sadistic delight.

My heart beats faster at the casual mention of Mario Rafa's murder. So she was the one who killed him—and now she has me in her clutches as well.

Scarlett's grip on the knife tightens. "But as much as I'd love to watch the life drain from your eyes," she continues, "you're actually worth much more to me *alive*."

She suddenly withdraws the knife, only to pat my cheek in a twisted parody of affection. "You see, *Alexis*, you're my biggest prize. The money I'll get for selling you off will make me a very, very rich woman."

My heart races as the full implication of her words sinks in. She doesn't want to kill me. She wants to *sell* me, carry on what her father intended. The thought of it makes bile rise in my throat.

"Damian will never let you get away with this," I spit, mustering as much defiance as I can.

Scarlett lets out a cruel laugh. "Oh, I'm counting on his trying to save you, *darling*." Her eyes gleam with malicious intent. "That's when I'll have him right where I want him—under my thumb."

I swallow hard, the reality of the situation dawning on me. Scarlett not only wants to get rid of me, but she also wants to take down Damian as well, making him into her puppet.

As Scarlett's fingers trail along my jaw, I have to resist the urge to flinch. "Soon, you'll be out of my hair, and I'll have Damian all to myself," she purrs. "We'll be the most powerful crime family in the country."

The thought of Scarlett and Damian together again, ruling over a criminal empire, makes me sick to my stomach. I have to find a way to stop her, to get back to Damian and protect our child. But trapped as I am, with no way to escape, I feel utterly helpless.

I stare at Scarlett in disbelief, my heart pounding. "You're insane," I whisper, my voice trembling.

Scarlett's eyes flash with fury, and before I can react, she seizes my jaw, forcing my mouth open. I feel the cold edge of the knife scraping against my tongue, and terror grips me.

"You know, I'm tempted to just cut out that pretty little tongue of yours," she hisses. "That way, you won't be able to talk back to your new master."

The mention of being sold off like property makes my stomach churn. I fight back the tears that threaten to spill, refusing to give Scarlett the satisfaction.

But this defiance only seems to enrage her further. Suddenly, she begins lashing out, her fists raining down on me. I cry out in pain, my vision blurring as the blows rain down.

Just as I feel myself slipping into unconsciousness, the door opens and a familiar voice cuts through the chaos.

"Scarlett, do calm down," Vincente drawls. "How can you expect anyone to want to buy her if she's black and blue?"

Scarlett pauses, chest heaving, and turns to the older man. "She needs to learn her place," she hisses.

Vincente raises a hand, silencing her. "And her new master will do that for her. We need her in one piece, remember?" He fixes me with a cold, calculating gaze. "After all, she's our most valuable asset."

As their discussion continues, the truth hits me. I'm nothing more than a bargaining chip to them—a prize to be sold to the highest bidder.

Something about Vincente is bothering me. Where have I seen him before? I take a closer look at his face.

Suddenly, a vivid flashback assaults my senses.

I see it all again—the closet door being wrenched open, my mother's terrified face as she's dragged out by a younger version of the man now standing before me. His features are unmistakable, even with all the years that have passed.

And then, the door closing, leaving me alone in the darkness as the sound of her screams faded away. When the closet door opened again, my mother was gone, and Vincente stood there, his eyes cold and unyielding as he stared me down.

The realization hits me like a punch to the gut. "You..." I whisper, my voice trembling. "You killed my mom."

Vincente pauses before he crouches down before me, an odd smile playing on his lips. His smile then widens, a twisted sense of satisfaction in his gaze.

"Yes, my dear Alexis. I killed your mother." He leans in closer, his breath hot on my face. "And now, as you're about to be sold off to a very rich man and leave this country forever, it's only fitting that you should know the truth. Damian's father never ordered the hit against your mother. It was *me*."

My heart races, a whirlwind of emotions flooding through me. Rage, grief, and a bone-deep terror grip me as the full weight of his confession sinks in. All this time, the man responsible for my mother's death had been right under my nose. And even worse, Damian *trusted* this man.

"And even better," Vincente continues, his eyes gleaming with malice. "It was *I* who eliminated my own brother, sister-in-law, and niece to pave the way for my rise to power. It was too easy."

I stare at him, utterly shocked by this revelation. The man who had taken everything from me is now poised to take even more. My child, my life with Damian—all of it is in jeopardy because of Vincente's twisted machinations.

"How could you?" I whisper, my words laced with anguish and disbelief. "Damian trusted you, and you betrayed him like this?"

Vincente lets out a cruel laugh. "Damian is a fool, just like his father. They're both weak, unfit to lead this Family." He leans in close, his breath hot on my face. "But with you out of the picture, I'll have Damian right where I want him. And soon, *I'll* be the one calling the shots."

The realization of Vincente's endgame sends a chill down my spine. He had orchestrated all of this—from my mother's murder to the attack at the mansion—all of it in a twisted bid for power. And Damian, the man I love, is completely unaware of the danger that lurks so close to him.

Before I can even process it, I feel a sharp pain in my neck, and the world around me begins to blur. Vincente's face swims before my eyes, his twisted smile the last thing I see before darkness claims me.

As consciousness slips away, one thought echoes through my mind—I have to get back to Damian. I can't give up, not when my baby's life is at stake. But with Vincente and Scarlett closing in, I have never felt more helpless.

The last thought that crosses my mind before the world goes black is a fervent prayer that somehow, some way, Damian will find me in time.

30

DAMIAN

My world descended into a waking nightmare ever since Alexis was taken, and I'm losing my fucking mind. The agonizing uncertainty of not knowing where she is or whether she is even alive is slowly driving me mad.

I can barely sleep or eat, my mind consumed by the horrific scenarios playing out on a loop—Alexis being tortured by Scarlett, being sold to some faceless man who takes her away forever, her blank, lifeless eyes after the sale, her spirit gone and only a hollow shell remaining.

I had stormed The Brotherhood's headquarters, desperate for answers, but it was completely abandoned. The eerie silence and emptied room only fueled my rage and despair. I interrogated their captured soldiers, but they either genuinely knew nothing or refused to talk.

In my unraveling state, I couldn't hold back. With my own hands, I ended their lives, slitting their throats as they pleaded for mercy.

Fucking coward.

The act provided no solace, only a momentary release from the all-consuming anguish threatening to shatter my sanity.

Alexis's disappearance has broken something deep within me. The cool, level-headed strategist is gone, replaced by a feral, single-minded creature driven solely by the need to find her, no matter the cost.

As days pass, I teeter dangerously close to the edge, unsure whether I will ever be whole again. All I can see are her lifeless eyes, her spirit snuffed out, and it's destroying me from the inside.

And I can't stop blaming myself. I never should have gone to that lunch with Uncle Vinny. I should have had Alexis spirited away to another safehouse. It's obvious now that Vinny figured out exactly who Alexis was the moment he saw her in the house.

But how could he allow the slaughter of our own people? How could he team up with The Brotherhood? This is a betrayal I will never forget.

The guilt is eating Edo alive. He keeps replaying that fateful day in his mind, berating himself for not doing more to protect Alexis. "I should have been faster, stronger, more vigilant," he tells me, his face twisted in anguish. "I failed her."

It's hard to not blame Edo for Alexis's disappearance. His only goal was to protect her and he failed. He allowed her to be captured.

But Nat doesn't allow me to pin the blame solely on Edo. "If you had only been more careful, more proactive, maybe you could have prevented this," she hisses at me after I snarl at Edo.

But I can't help it. Alexis's disappearance weighs on me. The not knowing where she is or whether she's even alive torments me endlessly.

As I pore over maps of Chicago, trying to figure out more Brotherhood safehouses, Nat slams her hands down on the table, startling me.

"What the fuck, Nat?" I snarl, looking up at my sister. "I'm busy."

"We need help to find Alexis," she insists. "We have to swallow our pride and call in Invicta."

"*Fuck no*," I snap. "They tried to fucking kill us not too long ago, Nat. Or do you not remember that?"

She scowls at me, dark circles under her eyes indicating she also has not been sleeping. "Don't fucking patronize me, Damian. I'm trying to get you to think as the Boss again, instead of a wet behind the ears idiot. But think of their resources—the weapons, the military-grade tech, the extensive network. If anyone can track Alexis down, it'll be them."

As much as it pains me to admit it, Nat is right. We're out of options, our own efforts proving futile. I've reached the end of my patience. I need to find Alexis *now*.

The phone feels heavy in my hand as I dial Bobby's number. I can practically feel the loathing rising in my chest, the memory of him ruthlessly murdering my parents and sister still haunting me. But I swallow my pride and bitterness because Alexis is all that matters now. When Bobby answers, I don't beat around the bush, asking to meet with him.

"Why the fuck should I meet with you?" Bobby's gruff voice cuts through the line, laced with disdain.

I take a steadying breath, steeling myself. "It's about Alexis Hartley."

The line goes silent, and for a moment, I wonder if he's hung up on me. But then his voice returns, clipped and devoid of emotion. "The Ballroom. One hour."

The call ends, and I let out a heavy sigh. Nat and Edo watch me with concern, knowing the weight of what I'm about to do.

"He agreed to meet us," I say. "The Ballroom, one hour."

They nod solemnly, understanding the risks we're about to take. Aligning ourselves with the Invicta Boss, our sworn enemy—it goes against every fiber of our being.

But for Alexis, there is no choice.

We soon arrive at The Ballroom, a lounge deep in Invicta territory. The message is clear—play nice or die.

As Nat, Edo, and I enter the dimly lit establishment, the tension is palpable. Invicta's men watch our every move, hands hovering near concealed weapons. I keep my own team close, ready to react at the slightest provocation.

This is Invicta's domain, and we are mere guests here at their sufferance.

As Bobby Shields emerges from the back, flanked by his most trusted lieutenants, I can't help but study him closely. He's a towering, muscular figure, every inch the quintessential Mafia Don. His hazel eyes bore into me with a piercing, calculating gaze, and I have to stamp down the loathing I feel when I look at the man who ruthlessly murdered my parents and sister.

His expression hardens as he approaches, sizing us up with a calculating gaze. "Damian," he greets, his voice even as he sits down, motioning for us to sit as well. "What do the Iacopellis want with Alexis Hartley?"

His tone makes me bristle, but I stamp it down. Alexis's safety depends on it.

"We need your help, Bobby. Alexis has been taken by The Brotherhood, and we've exhausted every other avenue. You have resources, connections—things we desperately need right now."

Bobby's brow furrows, and for a moment he looks... almost

concerned. "Alexis Hartley," he repeats slowly. "Why are you keeping that girl safe?"

I meet his gaze unflinchingly, determined not to show any weakness. "Because I've fallen in love with her."

Nat and Edo's eyes widen at my admission, though I know they've suspected as much for some time.

"The Brotherhood is going to sell her to the highest bidder, and I'll be damned if I let them take her from me forever."

Bobby is silent for a moment, his penetrating stare seemingly boring into my very soul. Then, he speaks again. "Let me see a picture of her."

Nat quickly pulls out her phone and shows him a photo of her and Alexis. In the image, Alexis stands tall, her slender frame belying the strength in her posture as she firmly grips the gun Nat is teaching her to fire. Her brow is furrowed in concentration, her hazel eyes alight with a fierce determination that makes my heart swell with pride.

For the briefest of moments, I swear I see Bobby's features soften as he gazes at the photo. But then it's gone, his face once again a mask of stone.

"How and why was Alexis Hartley taken?"

I straighten my shoulders, slipping back into the calculated, authoritative persona of a seasoned Mob Boss. "Alexis was targeted by The Brotherhood. They discovered she had escaped her foster family and boyfriend, who had sold her to them in the first place."

His brow furrows slightly, but he remains silent, gesturing for me to continue.

"My men and I have been sheltering her for months, ever since we found her being held at gunpoint by one of your soldiers." I pause, gauging his reaction. The tightening of his eyes tells me he doesn't appreciate that particular detail.

"When her abusive ex-boyfriend, Mark, tried to drag her back to the Carter house, Alexis was forced to kill him in self-defense." I meet Bobby's gaze steadily, refusing to show any sign of weakness.

"The Brotherhood has had a soldier stationed outside the Carter house—in *your* territory—for months now, hoping for any sign of Alexis." It takes everything in me to not ask Bobby how the fuck his men managed to miss a rival gang member in their territory, but I resist the urge.

This is for Alexis.

"And then," I continue, "my fucking traitorous uncle Vinny must have recognized Alexis when he came into my home unauthorized. He tipped off Scarlett, which is why they lured me and Nat to Basil and Olive—so Scarlett could storm my home, slaughter my men, and take Alexis."

Bobby's jaw clenches, a muscle twitching in his cheek. For a long, tense moment, he is silent. Then, finally, he speaks.

"Done," he says, his tone clipped. "Invicta will help."

I can't help but be taken aback at his ready agreement, given the long-standing animosity between our families. Edo voices the question on all our minds. "Why are you helping us? What's in it for you?"

The Don's expression hardens, his jaw clenching. "That's my business." He stands, his hulking frame casting an imposing shadow over us. "But know this—when I see Scarlett Rafa *and* Vincente Iacopelli next, I'm going to fucking kill them."

With a final nod, he turns and strides away, his lieutenants falling in behind him. "I'll be in touch."

As we withdraw, I can't ignore the sinking feeling in my gut. I've just made a deal with the devil, and I pray I won't live to regret it.

Edo and Nat remain silent, their expressions grim. We all know the risk we're taking, aligning ourselves with our sworn enemies. But for Alexis, we have no other choice.

Whatever the cost, we have to find her, no matter what it takes.

31

ALEXIS

I'm disoriented and confused as I slowly blink my eyes open, unsure of my surroundings. Gone are the familiar comforts of Damian's home. Instead, I find myself in a stark, windowless room, the only light filtering in from the hallway.

As my gaze sweeps the space, a sinking feeling settles in my stomach. The other women in the room are all dressed in skimpy, provocative attire, heavy makeup caked on their faces, likely to conceal any bruises or marks.

And to my horror, I realize that some of them appear to be barely more than children. One girl in particular looks no older than sixteen, while another is so small, she could be mistaken for an elementary school student.

Glancing down, I see that I'm also dressed in a short, red dress that barely covers my ass.

And then it hits me—the attack at the mansion, Scarlett finding me and tying me to a chair in another unknown location, Vincente coming into the room and bragging that he killed my mother and is the reason Damian's parents and sister are dead.

My stomach churns, nausea threatening to overtake me.

A gentle touch on my arm makes me jump, and I turn to see a young woman with red hair crouched beside me, her expression full of concern.

"Hey, you're awake," the woman whispers. "I was worried you might not come around. They just dumped you in here unconscious."

My brow furrows at the woman's words. "Where am I? What's going on?"

The woman glances around nervously. "We're in a hotel, I think. There are about a dozen of us here, all being held until…" She pauses, swallowing hard. "Until they sell us to the highest bidder."

My heart pounds in my chest as the realization dawns on me. I've been taken by The Brotherhood, just as I feared. These women—these *girls*—are being trafficked, and I'm trapped right alongside them. The realization makes my heart pound in my chest as panic rises in my throat.

"Oh, God," I breathe, panic rising in my throat as I take in the terrified faces around me. "How long have I been here? What are they going to do to us?"

The woman shrugs. "I'm not sure how long. A day, maybe two? But I know they're planning to auction us off soon. The door only opens when they bring in a new girl or food, and we're heavily guarded."

I swallow hard, mind racing. Damian, Edo, Nat—they must be searching for me. But will they find me in time? I can't bear the thought of being sold, of suffering the unimaginable horrors that await.

And then a terrifying realization hits me. I'm pregnant. My unborn child's life is now at stake as well.

The woman gives my arm a gentle squeeze. "I'll leave you to rest. We'll need to keep our strength up for what's to come."

As the woman moves away, I feel an overwhelming urge to break down, to give in to the paralyzing fear. But I force myself to take a deep, steadying breath. For my baby's sake, I have to remain strong. I can't let The Brotherhood break me.

Be the wolf.

Steeling my resolve, I force myself to take a deep, steadying breath. Damian *must* be coming for me, I'm sure of it. All I have to do is hold on a little longer.

Pushing past the nausea and fear, I begin to carefully observe my surroundings, searching for any possible means of escape. I have to get out of here, no matter what it takes. The lives of these girls, and my own unborn child, depend on it.

As I survey the other women in the room, I can't help but shiver at the sight of their vacant, haunted expressions. Some look absolutely terrified, their eyes filled with raw panic. Others appear strung out, their eyes dead and devoid of any trace of humanity.

The sight of them chills me to my core. Is that my fate as well?

Pushing past the crippling fear, my gaze lands on a small figure huddled in the corner, face streaked with tears. It's a little girl, no older than seven or eight, her once-vibrant eyes now dimmed with hopelessness, her mousy brown hair plaited into French braids going down her back.

The sight of her instantly tugs at my heartstrings. She reminds me of myself when my mom first died—scared, alone, desperately wishing for an adult to tell me everything would be alright and keep me safe. I know exactly how she feels, the overwhelming sense of vulnerability and the crushing fear of the unknown.

I'm filled with a fierce, protective instinct. This child should never have to endure such trauma, such violation of her innocence. I won't allow it. Somehow, some way, I have to get her out of here, to shield her from the horrors that await.

Forcing myself to move, I make my way over to the child and crouch down beside her.

"Hey there," I say softly. "What's your name, sweetheart?"

The girl sniffles, looking up at me with red-rimmed eyes. "K–Katie," she manages, her voice barely above a whisper.

"Katie," I repeat, offering her a gentle smile, hoping to convey that she can trust me. "It's nice to meet you. I'm Alexis. Are you hurt at all?"

She shakes her head, but the fear in her eyes is palpable. "I–I want my mom and dad." She hiccups, fresh tears spilling down her cheeks.

My heart aches for her. "I know, honey. I know." I reach out, gently brushing away her tears with the pad of my thumb. "But I promise, I'm going to do everything in my power to get you back to them, okay? You're not alone."

The girl clutches my hand, her small face fearful. "I was playing in my yard," she whispers. "Mom called me to come back inside, but a car pulled up and asked if I wanted to see their puppy. I love puppies. Mom and Dad say I can't have one yet."

Fresh tears spill down Katie's round cheeks. "Mom and Dad always told me I'm not supposed to talk to strangers, but he sounded so nice! But there was no puppy. T–they took me. T–they said I'll make someone else v–very happy."

As Katie buries herself in my side, sobs shaking her small shoulders, a swell of pure, unadulterated rages rises up within me. How dare they—The Brotherhood, Scarlett, *all of them*—prey on innocent children, tearing them from their families and selling them off to the highest bidder. It's repulsive, it's despicable, it's the very embodiment of evil.

For now, I'll be the adult she needs, the protector she deserves. I won't let anything happen to this child, no matter what it takes.

My blood boils at the thought of the horrors these women and girls have endured, and the utter violation of their childhoods. They should be carefree, playing in their yards, tucked safely in their parents' embrace—not huddled in fear, waiting to be auctioned off like cattle.

And Scarlett...

The mere thought of that vile woman makes my skin crawl. To think she and her father orchestrated this, that she takes pleasure in the suffering of these victims... it's enough to make me want to scream.

If I make it out of this alive, I vow to hunt her down to make her pay for her crimes in the most brutal way imaginable. No other woman or girl will ever suffer such a nightmarish fate at her hands, I'll make sure of that.

Clutching Katie tightly, I feel a renewed sense of purpose and determination. I have to get us out of here, no matter what it takes. This child—these women—deserve a chance at the life that was stolen from them, and I'll be damned if I let The Brotherhood or anyone else take that away.

With a deep, steadying breath, I pull back slightly to meet Katie's frightened gaze. "It's going to be okay," I tell her again, willing my voice to sound confident and reassuring. "I won't let them hurt you, I promise. We're going to get out of this, and I'll make sure you get back to your mom and dad, okay?"

Katie nods shakily, her small hand gripping mine. I know I'll do whatever it takes to protect her—even if it means going up against the full force of The Brotherhood itself.

They've made this personal, and I'll show them the true meaning of a mother's wrath.

The door suddenly bursts open, a Brotherhood soldier standing there with a gun in hand. "Line up, all of you!" he barks, his voice laced with menace.

Katie clings to me, her small body trembling with undisguised terror. I wrap a protective arm around her as the women slowly file out, herded toward a brightly lit stage at the front of the room.

As we take our places, I strain to make out the faces in the darkened audience, my heart pounding. There, in the front row, I spot Scarlett's cruel smirk and the vicious glint in Emma's eyes.

This is the revenge Emma has been waiting for.

A booming voice echoes through the hall, and I turn to see a slick-looking man step up to the podium. "Welcome, ladies and gentlemen, to our exclusive auction tonight!" he declares, his tone dripping with false charm. "We have a wonderful selection of merchandise for you, all ready to be claimed by the highest bidder. Let's start the auction with Lot 1."

My stomach churns as women are brought out one by one, paraded like cattle as the auctioneer rattles off their "attributes" in a sickening display. White bidder cards flash as prospective 'owners' bid on the woman of their choosing.

I watch in horror as the women are sold off, each woman's future now in the hands of a stranger. Katie and I are the only two left.

When Lot 44 is called, a Brotherhood soldier moves toward Katie. She screams and turns to me, her fingers scrabbling against my body as if I'm her lifeline, her eyes wide with terror.

Be the wolf.

White-hot anger roars through me, and I can't stop myself from lunging forward, using some of the self-defense techniques Edo taught me to land a solid blow. As the man grabs me from behind the waist, I quickly and brutally jab my elbow into his nose.

A sickening crunch fills the room as the man screams and lets me go, clutching his nose as blood runs down his face. The audience murmurs, all interested eyes turned in our direction, watching me fight off this soldier as if we are a spectator sport.

Two other Brotherhood soldiers swarm me. I do my best to fight them off, but they're stronger and quickly overpower me, dragging me to the stage as I fight and claw at them, doing everything I can to defend myself.

Hopefully, any prospective buyer will see that I'm not some docile woman who will do whatever he or she wants. The old Alexis would have done that, but she's gone now.

The new Alexis is a fighter, and I will *not* submit to anyone. I will not bow.

It doesn't even occur to me that some spirit—some *fight*—is exactly what some buyers are looking for, that breaking someone brings them delight.

"Well, well, what do we have here?" the auctioneer says, his beady eyes glinting with malice as his gaze roams my body. He turns back to the audience.

"Ladies and gentlemen, what a treat we have for you! As you can see, she is a feisty one and you will have an excellent time breaking her in."

Rough hands grab my waist and force me to turn around, showcasing my body to the interested crowds.

"Look at how well-proportioned she is, ladies and gentlemen! Long legs, perky breasts. Look at the curls on her, too!"

I glare at the audience, willing them to see my defiance even as panic claws my throat.

Damian, please hurry. I need you.

"Lot 45 is an extra-special artifact," the auctioneer says, lowering his voice theatrically. "As such, we will start the bidding at one million dollars. Not only is she from good breeding stock if that's what you're into, but if you've been recently fucked over by Invicta, just know you'll be the proud owner of Bobby Shields's daughter."

32

DAMIAN

I pace back and forth in my office, glancing repeatedly at my phone. I have been waiting days for Invicta to reach out, but so far, there's been nothing but silence.

"Where the hell are they?" I growl, running a hand through my hair in frustration. Alexis went missing over a week ago, and Bobby promised to be in touch when they got a lead. But if Invicta couldn't even bother to follow up, this might all be for naught.

"You need to be patient, Damian. Invicta knows what they're doing."

I whirl on Nat, eyes flashing with barely contained rage. "Patient? The longer we fucking wait, the more likely it is that Alexis has been sold and has disappeared forever!" I slam my fist down on the mahogany desk, causing the crystal tumbler on it to rattle.

"Excuse me for not being 'patient' enough when my girl's life is on the line!"

Nat lifts her glass in a placating gesture. "I know you're worried, Damian," she says with uncharacteristic gentleness, "but rushing in half-cocked could jeopardize everything. Invicta is our best shot at getting Alexis back safely."

I grit my teeth, warring with the part of me that knows Nat is right. But the fear for Alexis's wellbeing is overwhelming, drowning out all reason.

Just as I'm about to pour myself a stiff drink, my phone finally rings. I snatch it up hastily and place it on speaker so Nat can hear.

"This had better be good, Bobby," I nearly snarl into the phone as Nat leans in, her dark hair brushing against her shoulders as she places her forearms on her legs.

"Looks like there's an 'auction' going down tomorrow night at a hotel outside Chicago. The Brotherhood owns the place," Bobby's gruff voice says.

My fingers tighten around the phone. This may be the break we've been looking for.

"When and where, exactly?" I demand.

"Hotel Du Monde in Naperville, eight p.m."

Tomorrow night? Nat mouths to me, eyes wide.

"Tomorrow night?" I growl. "That's too damn long. Alexis has been missing for over a week already. Who knows what she's going through, what she's thinking?" I clench my jaw. The thought of her suffering cuts me to my core.

Does she even think I'm coming for her? The thought of Alexis losing hope, of her believing I have abandoned her, is almost too much to bear.

My nostrils flare as I shake my head. "The longer we wait, the more likely it is that she's been sold, or worse." I slam my hand on the desk again. "That 'auction' is our best chance, and we can't wait until tomorrow night. I can't just sit on my hands until then!"

"For fuck's sake, Damian, act like a leader," Bobby snaps. "Think about this logically. We can't just storm the place. We need to infiltrate and act like we're interested in buying. If we rush in, they'll just hide Alexis again and make it that much harder to find her. Use your goddamn head!"

Nat looks at me knowingly, nodding. I want to spit at her. How dare she agree with him?

I clench my fists, every fiber of my being screaming to charge in and tear the place apart. But I know Bobby is right. This requires a delicate touch, not brute force.

And Scarlett will be expecting me to do just that—storm the place. She'll have security galore waiting for me.

"Fine," I say curtly. "Text me the details."

As I hang up the phone, I let out a guttural roar of frustration and hurl my crystal tumbler at the wall. It explodes into a million glittering shards, the sound mirroring the turmoil raging within.

Nat watches me warily, wisely not saying one word.

For now, all we can do is wait and trust that Invicta's plan will work.

But my patience is paper thin, and Scarlett had better fucking pray she keeps Alexis unharmed until we can get to her.

∽

THE NEXT DAY, we converge on the opulent Hotel Du Monde, an exclusive luxury hotel just outside Chicago. As I stride through the lavish lobby, I can't help but wonder just how many of the well-heeled guests would be horrified to learn that human trafficking takes place within these gilded walls.

Or perhaps they simply wouldn't care, so long as it didn't affect them directly.

I push aside these thoughts as I spot Bobby and other Invicta capos, all of them dressed to the nines and exuding an air of casual wealth. Thanks to Bobby's impressive tech skills, their credentials have been expertly forged to make them appear as millionaires and billionaires —exactly the kind of clientele The Brotherhood would be eager to do business with.

With Nat and Edo flanking me, I follow Bobby and his crew into the hotel. Though every fiber of my being aches to find Alexis as quickly as possible, I know I have a more pressing issue to deal with first.

Uncle Vinny.

That fucking *traitor*. Nat's been right all along about him, and I've been too blind to see it for myself. I was so desperate to have some part of my father still around, I never saw that Vinny was using me.

It's time to turn the tables on him.

Discreetly tapping my earpiece in my ear, I scan the crowd of well-dressed people, searching for any sign of my uncle. Finally, I spot his familiar gray hair and sharp eyes across the lobby. With anger coursing through me, I make my way over, plastering a contrite expression on my face.

"Uncle," I say, inclining my head slightly. "I'm... glad you're here."

Vinny's eyebrows shoot up in surprise, then narrow in suspicion. "Damian. This is a surprise. What are you up to, boy? I hope you don't think you'll actually be able to rescue the girl. She belongs to The Brotherhood, and unless you plan on starting a war—"

I force a wry smile, even though I'm itching to wrap my hands around his neck and squeeze. "Actually, Uncle, I've been thinking. I've allowed myself to become too enamored with Alexis. It clouded my judgment."

I shrug, a rueful smile playing at the corner of my mouth. "She is a nice piece of ass, I'll admit. But in the process, I've put the Iacopellis in jeopardy."

Vinny's eyes gleam with triumph, though he tries to maintain an air of nonchalance. "Go on."

"It's time for me to step aside as Don," I continue. "The Family would be better off with you at the helm. I've been too soft. I should have turned Alexis over to The Brotherhood right away, instead of letting my emotions get in the way." I meet Vinny's gaze, my expression resigned.

"The Iacopellis deserve a stronger leader. And that's you, Uncle."

Vinny's grin widens, and he claps me on the shoulder. "Well, well, well. Looks like you've finally come to your senses, boy. I must say, this is the first correct decision you've made in a long time."

I nod stiffly, my stomach churning with revulsion and hate. Vinny doesn't believe me for a second—the fucker can smell a trap a mile away. But for now, I have to play along, lull Vinny into a false sense of security.

Once Alexis is safe, I'll deal with my traitorous uncle.

Vinny grabs me by the arm, steering me away from the lobby and toward the grand ballroom. A security guard nods at Vinny and pushes open the door for him.

"Come, nephew, let's get a closer look at this little auction of ours."

I follow, my stomach twisting with a mixture of dread and determination. As we enter the ballroom, my eyes immediately seek out Alexis, and my heart freezes when I see her.

She's one of the last two on the stage, standing next to a young girl, clearly no more than seven or eight years old. The child is shaking like a leaf, clinging to Alexis in obvious terror.

The auctioneer's voice booms through the ballroom. "And now, Lot 44—a rare and precious young flower, ripe for the plucking!"

Bile rises in my throat as Brotherhood soldiers move to grab the child. Human trafficking is bad enough, but to use children?

It's beyond the pale.

I glance at Vinny, who is watching the proceedings with sickening glee. Vinny leans in to nudge me. "Maybe I should bid on that girl. Make her into the type of woman I deserve. Children are just so… pliable. And they so easily want to please."

Rage courses through me, and I have to fight the urge to wrap my hands around his throat and squeeze until the life drains from his eyes. This is the type of man Vinny truly is—a twisted, heartless monster who preys on the innocent.

My attention is suddenly drawn back to Alexis as she fights against the soldiers, expertly breaking one man's nose. My lips curl into a proud, feral grin.

That's my girl.

Every fiber of my being aches to rush to her, to pull her to safety. But I have to remain patient, even as my body screams at me to rip, maim, and kill *anyone* who dares to harm her. I need to bide my time, wait for the right moment to strike.

Clenching my fists, my gaze never leaves Alexis, my heart pounding with a mixture of relief, fury, and love. I will get her out of this, no matter what it takes. And when I am done, Vinny, Scarlett, and the rest of The Brotherhood will pay dearly for their crimes.

But Alexis is soon overcome and is dragged toward the stage, kicking and fighting the entire way. The crowd murmurs as she's thrust into the spotlight.

"So much fight in her." Vinny chuckles, a cruel edge to his voice. "Just like her mother."

Time suddenly seems to freeze as his words echo in my ears.

Vinny's lips curl into a malicious smile as he continues, "Poor little Alexis had been *so* frightened after I killed her mother. I was supposed to kill Alexis too, but she managed to escape me. But now, I'm so glad I didn't. She's so much more useful to me now."

The blood drains from my face as the horrifying realization sinks in. My father never killed Alexis's mother. Vinny had. Which means...

Whirling on my uncle, I ignore the orders coming through my earpiece from Bobby. "Invicta didn't kill Mom, Dad, and Alessandra, did they?"

Vinny's smile widens, a twisted gleam in his eyes as he leans in closer. "Let me let you in on a little secret, Nephew. *I* killed Lorenzo, Josefina, and Alessandra."

A rushing, roaring sound fills my ears as I stare into the eyes of my family's killer. But then something clicks—Bobby had claimed Damian's father ordered the hit on his woman and child. Why would Vinny have killed Alexis's mother and tried to take out Alexis? What's the connection?

My stomach lurches as the auctioneer's voice booms through the ballroom. "—just know you'll be the proud owner of Bobby Shields's daughter."

All hell breaks loose.

The Iacopelli and Invicta crews surge forward, weapons drawn, as I whirl on Vinny, my vision going red with rage. "You fucking *bastard*!" I roar, my fist connecting with Vinny's jaw with a sickening crack.

Vinny stumbles back, clutching his face, but I don't let him, pummeling him with blow after blow. I can still see my parents' bodies lying on the floor, Dad in his study, Mom in the kitchen. And Alessandra? She had been gunned down in the foyer, her hand stretched out toward the door.

She had been so close to escaping.

"You killed them all! Mom, Dad, Alessandra—and for what? So you could rule the Iacopellis?"

Around us, the ballroom erupts into chaos as Invicta and the Iacopellis clash with The Brotherhood. People scream and attempt to flee the room, but I barely register it.

All that matters is making Vinny pay for his crimes.

In the midst of the pandemonium, I catch a glimpse of Alexis, her eyes wide with terror as she clings to the young girl at her side. My heart clenches, and with a monumental effort, I tear myself away from Vinny, intent on reaching her.

But as I surge forward, a new realization dawns. The auctioneer's words finally hit me.

Alexis is Bobby Shields's daughter.

33

DAMIAN

Behind me, the auction descends into an all-out war as the Iacopelli and Invicta crews surge forward, engaging in a brutal clash with The Brotherhood's forces. Potential buyers flee in a panic, some even trying to escape with their "purchases" in tow, but we show them no mercy, gunning them down without hesitation to help the terrified girls escape.

Once the initial shock of Alexis's being my most hated enemy's daughter wears off, I round on my uncle again, my eyes blazing with a fury Vinny has never seen before.

"You murdering *bastard*!" I roar, the veins in my neck standing out in stark relief.

Vinny's lips curl into a cruel smile, even as blood trails down his face from my earlier beating. "Now, now, Damian. We won't want to be hypocritical, do we?" He chuckles darkly. "After all, how many have you killed in the name of the Iacopellis?"

My hands clench into fists, every muscle in my body coiled and ready to strike. "I did what I had to for my family. But you..." My voice drops to a menacing growl as gunshots and screams erupt around me. "You killed them in cold blood for your own twisted ambition."

Without warning, Vinny whips out his gun, pistol-whipping me across the face. I stagger back, stars exploding in my vision, but I refuse to go down. I surge forward, tackling my uncle to the ground in a flurry of fists and fury.

We grapple, each fighting for the upper hand, but Vinny's years of experience give him the advantage.

If I make it out of here alive, I'm forcing Edo to fucking train me.

With a savage twist, Vinny wrenches the gun from my grasp and levels it at my head.

"Say goodbye, Nephew," Vinny hisses, his finger tightening on the trigger, his eyes full of hate.

But before he can fire, a blur of movement catches his eyes and he whirls just in time to see Nat barreling toward him, knocking the gun from his hand and sending them both tumbling.

I watch in amazed pride as my sister kicks the shit out of the man she's always hated, her fists flying with ferocious intensity. She may not know that Vinny killed our parents, but she saw him about to shoot me and that was enough for her to get involved.

Vinny manages to land a vicious right hook, sending Nat flying, but I can see the fear in the old man's eyes. He wasn't expecting Nat to be so strong, so unrelenting in her attack.

Vinny takes off running in the opposite direction, and rage courses through me. "You fucking coward!" I roar, my voice barely audible over the cacophony of the battle. I step forward to follow him, but Nat's hand on my forearm prevents me from doing so.

"Leave him, Damian! We'll get him later. You need to find Alexis!" she shouts, her face bleeding, as she pulls out another gun and shoots a

Brotherhood soldier straight in the head before she runs off into the heart of the battle.

Across the ballroom, Nat, Edo, and Bobby are holding their own against The Brotherhood's forces. Nat moves with a fluid grace, her handguns blazing as she takes down one enemy after another, her bleeding face a mask of cold determination. Edo, a hulking figure, fights with a raw, brutal efficiency, his assault rifle cutting a swath through The Brotherhood's ranks.

And Bobby—the cool, calculating Invicta Don—Alexis's *father*—is a veritable one-man army. His fingers dance along the controls of his modified M4 carbine, the weapon spitting a hail of high-velocity rounds that tear through the opposition with devastating precision. Wherever The Brotherhood tries to regroup, Bobby's relentless fire cuts them down, his tactical mind anticipating their every move.

The fight is a bloody, chaotic mess, dead soldiers and panicked buyers scattered everywhere. My head is pounding, blood trickling down my face, but I can't afford to slow down. I have to find Alexis. My sole objective is getting to her, my heart racing with a desperate urgency.

"Alexis!" I scream, my voice hoarse and strained. "*ALEXIS!*"

The battle rages on, the sounds of gunfire and agonized screams deafening. I push forward, my eyes scanning the chaos, searching for any sign of the woman I love.

But she's nowhere to be seen. The stage is empty.

A Brotherhood goon suddenly materializes in front of me, his face twisted in a malicious grin as he levels his weapon at me. But I'm quicker, my reflexes honed by years of ruthless combat.

With lightning speed. I dodge the first volley of bullets, my own gun roaring to life. The Brotherhood soldier staggers back, his eyes widening as the rounds tear through his chest, crimson blossoming across his suit.

I advance relentlessly, emptying my clip into the man, my face a mask of grim determination. There is no time for mercy or hesitation. I have to find Alexis, and I'll cut through an army of these fuckers if that's what it takes.

The lifeless body crumbles to the ground, and I whirl, my desperate gaze sweeping the chaotic ballroom. Where is she? Had Scarlett or another Brotherhood capo dragged her away?

Suddenly, a piercing screech cuts through the din of battle, freezing everyone in their tracks. All eyes turn toward the source of the sound, and my heart lurches.

There stands Scarlett, her face a twisted caricature of sanity, her fingers clutching Alexis's hair in an iron grip. A gun is pressed to Alexis's temple, and I can see the pure terror in her eyes.

"Any of you take one step, and Princess Alexis dies!" Scarlett howls, her voice shrill and unhinged as her red hair streams behind her. She pants, her eyes glittering with rage and malice. "I'm taking Alexis and the little *brat* and getting the hell out of here."

Her gaze sweeps the room, a manic gleam in her eyes. "Or maybe I'll use them as human bombs. I've been meaning to dabble in a little domestic terrorism."

Alexis whimpers, her body trembling, and my blood boils with impotent rage. I have to do something, but one wrong move and Scarlett will pull the trigger.

Time seems to slow to a crawl as Scarlett begins to retreat, using Alexis as a human shield. I watch in agonized helplessness, my heart pounding, as the woman I love is dragged away, her frightened eyes pleading with me to save her.

But just as Scarlett is about to pull her out of the ballroom, Alexis suddenly surges forward. In a desperate, instinctive move, she slams the back of her head into Scarlett's face, causing the deranged woman to cry out in pain and momentarily loosen her hold.

The world hangs suspended in that pivotal moment, every eye riveted on the scene unfolding before us.

Alexis, her eyes wild with terror, determination, and *rage*, seizes the opportunity. Her fingers close around the gun in Scarlett's hand, and with a fluid motion, she wrenches it free.

Scarlett's face contorts in a mask of fury as she realizes what is happening, but she's too late.

Alexis, her hands shaking, raises the weapon and pulls the trigger.

The thunderous report echoes through the stunned silence, and Scarlett's lifeless body crumples to the ground, crimson blood blossoming on her forehead.

Alexis stands there, the gun still clutched in her trembling hands, staring down at the woman who had terrorized her with a look of disbelief and horror. A deafening silence falls over the ballroom. All eyes are on Alexis, the gun still smoking in her grasp.

In the stunned silence that follows, I see the realization dawn on the remaining Brotherhood members and their "guests"—powerful leaders in their own right, indulging in the abhorrent practice of human trafficking.

Without hesitation, the Iacopelli and Invicta soldiers open fire, their weapons blazing with ruthless efficiency. I watch impassively as the so-called "respectable" businessmen and politicians are cut down, their cries of terror and pain echoing through the ballroom.

These are not innocent victims. These are the men and women who profit off the suffering of the weak and vulnerable. *Let the world see the true faces of these self-proclaimed pillars of society,* I think grimly. *Let them know the sick games these leaders enjoy.*

Our crews move with practiced precision, systematically eliminating The Brotherhood's forces and any of their "guests" who try to flee. My own weapon barks repeatedly, my aim unwavering as I methodically dispatch one target after another.

The chaos is deafening—the thunderous roar of gunfire, the agonized screams of the dying, the frantic shrieks of those trapped in the crossfire. As the last of The Brotherhood's forces fall, my eyes finally find Alexis, still clutching the smoking gun in her trembling hands.

She looks shell-shocked, her eyes wide and haunted, and a surge of fierce protectiveness washes over me.

I stride toward her, my expression grim but my movements gentle as I pry the weapon from her grip.

"It's over, Alexis," I murmur, my voice low and soothing. "You're safe now."

But as I envelope her in a fierce embrace, I know that the true battle has only just begun. The world will know the truth about these so-called "leaders" and their depravity.

And I will make damn sure that Alexis—my love, the reason I breathe—will never have to endure such horrors again.

34

ALEXIS

I ... I just killed someone.

Again.

But this time, I *meant* to do it.

My hands tremble as I stare down at Scarlett's lifeless body. I can't believe I just killed her. The gravity of my actions is only beginning to sink in.

But then, an even more shocking revelation comes crashing down on me. The Don of Invicta is *my father*.

How could this be happening? An Invicta member held me at gunpoint all those months ago when I first escaped from the Carter house. Did my father know who I was? Why didn't he try to rescue me?

I feel utterly disoriented, as if the world around me has shifted into an alternate reality. One moment, I'm a woman about to be sold in a human trafficking ring. The next, I'm a killer learning that my father is the Don of a criminal empire.

This can't be real, I tell myself as my eyes dart around the room, watching as Iacopelli and Invicta men round up the rest of the remaining Brotherhood members. *I'm going to wake up any minute now in my bed at the mansion. This has to be a nightmare.*

But the stark, unforgiving truth refuses to fade.

My father—the man I assumed had abandoned me and my mother—is the very embodiment of the darkness I have been running from.

A million questions swirl in my mind—was he involved in Invicta when I was born? What unspeakable acts has he committed? Did he truly love my mother? Why did he leave us?

I feel like I'm drowning, the weight of this revelation crashing down on me. I open my mouth, desperate to scream, to purge this nightmare from my mind, but all that escapes is a strangled sob, tears streaming down my face.

Nothing makes sense anymore.

Damian wraps me in his arms, the smell of his cologne enveloping me as he murmurs something about my being safe into my ear. Vaguely, I can feel him pry the gun from my hands, but I feel so cold.

Safe? How can I be safe when I've just taken another life? I was the one who pulled the trigger, who purposefully ended Scarlett's life. I'm the reason she's lying on the ground, dead.

A thought horrifies me. Am I more like my father than I ever realized? Does that make me just as much a monster as him?

The guilt and anguish threaten to consume me. I squeeze my eyes shut, willing this all to be a horrible nightmare that I can wake up from. But the stark reality refuses to fade—*I killed Scarlett Rafa.*

Damian's arms tighten around me, and I can feel the concern radiating off him. "Alexis, look at me. You had no choice. She would have killed you."

His words do little to ease the turmoil within me. I may have acted in self-defense, but that doesn't change the fact that I've taken a life. I'm no better than The Brotherhood.

"I'm a monster," I whisper brokenly. "Just like him."

I know Damian is trying to comfort me, to reassure me that I did what I had to do. But in this moment, all I can see is the darkness that now resides within me—the darkness that links me to my father, the Don of Invicta.

How can I ever be safe when I'm capable of such violence?

Damian's lips press against my temple, and I sag against him, watching the scene unfold before me with dull eyes.

Iacopelli soldiers capture a screaming Emma. She's thrashing and begging them to let her go, insisting that she's done nothing wrong, that she's innocent. But I feel nothing for my foster sister. I simply watch as they drag her away, her cries echoing in the ballroom.

Is this how she felt when Mark and her parents dragged me to the basement?

I should feel something—anger, sadness, maybe even a lingering twinge of protectiveness? But all I can muster is an eerie detachment, as if I'm watching this all unfold from the outside, disconnected from the gravity of it all.

Damian murmurs soothing words, trying to pull me back, but I can't seem to focus on anything beyond the hollow sensation coursing through me. I've taken a life, and now I'm witnessing the aftermath, yet I feel nothing.

Am I truly becoming like my father? Cold, calculating, unmoved by the suffering of others? The thought should terrify me, but it only serves to deepen the emptiness I feel.

Emma's screams fade as she's escorted out of the ballroom. I find I don't care what happens to her.

My father—*Bobby*—appears with a bound, gagged, and battered Vincente. He glares at us through bruised eyes with a mix of rage and fear. His gaze is especially pointed toward Damian.

Bobby yanks Vincente closer. "Found the rat trying to escape," he says grimly before turning to his men. "Take him and that screaming girl to the basement."

I shrink back as Bobby tries to approach me, pushing myself further into Damian's arms. The numbness I felt moments ago has given way to a deep sense of unease. This is all becoming too much to bear.

"Katie," I murmur. "Where's Katie?"

"Who's Katie?" Damian asks, smoothing my hair.

"The little girl—the one who was going to be *sold*" —I choke on the word— "like me. I promised her I would get her home. Damian, please, you have to help me get her home."

I can't bear the thought of Katie being caught up in this twisted web of criminal dealings. She deserves to be safe, away from this nightmare.

I promised her. I promised her I would get her back to her mom and dad. I'm not going to break that promise—not like all the other adults in my life did to me.

"We'll find her," Damian promises, stroking my cheek. "We'll get her home."

The Don of Invicta watches me impassively, his gaze unwavering. His hazel eyes—*my* eyes—bore into mine, seemingly searching for something.

I turn my head away, unable to look at him any longer.

All I'm focused on is finding Katie, even if it means risking everything. Katie's wellbeing is the only thing that matters. I will move heaven and earth to protect her, to make good on the promise I made to reunite her with her family.

Damian and I quickly begin our search for Katie, our eyes scanning the chaotic ballroom as we step over the bodies of fallen Brotherhood members.

"Katie!" I call out, my voice tinged with desperation. "Katie, honey, where are you? Please come out!"

The longer we search and can't find her, the more my panic builds. How can I ever be a good mother to my baby if I can't even keep this young girl safe? The guilt and self-doubt threaten to consume me.

Suddenly, Damian shouts from across the room. "Alexis! I found her!"

I rush over to where he's crouched, and there, huddled in a tiny space beneath the stage, is Katie. Her eyes are wide with terror, her small frame shaking uncontrollably.

"Katie," I breathe, my heart aching at the sight of her obvious distress.

Without hesitation, I reach down and scoop her into my arms, holding her close. Tears stream down her cheeks as she clings to me, her tiny fingers grasping at my clothes.

"It's okay, Katie," I murmur, my own tears falling as I rock her gently. "You're safe now. I've got you."

The relief I feel is palpable, but it's tinged with a deep sorrow for the trauma this child has endured. She shouldn't have to be this afraid, this broken. It's a harsh reminder of the horrors she's faced—the horrors she almost just faced.

Damian places a comforting hand on my shoulder. "Let's get her out of here," he says softly. "She shouldn't see the carnage."

I nod, tightening my embrace around Katie as we make our way out of the ballroom. The young girl's trembling subsides slightly, but the haunted look in her eyes is a reminder of the scars she'll have to carry.

As we step into the main hallway, Katie lets out a shuddering breath and looks up at me. "You found me," she whispers, her voice laced with disbelief and relief.

I press a gentle kiss to her forehead, unable to help myself as my own tears flow freely. "I promised I would, didn't I?" I murmur.

As Damian moves closer, Katie suddenly clings tighter to me, her terror returning. I can see the alarm in Damian's eyes, but he quickly recovers, holding up his hands in a calming gesture.

"Katie," he says gently, "my name is Damian. I'm one of the good guys, I promise."

I can't help but find a touch of irony in the fact that the Don of the Iacopellis is calling himself a "good guy", but I'll let it slide for now. The most important thing is making Katie feel safe and comfortable.

Damian pauses, considering his next move. Then, a small smile plays at the corner of his lips. "Hey, Katie," he says softly, "would you like to see a picture of my dog, Biscotti?"

Katie's eyes widen slightly, but she still refuses to let go of me. Damian simply nods and pulls out his phone, beginning to scroll through photos and videos of his girl.

As Damian narrates the pictures, his tone warm and inviting, I can see the tension slowly start to leave the child's body. She doesn't release her grip on me, but her eyes are glued to the screen, mesmerized by the images of the dog.

Damian chuckles as he shows a video of Biscotti chasing one of the Iacopelli soldiers, and I watch as a flicker of a smile crosses Katie's face. It's a small, fragile thing, but it fills me with a sense of hope.

"Biscotti looks like a fun friend," Katie murmurs, her voice barely above a whisper.

Damian nods, his expression one of genuine warmth. Is this how he was with Alessandra?

"She is," he says. "She's my best girl. She'd love to meet you, if you'd like."

Katie's gaze flits between Damian and me, as if seeking my approval. I offer her a reassuring smile, giving her hand a gentle squeeze.

"I think that would be nice," I say softly. "Biscotti is a very good dog. She would like you."

The tension in Katie's shoulders eases slightly, and I breathe a sigh of relief. Though she's still clinging to me, the sight of her relaxing, even if just a little, is a testament to Damian's compassion and patience.

He'll be such a wonderful father, I think to myself, imagining him holding a little girl with dark, curly hair and hazel eyes. It warms my heart.

As we continue to sit with Katie, sharing stories of Biscotti's antics, I can't help but feel a surge of love and gratitude toward Damian. In the midst of this chaos, he's found a way to offer comfort and solace to a traumatized child, proving that there is indeed a glimmer of light in the darkness.

35

ALEXIS

After we had tucked a sleepy Katie into a hotel bed, Damian received a text that set his face into a grim line.

"We're needed downstairs," he tells me after I reassure Katie that we will be back with some pizza and ice cream. "The interrogation has begun."

Damian, Nat, Edo, and I head down to the basement, where Vincente and Emma are being held in a windowless, soundproof room. The air is thick with tension as we enter, the gravity of the situation weighing heavily on all of us. Damian takes my hand in his, lacing our fingers together.

Vincente sits before us, his face bloodied and bruised, the evidence of his torture clear. Emma sits in the chair beside him, her face white with panic. When she sees me, her eyes bulge and her screams are muffled by the gag.

I turn my head away from her.

Bobby regards Vincente with a cold, unrelenting gaze. "Talk," he demands, leaving no room for defiance.

Vincente glares back, his expression defiant despite his battered expression. "I won't tell you a fucking thing," he spits.

Bobby raises an eyebrow. "No? Let's refresh your memory, then." He presses *Play* on a recording device sitting before him. Vincente's voice echoes through the basement room.

"Poor little Alexis had been so frightened after I killed her mother. I was supposed to kill Alexis too, but she managed to escape me. But now I'm so glad I didn't. She's so much more useful to me now."

As the recording cuts off, Bobby's gaze settles on Vincente, his expression transforming into something truly terrifying. The Don of Invicta is no longer a distant, unreadable figure but a true embodiment of menace and rage.

Damian's grip on my hand tightens, a silent gesture of support. I'm left reeling as I hear Vincente speak so callously about my mother's murder, to know that he had intended to end my life as well.

The air in the room seems to grow even thicker with tension, the weight of the revelation and the palpable threat of violence hanging heavily upon us all. I find myself holding my breath, bracing for whatever retribution Bobby has in store for Vincente.

"You let your own brother take the fall for your actions," Bobby says silkily, dangerously. I can't help but shiver at the pure fury in Bobby's voice. "Lorenzo had nothing to do with Rebecca's murder."

Nat's face crumples in anguish.

"Yes," Vincente snaps, his eyes wild. "But Lorenzo had proof that he didn't order the hit and was going to tell Bobby. I couldn't have that, especially when word got out that the Iacopellis and Invicta were going to form an alliance. I couldn't have that, especially if I wanted to take over."

"So you decided to wipe out your brother, his wife, and his children," Bobby says flatly.

Nat cries out, the anguish etched into every feature. "Why did you kill Alessandra? She was only a child!" she screams, her voice laced with raw, unrestrained fury.

Vincente shrugs. "She was collateral damage," he replies, his cold, callous words cutting like a knife. "She shouldn't have been home sick to be a witness."

Nat surges forward, her eyes wild with hatred, but Edo quickly moves to hold her back, struggling to keep her from lunging at Vincente.

I stare at Vincente in a daze, my mind reeling from the sheer callousness with which he describes the murders of my mother and his own family. It's as if he's talking about the weather, completely devoid of any remorse or humanity.

How can a person be so utterly twisted, so heartless in the face of such unspeakable acts?

Beside me, Nat is barely being held back by Edo, her anguished screams echoing through the basement. The raw pain and fury in her voice is palpable, a testament to the devastation that Vinny has wrought.

And then, there's Emma, who has somehow managed to get the gag out of her mouth.

"Alexis, please," she begs. "We're sisters. Have mercy on me. You know I didn't mean it."

I feel nothing but revulsion toward this woman who has tormented me for so long. Her pleas for mercy only serve to heighten my disgust.

"I'll show you the same mercy you showed me when you fucked my boyfriend and agreed to sell me to The Brotherhood," I reply, my voice devoid of any emotion.

Emma's face crumples, and I watch, unmoved, as she descends into tears and desperate, futile pleas. I can't bring myself to feel an ounce of pity for her, not when she has inflicted so much pain and suffering upon me.

In the face of such profound betrayal and anguish, any empathy I might have once felt has been extinguished. Their callousness toward my mother, toward me, has stripped me of my humanity, leaving me a mere shell of the person I once was.

I can feel Damian's gaze upon me, his concern palpable. But even his touch, his silent support, does nothing to alleviate the overwhelming sense of loss and isolation that envelops me.

Turning to Damian, my voice is laced with a weary finality. "I'm done with this conversation."

He looks at me with concern, no doubt sensing the shift in my demeanor. "Let's get you out of here. An execution is about to take place."

Emma's eyes bulge, and she starts to scream for help, but an Invicta soldier stuffs the gag back into her mouth. She whips her head back and forth, trying to remove the gag, but is unsuccessful.

I stand firm, my gaze unwavering. "I want to watch."

He looks at me with concern, no doubt sensing the shift in my demeanor. "Alexis, are you sure? This isn't something you need to see."

But I stand resolutely. "I need to see it, Damian. I need to see Vincente and Emma get what they deserve."

I can see the conflict in Damian's eyes, but he knows better than to try and dissuade me. He wraps an arm around me, pulling me close to him, but doesn't try to take me out of the room.

Out of the corner of my eye, I catch a subtle nod from Bobby. It's a silent acknowledgment, a tacit approval of my decision to stay.

And in that moment, I feel a strange sense of power, a twisted validation that I'm finally taking control of my own fate.

Bobby stands, his gaze sweeping over the room. Reaching down, he offers a second gun to Damian and Natalia.

"I told you that Scarlett and Vinny were mine to kill," he says, his voice cold and authoritative. "But I wasn't expecting the girl."

Nat's eyes blaze with a fierce determination as she seizes the weapon. "The kill is mine too," she declares, her grip tightening around the gun.

Damian glances at her, his brow furrowed with concern. "Nat, are you sure?"

But Nat's response is unwavering. "Yes," she says, her voice trembling with barely contained emotion. "This is for our parents. For Alessandra."

The weight of her words hangs in the air, the pain and anguish of their shared loss etched into every syllable.

As Bobby and Nat raise their guns, I steel myself, bracing for the inevitable. I don't flinch, not even as the shots ring out, echoing through the cavernous basement.

Vincente and Emma fall to the ground, their lives snuffed out in an instant. A part of me feels a twinge of satisfaction, a sense of justice being served. But it's quickly overshadowed by the overwhelming sense of loss and anguish that has become my constant companion.

I watch dispassionately as their bodies lie motionless, the finality of their demise settling heavily upon me. This is the end of a twisted chapter, but it offers little in the way of closure or relief.

Damian's hand finds mine, a silent gesture of support. I squeeze it in return, drawing strength from his presence. In this moment, I know that I'm not alone, that he will always be by my side as I navigate the uncertain path that lies ahead.

I *will* carry on, even if the road ahead seems shrouded in darkness. I have to for my baby.

With a deep breath, I turn to Damian, my resolve hardening. "Let's go," I say, my voice steady despite the turmoil raging within me. "There's nothing left for me here."

Damian nods, gently squeezing my hand. "Alright, let's go."

As Damian moves to guide me toward the exit, I hesitate, my gaze drifting back toward Bobby. My father—the Don of Invicta—stands there, his eyes pleading with me to stay.

But I'm not ready. Not yet. The weight of everything that has happened—the near-sale, Scarlett's death, the execution of Emma and Vincente—it's all too much. I feel raw, exposed, on the verge of shattering.

"I'm not ready," I say, my voice barely above a whisper. "I need time, Bobby. I need time to process all of this."

The hurt that flashes across his face is palpable, but I can't bring myself to feel sympathy. Not now, not when I'm barely holding myself together.

Damian squeezes my hand gently, but Bobby nods.

"Take all the time you need, Alexis. I'll be here when you're ready."

I nod, grateful that he won't push me. I see the desperation in his expression, the yearning to reconnect with me.

But the wounds are too fresh, the betrayal too deep. I need space, time to heal, before I can even begin to consider forgiving him, let alone build a relationship.

"I'll come back," I promise, though the words feel weighty, uncertain. "But not today. I just... I can't."

Bobby nods again. He knows, as well as I do, that pushing me now would only drive me further away.

With a final, lingering look, I turn and allow Damian to lead me out of the basement. Each step feels like a weight lifted, a chance to breathe, to process the maelstrom of emotions swirling within me.

As we reach the main level of the hotel, I feel a glimmer of hope, a fragile promise that I can move forward, one step at a time. With Damian by my side, I know I'm not alone in this journey. And that knowledge, more than anything, gives me the strength to keep going.

Damian guides me upstairs to a lavish hotel room, the weight of the day's events palpable between us. As the door closes behind us, the tension in the air is heavy, a silent acknowledgement of the profound experience we've both endured.

He reaches for me, his touch gentle and soothing. In his embrace, I feel a sense of comfort and safety that I haven't known in far too long. The fear, the anguish, the overwhelming sense of loss—it all seems to melt away.

We stand there, holding each other, drawing strength from the simple act of being together. No words are needed, for in this moment, our connection transcends spoken language.

Damian pulls back slightly, his dark eyes shining with a mix of tenderness and vulnerability. "Alexis," he murmurs, his voice thick with emotion, "When you were missing, I… I went crazy."

I listen, my heart aching at the pain etched into his features. "I couldn't sleep, couldn't eat, couldn't *function* without you at my side. I've never been so scared in my life as when I saw you on that stage, about to be *sold*."

His hand trembles as he cups my face, his thumb caressing my cheek with reverence. I lean into his touch. "I thought I was going to lose you, Alexis. I couldn't bear the thought of living in a world without you in it."

The raw honesty in his words catches me off guard, and I feel tears prick at the corners of my eyes.

"Damian," I breathe, my own hands reaching up to cover his. "I'm here, I'm safe. You found me."

He nods, his forehead coming to rest against mine. "I'll always find you, Alexis. No matter what, I'll never stop searching, never stop fighting to bring you home."

The depth of his conviction, the fierce protectiveness in his voice, ignites a fire within me. In this moment, I know with absolute certainty that Damian will be the constant, the unwavering anchor in the stormy sea of my life.

Closing the distance between us, I press my lips to his in a tender, searing kiss. It's a silent promise, a declaration of the bond that tethers us together.

He guides me toward the bed, our movements unhurried, almost reverent. As we sink into the plush mattress, I feel the weight of the world lift from my shoulders, replaced by a profound sense of tranquility.

Damian moves from my mouth down to my neck, his hot mouth lavishing kisses to my skin. I moan and plunge my fingers into his soft hair, tugging on the strands. I want more. I want to feel as close to him as possible after everything.

"Damian," I moan, arching against him, desperate for any friction as his hair tickles my chin. "Take me."

He stills and looks up at me, his eyes dark with desire. "Oh, I plan on it, Alexis."

He resumes his attention to my neck, his hands sliding down my breasts and stomach before reaching the end of the short red dress I was forced into. Breaking away from me, he yanks the dress off me, throwing it somewhere onto the floor, leaving me only in my underwear.

"I'm burning that fucking dress," he growls before capturing my lips in a heated kiss again, his tongue sliding along the seam. I immediately comply, opening my mouth eagerly as our tongues battle for dominance.

His hands slide down to my breasts, kneading them before taking a nipple into his mouth, rolling the sensitive bud between his teeth. I moan again, thrusting my hips up against him. I honestly feel like I could burst and all he's done is kiss me.

Damian removes his mouth from my nipple and the cool air causes it to pucker. I gaze at Damian through heavy-lidded eyes as he unbuttons his shirt and takes off his pants. His erect cock strains against his boxer briefs, and my mouth waters at the sight.

It's time for me to show him just how much I love him. How grateful I am for rescuing me. For being my everything.

Before Damian can kiss me again, I sit up, lightly pushing him back until he's lying on the bed. His eyes are wide as he looks at me.

"Alexis, what the...?"

I pay him no mind as I kiss down from his neck, down to his sculpted yet scarred body, my tongue swirling over some of the scars mapping his torso. I rain kisses past his belly button, my chin moving against the rough material of his boxer briefs.

"You're wearing entirely too many clothes," I murmur, ignoring the fact that he and I are equally clothed. I pull his underwear down slowly, watching with delight as his giant dick stands at attention before I toss his boxer briefs onto the ground.

Reaching out, I run my hand down his shaft, smiling as I hear Damian hiss and tip his head back.

"Fuck, Alexis."

Encouraged by that reaction, I lean down and press kisses to his head, licking up any precum leaking from the tip. Damian moans, his back arching as he brings his penis closer to my mouth.

I've never really done this before, but that's not going to stop me. I want Damian to feel *good*.

I relax my throat as I take him deeper into my mouth, moving my lips up and down his shaft as my tongue swirls around his hard length. My hands cup his balls as I roll them between my fingers.

"Oh, *fuck*, Alexis!" Damian moans before seizing my hair and guiding me up and down his shaft. "Holy fuck, *yes*. Yes, right *there*. Oh, *fuck*, don't stop."

He's gripping my hair so tightly, my eyes are watering, but I refuse to quit, sucking his penis with all I have, bobbing my head up and down in the way he seems to like. I take him deeper into my throat, breathing through my nose as my lips nearly touch his balls.

Damian's moans and hisses are music to my ears. *I'm* making him feel this good. *I'm* the reason he's getting so much pleasure from this.

He continues to spasm and groan as I work his shaft, his fingers digging nearly painfully into my hair, but I don't care. His hips move rhythmically as he fucks my mouth. I slow the pace a little before speeding up again, smiling as he moans loudly.

"Fuck, I'm going to come, Alexis," he pants, his hips moving wildly.

Oh, no. We can't have that.

I remove my mouth from his penis, releasing him with a wet *Pop*. He glares at me. I smile sweetly at him.

"That was just an appetizer," I respond.

Growling, Damian pounces on me, pinning me to the bed. Our skin touches, and goosebumps erupt on my flesh. His touch always causes such reactions in me.

Damian kisses me, his hands caressing my breasts again. He's moving deliberately slow, taking his time. I feel like I could burst. I'm ready and eager, but he's savoring every single touch.

It excites me how he looks at me like I'm a valuable treasure. It fills me with such joy and confidence.

It looks like he really loves me.

His hand moves between my thighs before ripping my underwear off me. I gasp, but it turns into a moan as his fingers rub against my clit. I convulse as he increases speed, sending jolts of pleasure through me.

I grab him by the arms. "Take me, now," I pant.

Damian smirks but does as I ask, sliding his throbbing erection into me effortlessly. He fits perfectly.

He looks at me as he begins to thrust. He pushes hard and then slowly pulls back. Harder, and then gently pulls back, again. It's exciting and frustrating at the same time. I moan into his ear.

His hands move up to my face, and he holds my head in his hands as he grinds in and out of me. My fingers begin to claw at his back as he increases his speed.

Damian releases my face and moves his hands to my breasts, gently massaging and squeezing them before clamping his mouth over a nipple and sucking eagerly.

The stimulation overpowers me, and I twitch beneath him, arching my back and gripping him against me.

"Yes, Damian, don't stop!" I cry.

Damian increases his speed again, pounding enthusiastically as I moan and squirm. I never want him to stop.

"More, Damian. Harder!" I beg, and he happily obliges. The more I cry out, the more aggressive he becomes. Finally, his mouth moves up to my throat, and he bites me playfully, causing me to gasp.

"Yes, Damian!" I cry out breathlessly.

Damian abruptly pulls himself out of me.

"What are you doing? No, please don't stop." I whimper, and he flashes a devilish grin before getting to his knees and flipping me onto my stomach.

I gasp again, and he chuckles before putting his hands on my hips and moving me up on all fours. "You're mine," he purrs before he enters me from behind.

Damian pushes harder and more profoundly than before, and I cannot control my screams of pleasure.

"Yes, Damian! Yes, take me! I'm yours!"

His skin slaps against my ass as he grinds into me over and over. His fingers dig into my hips. I've never felt like this before. He brings me to new levels of ecstasy.

I feel my orgasm growing inside me, and Damian seems more excited the harder he pounds me.

"I'm going to come," I whimper as I can no longer keep it inside. I cannot fight this one. It's overtaking me. I am at its mercy.

"Me, too," he pants as he growls, spilling his seed inside me.

I scream as my muscles contract against his stiff shaft. Finally, the warmth spreads inside me, and I feel satisfied. Complete.

Damian collapses over my backside, his skin slick against mine as he catches his breath. My arms are shaking from holding my body weight up, but I wouldn't change it for the world.

That was *amazing*.

Slowly, Damian pulls himself out of me and lies down beside me.

I rest my head against Damian's chest, feeling the comforting thrum of his heartbeat. His arms are wrapped around me. I can't help but marvel at the profound change I've witnessed in him. I remember vividly the first time we had sex, how he had retreated afterward, refusing to partake in the simple intimacy of post-sex cuddling.

At the time, I had been confused and hurt, unsure of how to navigate this man who seemed to keep me at arm's length.

But now, as he holds me close, his fingers tracing gentle patterns along my skin, I realize just how much he has grown, how he has allowed himself to be vulnerable in a way he'd once resisted.

Damian's walls have come down, and in their place, I see the depth of his love and devotion. The fierce protectiveness he displayed earlier, the raw honesty with which he confessed his fears of losing me—it's a stark contrast to the guarded, distant man I first knew.

I reach up to caress his cheek, marveling at the softness in his expression, the warmth that radiates from his very being. This man—this man who has become my everything—has truly opened his heart to me.

"Damian," I whisper, my voice laced with reverence. "You've changed so much."

He turns his head slightly, pressing a gentle kiss to the palm of my hand. "For you, Alexis," he murmurs. "Always for you."

In that moment, I'm struck by the realization that our journey, our bond, has been a transformative one—not just for me, but for Damian as well. He has shed his armor, his defenses, and in doing so has allowed me to see the depth of the man he truly is.

Damian deserves to know the truth. I can no longer keep this secret from him, not when he's proven time and time again that he is my unwavering rock, my fiercest protector.

Summoning my courage, I lift my head to meet his gaze. "Damian?" I murmur, my voice soft yet resolute.

He looks down, his eyes filled with warmth and adoration. "Yes?"

Taking a deep breath, I hold his steady gaze. "I'm pregnant."

36

ALEXIS

The minute the words leave my lips, I see Damian's expression shift from one of concern to utter joy. Before I can blink, he's sweeping me up into his arms and jumping off the bed, spinning me in delighted circles.

"A baby?" he exclaims, his eyes shining with an unbridled happiness. "Alexis, this is… holy fuck, this is incredible!"

I can't help but laugh, even as a wave of relief washes over me. How could I have ever doubted his reaction? This man—who has proven time and time again to be my steadfast protector—is overjoyed at the prospect of starting a family with me.

He suddenly stops spinning me and gently sets me down. "I need to be careful," he murmurs. "I don't want to jostle the baby."

I laugh again as his hands come to rest reverently on my abdomen. "You can't jostle the baby," I tell him. "He or she is pretty well protected in me."

"She," Damian corrects me, his voice thick with emotion. "But I don't want to do anything that could hurt you or our baby."

I'm struck by the depth of his devotion, the fierce protectiveness that radiates from him. This man—this *Don* of a powerful Mafia organization—is utterly captivated by the thought of our growing family.

And he's also convinced this baby is a girl. God help anyone who tries to harm her.

"I love you, Alexis," Damian breathes, his forehead coming to rest against mine. "With all that I am, I love you. And now..." His gaze flicks downward, a tender smile playing at his lips. "Now we have a child to love, too."

The confession—so raw and genuine—causes tears to well in my eyes. For so long, I've yearned to hear those words, to feel the weight of them as they settle into the very depths of my soul. To have Damian declare his love so freely is a gift I had scarcely dared to hope for.

"I love you too, Damian," I whisper, my voice thick with emotion. "So much."

The words spill forth, unbidden, as a few stray tears slip down my cheeks. This man, this fierce, unyielding force in my life, has somehow found a way to crack open the walls I'd so carefully constructed around my heart.

His eyes widen with delight, and in the next moment, I'm enveloped in his strong, familiar embrace. As I melt into his arms, I feel a weight lift from my shoulders, a burden I hadn't even realized I was carrying. Damian's unwavering devotion, the way he cherishes me, is a balm to my battered soul.

He pulls back slightly, his eyes shining with emotion. "Alexis," he murmurs, his voice thick with affection, "now that we have finally said we love each other *and* with a child on the way..." He pauses, a boyish grin spreading across his face. "Will you marry me?"

The proposal takes me by surprise, but I feel a surge of warmth spread through my chest.

"Where's my engagement ring?" I ask playfully. "A girl deserves to have a beautiful engagement ring and for the man to be on one knee."

Damian growls, but his dark eyes dance with amusement. "I'll get you the biggest fucking ring imaginable," he proclaims, cupping my cheek with his rough hand. "Just say the word and we'll go to the best jewelry store in Chicago."

He searches my face. "So, what's the answer? You can't keep me waiting."

I laugh again, my heart fluttering. "Yes, Damian. Yes, I'll marry you."

He lets out a delighted laugh, pulling me into another fierce embrace. "You've made me the happiest man, Alexis," he murmurs against my hair. "I can't wait to call you my wife."

As we hold each other, I can't help but marvel at the whirlwind of emotions swirling within me. Just hours ago, I was facing unspeakable horrors, about to be sold to someone who would keep me a prisoner forever.

And now, here I am, pledging my life to the man I love, a child growing within me.

It's all so overwhelming, so breathtakingly fast. Yet, in the safety of Damian's arms, it feels like the most natural thing in the world. This is where I belong, with the man who has become my protector, my constant in the chaos.

We decide to find Nat and Edo to tell them the news. Edo was in the hotel lobby, phone pressed to his ear as he murmured something in a low voice, while Nat was at the bar, a drink clutched in her hand as she stared into nothing.

When we tell them, she nearly drops her glass.

"You're... you're pregnant?" Nat stammers, her eyes wide. "And you're getting married?"

Damian nods, his arm wrapped firmly around my waist. "That's right."

Edo lets out a low whistle, a smile spreading across his face. "*Mio Dio*, I never thought this would ever happen. Congratulations, you two."

But even as they offer their heartfelt congratulations, I can see the haunted look in Nat's eyes, the lingering shadows of the day's events. The loss of her family, the betrayal of her uncle... it's a wound that will take time to heal.

Still, in this moment, I see a glimmer of hope, a promise of a future worth fighting for. With Damian by my side and our child on the way, I feel a renewed sense of purpose, a determination to forge a life filled with love, security, and the chance to right the wrongs of the past.

In this child—in this union—I see the chance to break the cycle of darkness that has plagued us all.

"I also have good news," Edo says. "I was able to track down Katie's parents. There's a manhunt for her. We can take her home on our way back to Chicago."

I let out a shaky breath, relief flooding through me. "What about the other women? Were you able to rescue them all?"

Nat nods solemnly. "Yes, we got them all out safely. They're all going to be reunited with their families. Most of them were just innocents who were caught up in this against their will."

"Thank goodness. I'm so glad to hear that. Those poor women have been through enough."

Nat nods and looks down at her hands.

I remove myself from Damian's embrace and move closer to Nat, gently touching her arm. "Are you okay?"

Nat inhales sharply and her eyes meet mine. I can see the pain lurking in her dark orbs. "No," she says abruptly. "But I'll be okay. Eventually. Today was just... it was a lot."

She tips back her drink into her mouth before slamming the tumbler down.

I pull Nat into a tight hug, ignoring her squawk of surprise. "I'm here for you, Nat. We're all here for you."

Nat tentatively returns the embrace. "Thank you, Alexis. That... that means a lot."

∽

AFTER COORDINATING WITH THE AUTHORITIES, we're able to safely return Katie to her overjoyed parents. The moment they see their daughter, they rush forward, pulling her into a fierce embrace as tears of relief stream down their faces.

"Oh, Katie!" her mother cries, showering her with kisses. "My baby!"

Katie sobs into her mother's shoulder, her small body trembling.

Her father looks up at us, eyes shining with gratitude. "Thank you, thank you *so much*. We can never repay you for bringing our little girl back to us."

Katie turns to me, her eyes wide and shining, "You're my guardian angel!" she declares, throwing her arms around me.

I blink back tears, hugging the child tightly. Somehow, this has healed some part of my inner child, knowing I was able to fulfill a promise. "I'm just happy you're safe now, sweetheart."

Damian steps forward, clearing his throat. "We're glad we could assist to bring Katie back home to you."

The child pulls back, beaming up at him. "Will you come visit me? And can you bring Biscotti next time?"

Damian laughs, a broad smile on his handsome face. "Of course, Miss Katie. Biscotti would love to meet her new friend."

As Katie's parents usher her away, their heartfelt gratitude and overwhelming relief are palpable. I watch them go, my heart swelling with bittersweet joy. We may have been able to rescue Katie, but there are still countless others still trapped in a living hell.

But for now, this small victory is enough to give me hope.

We finally get back to the Iacopelli compound, and my heart swells as I see the familiar mansion come into view. I'm finally *home*.

As we enter the foyer, I stop in my tracks when Bobby Shields emerges from the shadows.

Damian hisses and glares at his head of security. "What the *fuck*? How was he allowed in?"

I don't hear what the head of security stammers out as Bobby's gaze immediately zeroes in on me, his expression unreadable.

"Alexis," he says, his deep voice rumbling. "I need to speak with you. Alone."

Damian immediately stops bitching out his security, and I glance at him, bracing myself. I know my father won't leave until he's had his say, and the look in his eyes tells me this won't be an easy conversation.

Damian steps in front of me protectively. "I'll join you," he insists.

I place a hand on Damian's arm, shaking my head. "No, it's alright. I can handle this."

Turning to Bobby, I speak in a measured tone. "I'll speak with you. Alone."

Damian doesn't look convinced, but a sharp look from Bobby and a nod from Nat convince him otherwise. "Fine," he grumbles, "but if it lasts longer than ten minutes, I'm busting down the door."

I guide Bobby into the sun room, softly closing the door behind me.

The tension in the air is palpable as we face each other, the years of distance and unspoken history weighing heavily between us. I gaze at his face, finding traces of myself in him—the hazel eyes, the slope of our nose, the high cheekbones...

I'm not even sure where to begin with this man. I haven't seen him since I was a small child. But he seems to sense my hesitation, and he takes the first step.

"You look so much like your mother," he says, his deep voice tinged with emotion. "Your mother... I loved her more than anything in this world. And you..." He pauses, his brow furrowing. "You were the light of my life."

The raw sincerity in his words catches me off guard, and I feel a lump forming in my throat.

"Why don't I remember you?" I ask in a whisper. "You... you weren't around."

Bobby sighs, suddenly looking much older. "It was dangerous," he admits. "As the Don, I have a target on my back at all times. That includes my loved ones." He meets my gaze, his hazel eyes filled with regret. "I was trying to keep you and your mother safe by keeping my distance. But I never stopped thinking about you, my darling girl. Not a day went by that I didn't wonder how you were, if you were safe and happy.

"When I was told you and your mother had died..." Bobby shakes his head, a pained expression crossing his face. "It devastated me. I thought I'd lost everything."

I open my mouth, wanting to ask the question that's been weighing on my mind. "But how could you have believed Vincente? Without even seeing..." I trail off, unable to finish the sentence.

Bobby grimaces, his jaw tightening. "The grief," he says simply. "It clouded my judgment. I never looked closely at the body of the child Vinny produced. I just... assumed it was you."

I feel a shudder run through me at the implication. To have lost us so completely, only to find out later that it was all a lie? I can only imagine the pain and anguish he must have felt.

"But The Brotherhood," I say, something about this not adding up. "How do they play into this if Vincente was the one who started the rift between Invicta and the Iacopellis?"

A ghost of a frown plays across Bobby's face. "Vinny Iacopelli and Mario Rafa have been conspiring for years," Bobby says. "It's why they pushed Damian and Scarlett to be together."

My heart lurches at the mention of Scarlett Rafa, her cold blue eyes and twisted smile flashing in my mind. I can almost feel the cool knife blade on my tongue as Scarlett taunted me, threatening to cut it off.

"When your foster family tried to *sell* you..." Bobby spits the word out as if it were poison. "Vinny Iacopelli was there and let Mario know who you were. That's why The Brotherhood pursued you so badly. They knew having you would bring me to my knees."

My head is swimming with all this new information. "But how did you find out I was alive?"

"Our intel heard about this girl The Brotherhood was pursuing. Some fucking Brotherhood soldier couldn't keep his mouth shut. Once I saw your picture, I knew who you were and I did my best to find you."

I freeze, remembering how the gun felt against my temple. "The soldier..." I whisper. "He–he was trying to rescue me?"

Bobby scowls, his face turning truly thunderous. "No," he says shortly. "No. *That* soldier was disloyal and has been eliminated."

The thought *should* terrify me, that the soldier was planning on doing something horrible to me, but I find that I'm more annoyed than anything else.

"Good," I finally say. "It's better to cut off the diseased tree than try to treat it."

Bobby cocks his head at my response, his expression serious. "You have what it takes to become the next Donna of Invicta."

My eyes widen, and I nearly choke on my saliva. "A *Donna*? But... is that even possible for a woman?" I ask hesitantly.

Bobby gives me an odd look. "Of course it is," he replies matter-of-factly. "There have been powerful women leading Mafia families for generations. Don't sell yourself short, my girl."

I take a moment to process his words. The weight of the responsibility he's offering me is daunting. "I–I appreciate the offer, but I..." I pause, steeling myself. "I don't think I can accept it. I'm not a killer. Even though I've taken lives, I... I don't want that to be my path."

Bobby is silent for a long moment, looking contemplative. Finally, he speaks again. "What if we used Invicta for good, Alexis? To clean up the streets, to protect the innocent?" He looks at me intently. "You have a good heart. Perhaps together, we could make a real difference."

I contemplate my father's proposition, the idea of using Invicta's power for good rather than the ruthless violence I've witnessed intriguing me.

"That's an interesting idea, Bobby," I muse. "But what would happen to The Brotherhood?"

Bobby's expression darkens. "Anyone still loyal to Scarlett's methods would be executed," he states matter-of-factly. "The rest would be absorbed into Invicta and the Iacopellis."

His words hit me as I realize the full implications of his plan. The child I carry would one day potentially be the head of Invicta *and* the

Iacopellis as well—a combined criminal empire under my child's control.

A wry smile tugs at the corner of my lips. My child will have everything Vinny, Scarlett, and Mario so desperately wanted—*power*.

Bobby studies me closely, a hint of hesitation in his eyes. "Alexis... may I?" He extends his arms slightly, silently asking permission to embrace me.

I consider his offer for a moment, still not quite ready to call him "Dad". But I nod, desperate for some parental affection.

As he envelops me in his strong arms, I can't deny the healing warmth that spreads through me—a part of me that's been festering for fifteen long years.

EPILOGUE: ALEXIS

The last five years have been the happiest I've ever known. Life has never been better.

Damian and I got married a few months after I was rescued from the human auction. It was a small, intimate ceremony at the church his parents married in—just the close family and friends who have stood by us through it all. The look of pure joy on Damian's face as he said his vows is a memory I'll cherish forever.

Just three months later, our daughter Alice was born. Named in memory of Damian and Nat's sister, she has brought so much light and laughter into our lives. Damian is the most doting father I could have ever imagined, and watching him with our little girl makes my heart swell with love.

Two years after Alice, we welcomed our son Luca into the world. With two tiny terrors keeping us on our toes, Damian and I have our hands full. But we wouldn't have it any other way.

Juggling the responsibilities of raising our growing family has certainly been a challenge, But we have a strong support system with

Nat, Edo, and the rest of our trusted inner circle always there to lend a hand.

Part of that inner circle contains my father, Bobby Shields.

I've come to call Bobby "Dad" over these past five years. He's made good on his promise to use Invicta's power for good, and we've made significant progress in cleaning up the streets. We've teamed up with the Santiagos in Milwaukee and have done our best to stamp out any human trafficking rings in the area.

It's my personal mission.

Of course, we still deal in weapons—we have to make money somehow. But the animosity between the Iacopellis and Invicta is officially over. There aren't any needless wars being fought anymore, which has been a relief.

Although, I did authorize a hit against Suzanne and Dennis Carter about six months after I gave birth to Alice. They were executed swiftly and efficiently in Boca Raton, Florida, where they had been hiding out, desperate to escape The Brotherhood.

Too bad they should have been more afraid of me.

Overall, I'm proud of the work we've done. Dad and I have made a real difference in our community. We're cleaning up the streets, protecting the innocent, and ensuring the criminal element knows there are consequences for their actions.

Damian has been an incredible partner in all of this. He's fully on board with our mission, using his resources and connections to bolster our efforts. And of course, our children, Alice and Luca, are the light of our lives. Seeing them grow up in this new era, free from the constant threat of violence, fills me with hope for the future.

There are still challenges, of course. Old habits die hard, and we've had to ruthlessly eliminate any pockets of resistance. But I firmly believe that what we're doing is right. We're using our power and influence to make a positive impact, to create a safer, more prosperous world for our family and community.

As I wrap up my day at the Invicta headquarters, I can't help but feel a sense of accomplishment. The negotiations with a Cuban Mafia Family for new weapons were long and exhausting, but I managed to secure an excellent deal for Invicta.

Just as I'm about to head home, Dad stops me.

"Alexis," he says, a stern look on his face, "you know you're not allowed to come here unless you bring my grandbabies with you."

I can't help but chuckle at his playful demand. Ever since Alice and Luca were born, Dad has been completely smitten. He insists on seeing them as often as possible, and I have to admit, it's one of the sweetest changes I've witnessed in him over the years.

"Don't worry, Dad," I assure him. "I'm headed home now. Katie will be joining us for the barbecue, and you know how much she loves spending time with the kids."

Ever since we rescued Katie from the auction all those years ago, we've kept in close contact. Her parents were initially horrified to find out their daughter's "guardian angel" was the girlfriend—now wife—of the Iacopelli Crime Family's Don. But they've come to accept it, especially since Damian seeds an armored car to pick Katie up whenever she wants to visit our mansion.

As I step into the back yard, I can already hear the joyful laughter of my children. Damian is *attempting* to grill some food while Edo shit talks about Damian's grilling abilities. Katie chases after Alice and Luca, her face alight with pure happiness as Nat hurries after them, ordering the children to come here so she can feed them a snack.

It comes as no surprise to anyone that Edo and Nat have finally gotten together after years of dancing around the topic. Their chemistry and close bond have been obvious to us all, but they've always been content to keep things professional—until now, that is.

Watching them together, it's clear they're a perfect match. Nat's fierce determination and unwavering loyalty complement Edo's calm, methodical approach, and the way they look at each other with such affection and trust. It's really quite adorable.

What's perhaps most surprising is that they've decided not to have children of their own. With Alice and Luca keeping them more than busy as the doting aunt and uncle, they seem perfectly content to pour their love and energy into our little ones.

I can't help but smile whenever I see Edo and Nat playing with the kids, their faces alight with joy. They may not have chosen the traditional path, but the love and care they show is no less meaningful.

In a way, our children have become the shared legacy that binds our Families together.

My two whirlwinds of energy come barreling toward me, their little faces alight with excitement.

"Mama! Mama!" Alice shrieks, her tiny arms reaching up. Luca toddles along beside her, his chubby cheeks dimpled in a wide grin.

I scoop them both up, peppering their faces with kisses as they giggle and squirm.

"Hello, my darlings! Did you have a good day?"

Before they can answer, Nat swoops in, snatching Luca up and tossing him over her shoulder. "Alright, you little terror. Time for your snack," she declares, eliciting more delighted shrieks from my son.

"Auntie Nat!" Luca protests, though the laughter in his voice betrays his mock outrage.

Nat grins mischievously. "A growing boy needs his nourishment, little man. Can't have you wasting away on us, can we?"

As she carries Luca off toward the table, I turn my attention to Alice, brushing a stray lock of hair from her face. "And how about you, my sweet girl? Were you good for Daddy today?"

Alice nods emphatically, her big hazel eyes shining. "Uh-huh! I helped Daddy in his office, and then we had a tea party with Biscotti!"

I chuckle, picturing the scene. My fearsome Don of a husband, patiently sipping imaginary tea with our daughter and the dog. It's a sight that never fails to melt my heart.

Katie approaches me as Alice runs off, a bright smile on her face.

"Alexis!" she calls out, rushing over to wrap me in a tight hug.

I can't help but marvel at how much she's grown in the years since I rescued her. At thirteen years old, she's blossoming into a beautiful young woman, her features softening into graceful lines.

"Hello, Katie," I say, affectionately smoothing a hand over her hair. "My goodness, look at you. You're practically a grown-up now."

Katie beams up at me, her eyes sparkling with joy. "I've missed you! And the kids, of course. Can you come to my soccer game next week?"

"Of course I can! I'll bring the kids."

Katie sneaks a glance at Damian who is throwing his spatula at Edo, a scowl on his face. "But don't bring Damian, okay? The boy I like is going to be there, and Damian is... scary."

I laugh. Damian and Katie's father have gotten along in the years since Katie's rescue since they both have a common goal—protecting Katie. Katie's father loves the fact that Damian can make any boy disappear "like Jimmy Hoffa."

Damian appears at my shoulder, a steaming plate of hot dogs and hamburgers in his hands. "I heard that, Katherine," he says sternly, though his eyes show amusement. "And I resent the implication."

Katie groans, rolling her eyes good-naturedly. "Damian," she whines. "Nat's been teaching me how to shoot, and Edo's teaching me self-defense, too. I can take care of myself."

"I know you can," Damian responds, ruffling her hair, smirking at Katie's indignant squawk. "But I'm still going to that game."

As I watch the exchange, I'm filled with a sense of gratitude and wonder. The little girl I once rescued is now a thriving, confident young woman, and I'm honored to have played a part in her journey. And knowing that Damian and the rest of our Family will always be there to protect her? Well, that just makes my heart swell with love.

LATER THAT EVENING, after Katie had been taken home and Alice and Luca are tucked into bed, Damian and I collapse into our bed, exhausted.

Damian pulls me close, his strong arms wrapping around me as we sink into our mattress. "You okay?" he murmurs, his voice low and soothing.

I let out a contented sigh, relaxing into his embrace. "I am now." I tilt my head back to meet his gaze, a small smile tugging at my lips. "Being with you always makes everything feel right."

He brushes a stray lock of hair from my face, his touch gentle. "You're the best thing that's ever happened to me. I don't know what I'd do without you."

"Probably get into a lot more trouble," I tease, my fingers tracing the lines on his face.

Damian chuckles, the sound rumbling in his chest. "Probably." His expression turns serious as he cups my cheek. "But I mean it. You and the kids... you're my whole world."

I lean in, pressing a soft kiss to his lips. "And you're ours. Always."

Our kiss deepens, filled with a familiar heat and urgency. Our hands roam, reaffirming our connection as we lose ourselves in each other's embrace.

All I want is for him to be inside me. I want to feel every inch of him.

He pulls back. "Sit up," he commands.

I slowly move myself into a sitting position. He reaches down and removes my shirt, and I unhook my bra as he undresses himself.

As soon as my breasts are exposed, he wastes no time and presses himself onto me. His lips trail down my neck, eliciting shivers and anticipation.

I can feel his hardness against me, making me ache for him even more.

With effortless grace, he slides my pants down my legs, his fingers trailing lightly over my skin. My breath catches in my throat, and I gasp as his hand grazes my clit while he works his way back up.

"I love it when you react like that," he whispers with a mischievous grin.

Without hesitation, I pull him back on top of me, feeling the weight of his body press against mine. My arms wrap around his broad, muscular back as I subtly move my hips toward him, hoping he'll pick up on my desire.

"Impatient," he growls seductively in my ear.

"Please, Damian," I plead with him. "I need you now."

As soon as I utter the words, a spark of desire ignites in his eyes and he plunges into me. His hot tongue swirls around my mouth while he thrusts in and out with slow, deliberate movements.

I can't resist arching my back in pleasure as he continues to ravish me with his passionate lovemaking.

As he picks up speed, our bodies move together in perfect harmony. I can't help but dig my nails into his strong back as he fucks me with both passion and tenderness. In this moment, there is nothing else but us and the electrifying connection between our bodies.

The sensation is intense, our bodies pressed together in a frenzy of desire. It's like we are melding into one another, giving ourselves over completely. Nothing else matters but this moment, this connection between us.

Our breaths mingle and our hearts beat in unison as we reach the peak of ecstasy together. Our bodies tremble with pleasure and release, leaving us both drenched in sweat and gasping for air.

We lie here, unable to move, basking in the aftermath of our passionate union. Damian kisses my head and tucks me against his chest. "I love you, Alexis."

I smile sleepily, snuggling into him. "I love you, too."

As I drift off to sleep, cradled in the safety of Damian's embrace, I can't help but marvel at how my life has unfolded. Never would I have imagined that my happily ever after, the family I so desperately craved, would come from within the world of the Mafia.

And yet, here I am, a powerful figure in my own right, leading with a compassionate heart while also surrounded by a devoted husband and beautiful children. It's a far cry from the uncertainty and fear that once consumed me.

As sleep claims me, I can't help but feel a deep sense of gratitude. This life, this family, it's more than I ever could have dreamed of. And I know, without a doubt, that I'm exactly where I'm meant to be.

Loved Evelyn and Alessandro? **Get the next book in the series here.**

tangled loyalties

AN ARRANGED MARRIAGE SECRET PREGNANCY DARK MAFIA ROMANCE

AJME WILLIAMS

bulletproof baby

AN AGE GAP SURPRISE PREGNANCY MAFIA ROMANCE

AJME WILLIAMS

WANT MORE AJME WILLIAMS?

Join my no spam mailing list here.

You'll only be sent emails about my new releases, extended epilogues, deleted scenes and occasional FREE books.